HANDFULS OF YESTERDAY
BY
SHENEEN MONIQUE SOARES

Handfuls of Yesterday

Trilogy Christian Publishers A Wholly Owned Subsidiary of Trinity Broadcasting Network

2442 Michelle Drive Tustin, CA 92780

Copyright © 2022 by Sheneen Monique Soares

Unless otherwise indicated, all scripture quotations are taken from the King James Version of the Bible. Public domain.

No part of this book may be reproduced, stored in a retrieval system, or transmitted by any means without written permission from the author. All rights reserved. Printed in the USA.

Rights Department, 2442 Michelle Drive, Tustin, CA 92780.

Trilogy Christian Publishing/TBN and colophon are trademarks of Trinity Broadcasting Network.

Cover design by: Jeremiah Diaz

For information about special discounts for bulk purchases, please contact Trilogy Christian Publishing.

Trilogy Disclaimer: The views and content expressed in this book are those of the author and may not necessarily reflect the views and doctrine of Trilogy Christian Publishing or the Trinity Broadcasting Network.

Manufactured in the United States of America

10 9 8 7 6 5 4 3 2 1

Library of Congress Cataloging-in-Publication Data is available.

ISBN: 978-1-68556-374-5

E-ISBN: 978-1-68556-375-2

DEDICATION

To my mother, Shelia Soares: without you, this book would not be.

To my father, Durvin Soares, who has always encouraged every dream of mine.

TABLE OF CONTENTS

Prologue 7

Chapter 1 9

Chapter 2 17

Chapter 3 33

Chapter 4 55

Chapter 5 79

Chapter 6 93

Chapter 7 105

Chapter 8 119

Chapter 9 161

Chapter 10 177

Chapter 11 185

Chapter 12 199

Chapter 13 207

Chapter 14 221

Chapter 15 231

Chapter 16 251

Chapter 17 273

PROLOGUE

"Child, take the flower."

He looks at her. The only familiar face he has ever known. Begging him. Beseeching him to take what isn't his. He looks at the field of pink flowers. He glares at his tiny hands. He looks back at her. His palms begin to sweat.

"But," he attempts to speak, but his voice seems to be on vacation. "This is…this is not our home. This is not our garden," he manages to spew.

The woman kneels to the level of the six-year-old child. "Listen to me," she says. She gently lifts his head to the level of her own. "The owner of this home is in no dire need of these flowers," she continues.

"Are we in need of them?" the boy questions.

"Yes," she answers, then contemplates for a moment. "It's my birthday. Take it for me, won't you?" The youngster debatably bows his head in response.

"Look at me," she says as she lifts his head again. "In life, there are people who need things and cannot have them, and then there are people who have things but do not use them. It is quite alright for you to take the flower, and if anyone asks you what you're doing with the flower, you tell them that you are going to give it to an underprivileged person."

He stares into her eyes, green as the grass beneath him. He nods and grips the nearest flower. He looks at her, and she smiles. To him, she looks more beautiful than the sunset. He uproots the flower.

"Good boy," she says with a grin.

They leave the garden unnoticed and start walking down the sidewalk. Flower in hand, the youth looks up at the lady and asks, "Are you proud of me?"

"Yes," she says, smiling. "Now more than ever."

He breaks into a grin, and then he hands the flower to his mother. "For you."

CHAPTER 1

Farook watches from the fourth-story window as the workers push the snow off the driveway. They work absent-mindedly, much like he did when he was their age. He watches as one of the workers breaks the melancholy mood and garbs a handful of frozen sky water, throwing it at the other. The simple act slowly escalates into a gleeful and frigid fight. Farook laughs, knowing he should stop them but decides to let them enjoy a little entertainment on such a cold day.

Eventually, Farook retires from watching the workers and takes a seat at the dinner table, aimlessly reading his newspaper. He anxiously awaits the arrival of his grandchildren. Farook looks across the table at his wife, who gracefully balances a cup of tea in one hand and a thick book in the other. This woman had stolen his heart at the age of twenty-one. He remembers how they meet. He, gun in hand, playing Russian roulette and hoping to hit the target. She, talking him into putting the gun down and holding him as he cried. Not the most romantic meeting, but a meeting that drew them closer than they ever thought they could be. *It's amazing*, he thought, *how destiny could pull two people from two different worlds together in such a magnificent way.*

Farook, bored with reading the same article fifteen times, returns to the window and begins watching the workers again as he waits for the familiar minivan to pull into the driveway.

"Dear," Farook utters to his wife as he continues to look out the window. Zahra puts down the teacup she had meaningfully placed at her lips and stares at her husband with laughter in her eyes.

"Don't fret yourself, Farook. They will be here in due time," Zahra scolds and reassures.

"But it is already after nine in the morning, and they are not here as yet," Farook states matter-of-factly.

"Have a seat, Farook." He obeys and sits back down at the table.

"Stop being anxious. They will be here soon. It is an icebox out there. Nadya and Niran have to be careful on the road with the children." Farook nods and begins to read the same article once more.

"Farook," Zahra calls questioningly.

"Yes, dear," Farook answers without looking up from the newspaper.

"What will you do with the children once they have arrived?" Zahra inquires.

"I really don't know. What do you suggest?" he replies without looking up at his wife.

"How about you tell them a story," Zahra proposes.

"What story?" Farook asks, still immersed in the familiar prose.

"Your story," Zahra replies. Farook feels as if his superior vena cava caved in. He slowly looks up to behold his wife.

"Zahra," Farook says slowly. "Honey, my love, have you…have you lost your mind? They are but children! If I were to do such a thing, they would hate me. Nadya, my own flesh and blood, would detest me!"

Farook shakes his head. "No, I will carry them shopping like I always do. They seem to enjoy that activity."

Zahra looks her husband lovingly in the eyes. "Dear, my love, you know I do not mean to upset you. I understand that they are children and that it would be a salient tale to tell, but I reason that it would be a good thing to give them that piece of you they don't already possess."

Farook stares at his wife with a mixture of love, anger, frustration, and fear. Zahra continues, "You could perhaps reveal your past to them in the form of a tale. You could be the protagonist and tell your story in a third-person manner so that they don't know whom you speak of and—"

"No," Farook says, cutting his wife's statement short.

"But dear—" Zahra lovingly beseeches.

"No!" Farook exclaims as he slams the newspaper down onto the table top. He returns to his post at the window. Zahra slowly gets up from around the dining room table. She walks over to her husband and wraps her arms around him.

"Farook," she says dotingly.

"Yes, my love," Farook answers in a muffled voice.

"Tell them."

"But—" Farook tries to interject almost inaudibly.

"Tell them," Zahra repeats. "You have to let it go. You love those children, and telling them about you in a meticulous way will do wonders for your heavy heart, my love. Remember when you told me your story?"

"Yes," Farook replies.

"Do you remember the way you felt when you did?" Zahra inquires with her arms still draped around her husband.

"Yes," Farook responds.

"Tell them. Don't try to keep it in. Let it go. The only way to let it go is to let it out."

Farook is about to answer his wife when he sees the familiar blue minivan. A brilliant smile spreads across his face. He hurriedly leaves the dining room, walks down the hallway to the elevator, enters the elevator, and begins the descent to the first floor. The elevator ride seems like an eternity to him.

****

The old house looks the same to Nadya. She soaks in the memories of laughter and joy that coming back home brought to her. Nadya closes her eyes and breathes in the fragrance of her childhood from the slightly agape blue minivan windows. It smells wonderful to her. The memories so close, but yet so far. So real, but yet so imagined. Akin to another world in which she was a pilgrim.

The sweet moments of grasping mental memorabilia are diluted as the sounds of reality seep in. She begins to listen to her children's conversation.

Whispering as if sharing a life-changing secret, Olathe states, "I'm going to ask Grandpa for a cell phone." A bright smile spreads across Olathe's face as she thinks about being the first out of all her friends to have a cellular device. Olathe's siblings, Perri and Halia, both shoot their sister a look.

"What are you going to do with a cellphone?" Halia asks her sister.

"Who are you going to call?" Perri follows.

"Ghost Busters," Olathe replies, then laughs at her own cultured joke. When she realizes that her joke has left a humorous mark on herself alone, she ceases laughter and says, "I don't know. You two have phones, so why not I?" Olathe reckons that her argument is reasonable.

"Because you are a child," Perri retorts.

Olathe looks at her brother quizzically. "And you are an adult?"

"I'm closer to one than you are," Perri debates.

Olathe raises her arms in disbelief. "You're fifteen!"

Perri mimics her by raising his arms in the same manner and responds almost immediately, "You're nine!"

"Children, behave yourselves. Your grandfather is not an ATM machine. Olathe, you will not ask him for a phone. We did not give you one, and your grandparents will not be giving you one either. Are we clear?" Niran admonishes his children as he steps out of the driver's seat of the van.

"Yes, Daddy," they all recite in harmony.

Nadya smiles at her husband as she continues to breathe in the fresh scent of her childhood mixed with the all too familiar fragrance of the tulips that dance around the beige brick mansion of her parents. Nadya follows the lead of her husband and children and begins to exit the blue minivan. The side door of the home opens, and out comes Farook with a radiant grin. Nadya's heart leaps at the sight of her father. The father she so respects and loves.

"Papa!" Nadya says lovingly as she embraces her father. Farook kisses his daughter tenderly on the forehead.

"How have you been, my child?" Farook asks his daughter.

"I am well, Papa. How are you?"

"I am well now that you are here." A board smile spreads across Farook's face, and its infectious nature catches Nadya. Zahra emerges from the side door and joins her husband as they greet their family.

"Mother!" Nadya gleefully bellows as she embraces Zahra, "How are you?"

Zahra holds her child close to her, knowing how much of a miracle having her was. "I am well and delighted to see you," Zahra responds with a smile. Zahra shifts her focus to her son-in-law and approaches him for a hug. "Niran, what a pleasure. How are you, my son?"

Niran smiles and hugs his mother-in-law. "I am well, Mum, thank you."

Perri, Halia, and Olathe run into the tender arms of their grandparents. The embrace explodes into a festival of kisses. The atmosphere reeks of love. True and honest love. With a smile larger than the Arabian Peninsula, Farook embraces his son-in-law with a full heart.

"How are you, Niran?" Farook asks.

"I'm doing well, Dad. Yourself?"

The Arabian Peninsula cracks, and a vivacious laugh escapes from the inner crevices of Farook's heart. "I am more than overjoyed about spending the day with these three," Farook retorts while trying to tickle Olathe, whose laughter fills the air.

"Well, Dad, you have the entire day with them. Niran and I have several business meetings to attend," Nadya states as she and Niran hug the children and her parents again before heading to the minivan.

"Bye, you three. Behave yourselves," Niran warns. "We'll be back around seven thirty."

"Bye, Mum! Bye, Dad!" the children sing.

Perri pats his empty pockets and then begins to run towards the gate where the van has now reached. "I left my wallet in the car, Grandpa. I'll be—"

"You won't need it today, son," Farook interrupts Perri, who is in mid-sprint. Farook looks over his shoulder to give his wife a loving glace. "Today, I'll be telling you a tale."

Zahra gives her husband a modest smile. Perri begins to walk back slowly. He gives his grandfather a questioning look. Olathe looks disappointed. Halia looks intrigued.

"Come, children, let us go inside," Farook says as he ushers his family into the familiar house through the heavy oak doors.

****

Farook laughs as the children press all the buttons in the elevator. He wishes he had experienced childhood as such, filled with laughter and a carefree spirit.

After stopping at every floor, they finally reach the fourth floor and the children dash for the game room. Farook follows his grandchildren. By the time he gets inside the game room, all three of them are immersed in their favorite game. Olathe plays her fashion game. Halia is taken by her vocabulary game. Perri plays one of his many Black Ops games. Farook smiles at the children. He had the room constructed and designed just for them.

Farook suddenly feels a gentle touch on his arm. He turns around to see his wife with her cell phone in her left hand and her right hand on the bend of his arm.

"Honey, I just got a call from the office. Roger is at the office sobbing and beating on my door. I must go."

Farook smiles at his wife. Her occupation as a therapist is so noble and so illustrative of the kind of woman he married forty years ago. Even though she has no need to work and has served faithfully in that occupation for over thirty-five years, she still goes voluntarily. Her practice cannot find anyone else like her. She cares so deeply about the well-being of her patients. She is moved with compassion for the cares and concerns of other human beings.

Farook kisses his wife gently on the cheek. "Alright, dear, I know Roger won't see any other therapist. I will be praying for you and especially for Roger." Farook places his hand gently on Zahra's face and whispers, "No other human being has a heart bigger than yours."

A radiant smile spreads across Zahra's face. "Thank you, Farook," she says as she kisses her husband's cheek. "I love you, and I'll see you soon." Zahra quickly gets her purse from the living room, says goodbye to the children, and departs.

"Children," Farook calls.

"Yes, Grandpa," they reply.

"Join me in the living area, won't you?" It takes them a few minutes, but they eventually make it to the living room.

"Grandpa, are you going to tell us the tale now?" Halia asks with avid anticipation.

"Yes, Halia, I am." The children sit on the soft and well-woven Tabriz carpet in front of the lazy boy their grandfather perches upon.

"I am excited for this tale, Grandpa," Halia states gleefully. Her love for words and the use of them still rich as ever.

"I am equally as excited to tell you, my dear," Farook states. "But I must warn you, some portions of the tale are quite gruesome," Farook says as he wears a grim expression on his face.

"Really?" Olathe inquires; her interest finally peaked. "How morbid? To the level of zombies?"

Farook laughs, then feigns a serious face. "Maybe even more morbid than zombies," Farook retorts. Olathe now looks genuinely intrigued.

Farook reclines in his chair. "Now, I am going to tell you a story about a young man. His name is—" Farook pauses to consider the name for his main character. "Peter. His name is Peter."

CHAPTER 2

Peter grew up without knowing his father, but he always had his mother. His mother was different than most women of that time. She was extremely independent. Growing up, she didn't have much, and when she found out she was with child, she concluded that she didn't want her offspring to live in the conditions she did. While pregnant with Peter, she worked at a diner. She stole ten pence every night before closing. When the boss's suspicions began to rise, and he started questioning the employees, she stopped stealing the sterling.

A few weeks later, she announced to the diner that she was fundraising for an organization that specialized in helping single mothers. Seeing that she was five months into her pregnancy and sporting an obvious baby bump, the diner believed her and donated to the phony organization. She even made flyers for the false liaison on her days off. Customers at the diner started to donate more and more until she had enough money to move to Liverpool.

The apartment she bought was small, but she loved the feeling of living on her own. She eventually bought a little red car. She was driving the car when her water broke. In tremendous spurts of pain, she drove to the hospital. She ran red lights and swerved as the pain increased in span and severity. As she neared the parking lot of the hospital, she sped up and morphed two parking spots into one with her vehicle. She got out of the car and wobbled into the hospital. She immediately caught the attention of medical personnel. She gave birth to Peter that night in March.

****

"Grandpa, are you saying that Peter's mother bought an apartment and a car with illegitimate funds?" Halia asks.

"Yes, she did," Farook replies.

"Grandpa, what's the name of Peter's mother?" Olathe asks.

Without hesitation, Farook replies, "Her name is Adela."

"That's a pretty name," Olathe comments with a smile, then her face drops. "But her deeds are not so pretty." Farook laughs at his granddaughter's animated personality.

"What happens next, Grandpa?" Perri asks. Farook reclines in his lazy boy.

****

Adela watched as Peter grew up before her eyes. She thought it riveting how days morphed into months and months into years. Before she knew it, the baby she once rocked to sleep was conversing with her in far from rudimentary speech at a very young age. She looked at the boy. So innocent, so impressionable, but yet so brilliant and beyond his six years. He looked up at her and smiled, then continued to play with his toy cars in their exceptionally small living room. His eyes were brown like his father's. The father he didn't know. His father the mystery.

Adela's bogus charity was losing funds. Peter was now six and a half years old, and customers and employees at the diner had grown weary of giving to the same charity, regardless of the new fundraising ideas Adela had concocted. Adela had a new idea.

"Peter," Adela spoke softly to her child.

"Yes, Mother," Peter answered without looking up from his toys.

"What do you desire to be when you grow up?" Adela inquired.

Peter smiled as he shifted his attention to his mother and replied, "A firefighter." Peter gleamed at his mother, then shifted his attention back to his toys.

"A firefighter, aye?"

"Yes."

"And why is that?" Adela pushed.

A brilliant smile came across Peter's face, "I want to help people. Just like Jack's dad."

"Jack's dad is a firefighter?"

"Yes, he is. He came to our class last week and spoke to us about being a firefighter. It was so intriguing because he came to class in his firefighter clothes. I really liked that presentation. It was my favorite. So, I have decided to be a firefighter."

"Have you ever thought of being an actor?"

"An actor?" Peter asked with a confused crinkled nose. He was more than sure that he had just moments ago confirmed with his mother the desire he had to be a firefighter. He wondered how she fetched acting from the pool of fighting fires.

"Yes, I think you'd make an excellent one," Adela said as she gleamed at her son.

Peter looked at his mother's sort of eerie gleam and thought about it for a moment. "Like the ones on television?" he asked, still perplexed.

"Not exactly…more everyday acting."

"Everyday acting?" Now Peter was really confused.

"Yes, it is when you act off the stage."

"Why would anyone act off stage?" Peter asked slowly with involuntarily narrowed eyes.

"It is difficult to explain, Peter," Adela thought for a moment before speaking further. "Would you like me to show you what it is?"

Peter looked at his mother with curiosity and confusion. *What is everyday acting?* he questioned within himself. Curiosity battled with confusion. Curiosity prevailed.

"Yes, Mother, I would like to see what everyday acting is."

Adela held her hand out to the child. He took it, and they grabbed their coats, then walked outside and got into their little red car. Peter watched as his mother adorned herself with her driving scarf and sunglasses. She was radiant, he thought. They drove for miles into areas unknown to Peter. Peter thought they were going to drive forever until he heard his mother mumble something under her breath and then parked the car across from an elegant home. Peter looked at the house. He'd never seen a house so grand in his life. It seemed to take up every area of land that his eyes could behold.

"Where are we, Mother?" Peter asked.

"We are at the set where you will learn to be an everyday actor," Adela said as she took off her sunglasses and driving scarf.

Adela began to exit the car, and Peter followed suit. As Peter found the hand of his mother, they walked towards the house that seemed to span for miles. Then it struck him. The field. Never before had he laid eyes upon a field of such radiant pink flowers. The sight of it was truly captivating. The color of the flowers matched beautifully with the light pink curtains that blew majestically in the wind from the fourth-story windows of the grand home. Peter was in awe. He fell in love with the house. They approached it tentatively. The distance between them and the field of flowers closed, and suddenly they were there, standing in the field.

"Alright, Peter, today will be your first lesson in everyday acting."

He looked up at her. He felt a little uneasy, but why should he be uneasy? He thought, of course, he could trust his mother.

"What am I supposed to do?" Peter asked.

"Take one of these flowers," Adela said dubiously but affectionately simultaneously. Peter didn't know what to do. The whole situation made him feel strangely apprehensive. He knew he was supposed to be acting, but he couldn't help but feel that what he was being told to do was wrong.

"But—" Peter tried to argue.

"Child, take the flower!" Adela sternly interrupted but then softened her face so as not to alarm the child.

He looked at her. The only familiar face he had ever known. He looked at the field of pink flowers. He glared at his small hands. He looked back at her. His palms began to sweat. "But," he attempted to speak, but his voice appeared to be off duty. "This is…this is not our home. This is not our garden."

The woman knelt down to the level of the six-year-old child and said, "Listen to me." She gently lifted his drooped head to the level of her own. "The owner of this home is in no dire need of these flowers."

"Are we in need of them?"

"Yes," she contemplated for a moment. "It's my birthday. Take them for me, won't you?" The youngster debatably bowed his head.

"Look at me," she lifted his head again. "In life, there are people who need things and cannot have them, and then there are people who have things but do not use them. It is quite alright for you to take the flower, and if anyone asks you what you're doing with the flower, tell them that you are going to give it to an underprivileged person."

He stared into her eyes, green as the grass beneath him. He nodded and gripped the nearest flower. He looked at her, and she smiled. To him, she looked more radiant than the sunset. He uprooted the flower.

Little did he know that the field had become his personal place of tarnish.

"Good boy," she said with an approving grin. She lifted herself from the earth and swiped the dirt from her knees.

They left the garden unnoticed and started to walk down the sidewalk. Flower in hand, Peter looked up at Adela and asked, "Are you proud of me?"

"Yes," she said, smiling. "Now more than ever."

****

"So, Grandpa, is Adela truly training Peter to be a thief?" Halia asks.

"Yes, Halia, but in a more manipulative way because she is teaching him that those deeds are alright once he is in character."

Olathe shakes her head. "That's terrible," she comments.

Perri looks puzzled. "My question is, Grandpa, why would she do that to her son? If she is that way, she chose to be that way as an adult. It is not fair for her to do that to her child," Perri interjects.

Farook soaks the comment in. "You are correct, my son; it truly wasn't fair to Peter."

"What happens next, Grandpa?" Halia inquires.

****

Months after the stealing of the flower, Adela drove Peter to a town eighty miles away from where they lived. She had ripped his oldest clothes, soiled them, and dressed him in them to make him appear to be a homeless boy. She had also decked him with a container to use to beg for money. Peter did not argue about the trips anymore because he was trained into thinking they were merely acting sessions, just everyday acting. Adela drove him out to different towns every weekend. People would pity Peter and give him an abundance of money because of his age and soft appearance. Adela had rehearsed with him the story he was to tell the people of himself. In one town, when Peter told a young woman the rehearsed tale that he was homeless and that both his parents were dead, she offered to help find him a home. They never went back to that town.

This went on for three years. As Peter aged, the people started giving less and less, and Adela had to formulate a new plan. She was enjoying the money that Peter brought in from the begging, but her greed called for more. The job at the diner was not going to be sufficient for the extravagant life that she had planned. The desire for riches was the stream of Adela's consciousness and the motif of her life. She set out to accomplish her next scheme on a loftier level.

Adela searched and inquired about ways people without a college education could attain vast amounts of money. Some dubious person advised Adela to step into scam calling. Adela began to do a great deal of research regarding scam calling. Her reading ability was slow and rudimentary, but she fervently pressed through it. The smell of future money filled her nostrils and her cranium.

Adela began taking communication courses at the local college, and for four years, Peter got the taste of what it was like to be a regular, carefree child. No abnormal demands. No "everyday acting," which made him apprehensive.

As Adela's knowledge developed, she started to call on various numbers to offer non-existent spa treatments and exotic trips.

One day when Peter arrived home from school, he saw his mother hurriedly setting up a telephone. "Peter, give me a hand with this, won't you?" Peter slowly approached his mother after closing the front door of their small apartment.

"Mum, why are we setting up another house phone?" teenage Peter asked as he placed his backpack on the ground.

Adela smiled at her son. "Well, my dear, I have started a new business, and I need one phone for business and one for the house."

Peter was stunned. "How come I didn't know of such a business? What do you do? You're not working at the diner anymore?"

"I'm still working at the diner," Adela retorted as she worked on setting up the phone. "I hope that this business will take off so I won't have to."

Adela smiled as she finished setting up the phone and listened for the dial-tone. Her smile broadened as she heard what she was anticipating. Seeing that his mother had gotten through with the phone, Peter took a seat on the armrest of the sofa in their petite living room.

"So, Mum, what is this business?"

Adela turned to face her son. "Well, Peter, it is a business in which I advertise certain things, and clients will call me on this new phone, and I will get the money from them."

"So, what are you selling, Mum?"

Adela touched the peak helix of her ear. It was an impulsive thing she did when she was deep in thought. She smiled at her son. "I'm selling vacations, honey," Adela quickly retorted. She went into their small kitchen and started to put a meal together so as not to meet the questioning glance of her son.

"So, where are you sending them?" Peter asked as he approached the kitchen and leaned against the doorframe.

"A variety of places," Adela replied as she chopped onions into fine pieces.

"Who is giving you the tickets for these trips?" Peter asked as he shifted to the other side of the doorframe.

"An agency that I'm working with," Adela responded as the pieces of onion became mush.

"What's the name of the agency?"

Adela tried to ignore her son. She reckoned that maybe if she ignored him and continued to focus on cooking the meal, he would stop questioning her. For a few moments, she thought she was free of her son's interrogation. Peter passed by her to grab a soft drink out of their narrow refrigerator, then returned to his post at the kitchen door.

"Mum, you didn't answer my question. What's the name of the agency?" Peter inquired again, almost casually, as he popped open his auburn-colored soft drink.

Again, Adela tried to ignore the pestering of her son because she didn't have an answer. Her face reddened as she broke the spaghetti with more force than warranted. She took the lid off of the pot of boiling water, and she placed the spaghetti in.

"Mum?"

Anger and shame crept up Adela's throat and out of her mouth. "Stop asking me all these questions, Peter!" Adela yelled at her son. Peter stared at his mother, absolutely flabbergasted.

"Peter, don't you trust me?" Adela said, to which Peter nodded. "Good, then just trust me."

****

"What is your account number?" Peter asked the woman calling on his mother's business phone. He wrote swiftly in his mother's little floral notebook.

"Thank you; I hope you enjoy your trip. Have a wonderful day." Peter hung up the phone and stared at it for a while. He knew that woman would never enjoy the trip. There was no trip. He knew what he was doing was wrong, but he had been his mother's right-hand man for the past six months, and he didn't know how to tell his mother that he didn't want to live that kind of lifestyle anymore, constantly lying and deceiving people, and taking their hard-earned money.

"What are the numbers?" Adela asked her son, which interrupted his train of thought. He looked up from the phone, opened the floral notebook, and read his mother the numbers. Adela smiled. She'd become immune to shame and natural affection because it had been devoured by her greed.

Peter left the room and went to get his backpack. "Bye, Mum," he said as he placed the bag on his back.

"Bye, Peter," his mother replied. He looked back at her, and a blend of shame, anger, frustration, and despondency filled his heart and emanated onto his face.

Peter left the house. While he walked to school, he contemplated running away, but where would he go? Shame and anger had built armies in his heart and decided to rage a civil war on this day. Tears streamed down his face unconsciously. He left disconnected from his body as if everything he did was controlled by another. He felt dirty and manipulated.

He crumbled to his knees on an isolated street on his way to school. He wept bitterly. He didn't want to live like that anymore, but he didn't know how to get out of the situation. His mother was all he had. After wiping his tears, he continued his journey to school. He went through the day with absolutely no emotion. In every class, he gazed ahead. His ears were functioning, but he could not hear anything. He couldn't feel anything. He ate at lunch but couldn't taste anything. Eventually, the last bell rang, and he walked despondently out the doors of the school. Just as he was about to step off the school grounds, a heavy hand rested on him and broke his depressed daze. He looked up to behold a grandiose man towering over him.

"Are you Peter Davies?"

"Yes," Peter answered, perplexed.

"We would like to ask you a few questions about your mother." Peter watched as two other men approached him.

"Who are you?"

"We work for the government, young man. Can we ask you a few questions?"

"About my mother?" Peter asked, trying his best to look perplexed even though he knew what it was about.

"Son, have you seen your mother frequently using telephones over the last two months?" the second grandiose man asked.

Peter activated the acting skills he had developed over the years. "Not more than usual."

"You see, Peter, someone in your apartment complex is running an illegal operation. Someone on your floor." Peter's poker face prolonged.

"Your mother and two others are the only ones on your floor who own a telephone."

"Well, I don't know anything about that, sir. My mom works at the local diner if you would like to speak with her," Peter said, trying his best to keep his composure.

"Well, alright, son, we will do that." The men turned to leave. Peter turned in the opposite direction. Head and heart pounding in sync. What manner of life had his mother given him?

****

"So, Grandpa, the government started getting involved?" Perri asks, intrigued.

"Well, they tried to get information from Peter as to what was going on in his home. They were inquiring about Adela's telephone usage, but Peter put on a pretty impressive front of cluelessness," Farook retorts. "Adela also shared the telephone line with her two neighbors, so there was ambiguity as to who was using when."

"Grandpa, what does ambiguity mean?" Olathe asks.

"Ambiguity is when there is uncertainty regarding the specifics of something," Halia answers before Farook gets the chance.

"You are extraordinary, Halia," Farook commends his granddaughter. Halia's eyes grin at her grandfather's compliment.

"Did those men talk to Adela?" Perri questions as the tale begins to pull him deeper and deeper into the abyss of suspense.

"Yes, they did," Farook responds.

****

Peter awoke startled and drenched in water. He opened his eyes to see his mother over him with an empty bucket. She looked deranged. That wasn't his mother, but it looked like her. Not knowing what else to do, Peter slowly slid off the bed, not wanting to make any sudden movements. He was a gazelle in the presence of a lion.

"What did you do?" Adela angrily questioned her son.

"Mum, what's going on?" Peter asked. He looked at the empty pail in his mother's hand. He looked at his drenched shirt. The daze of slumber wore off, and Peter suddenly came to the realization that his mother had thrown a bucket of water on him while he slept. This behavior was uncommon for his mother, he thought. He had never seen her behave so strangely. Peter watched as his mother aggressively rubbed her nose. He noticed that her green eyes were well past the point of dilation. Her once soft pupils were stone cold as she stared at him. Her irises, which he once equated to a beautiful field, now looked like a frightening forest. Peter's tiny bedroom seemed to envelop him. He felt as if he was suffocating.

"What did you say to them?" Adela yelled, her voice echoing off the beige walls.

"Who, Mum? What did I say to whom?" Peter asked, genuinely perplexed.

"What did you say to those men today?" Adela paused to wipe her nose with her sleeve. Peter tried to think about who his mother may be speaking of. Peter looked at the clock. It was two thirty in the morning.

"What men?"

"The men from the government."

Flashes of the earlier conversation after his last class flashed into Peter's memory. The men from the government that were investigating his mother and two others from the apartment floor. "Mum, I didn't say anything to them. I did what you told me to do. I said the things you told me to say," Peter tried to reason with his mother.

For a moment, his mother looked like her usual self, then suddenly, the pail from her hand was colliding with his forehead. He felt the warm liquid of his inner content flow from the impacted spot. He looked up at his mother in disbelief. She looked so wild and deranged. *Who is this woman?* he thought. Adela glared at her son for a moment, then swiftly walked out of his room. Slamming the bedroom door behind her.

****

Farook stares out the window in reminiscence. Even in telling the story, he felt like he could still feel the impact of the water pail. Farook touches his forehead. Fortunately, his hair covered the scar.

"So, Grandpa, what's wrong with Adela?" Olathe asks, breaking her grandfather's daze.

"Is it drugs, Grandpa?" Halia inquires.

"Yes, it was," Farook answers, a little wearily.

Olathe contorted her face and gestures enthusiastically. "Drugs are an abomination! I learned that in school."

"They are, my love." Farook smiles at his granddaughter, taken by her dynamic personality.

"Does it get better for Peter, Grandpa?" Perri asks. Perri is now fully enthralled by the tale.

****

After the incident, there was an awkward air between Peter and his mother for the entirety of a week. They seemed to tip toe around each other. At the end of that week, they sat at the dinner table in silence.

"Mum, is everything okay with you?" Peter asked, breaking the silence between them.

Adela gave her son a weary smile. "I'm well, Peter." Peter looked worriedly at his mother. "Truly," she said to affirm her previous statement.

After a few moments, Peter asked, "What happened the other night? Why did you pour water on me?" Peter made circles in his mash potatoes with his fork and then added, "You weren't yourself."

Adela covered her face with her hands so as to hide the shame she felt. She had shared a lot with her son over the years, but she wasn't going to share this portion of her life with him, even though he witnessed her in mid-trip. She uncovered her face and painted on a feigned smile.

"It was a mixture of fatigue and frustration, Peter."

Peter shook his head in disbelief. "Mum, I've seen you both tired and frustrated. That's not it."

Adela contrived an expression of sudden remembrance. "And I also had a couple of drinks after work."

Peter looked into his mother's eyes. Green as grass. Sane and healthy.

"I guess I had too much to drink," Adela said, breaking eye contact with her son and releasing a fake chuckle. She realized that the laugh sounded creepy instead of the casual chuckle she was aiming for. They ate in silence for a few more minutes.

"Mum," Peter said lovingly.

"Yes, Peter."

"Promise me you won't drink that much again." Peter looked desperately at his mother for reassurance that her frightening, maniac behavior would not happen again.

Adela put on her best smile and said, "I won't, Peter. I won't drink like that ever again." Adela was smiling, but she knew in her heart that she hadn't had a drink in months. It was easier for her to tell her son she had a drinking problem rather than to tell him the truth. Peter's face softened. He wanted to believe her. He had to believe her. She's all he had.

****

For two years, Adela placed her scamming on hold. Adela tried to live a normal life. In those two years, she worked harder than anyone else at the diner, but something was trying to pull her back into her old nature of con-artistry. She tried to formulate a plan that would not easily be traced back to her. She sought inspiration in the white powder hidden in the cluttered cupboard of her small kitchen. She rummaged through the cupboard and then held the bag in her hand. She had promised her son that he would not see her so deranged ever again, but she felt as if she needed it. Peter was at his friend's house for the night, and Adela deemed it the perfect opportunity. She denied the voice that was telling her that she had an addiction.

She placed the bag on the countertop and stared at it for a few moments. She debated her intentions. She tried to distract herself by cleaning the kitchen. She ironed clothes that didn't need ironing. She drowned the house plants in water. The container started to repulsively vomit up soil. She was trying to distract herself from the pull of the kitchen.

She sluggishly walked back to the familiar countertop. Her entire body rejecting what her mind wanted her to do. She walked into the smallest kitchen known to man. She looked at the bag. In a sharp twinkling, the substance in the petite, clear plastic was making its rounds in her bloodstream. The dipping of water from the faulty faucet sang in her ears with tremendous vibrato.

CHAPTER 3

Peter returned home at eleven the following morning. He opened the door, and he could feel a difference in the air. It was inexplicable to him, but he knew something was wrong. He put his backpack on the floor and headed to the kitchen for a snack. As he headed to the kitchen, he spotted his mother on the living room sofa.

"Mum, is everything okay?" Peter inquired.

"Hello, my love. Yes, I'm quite delightful."

She looked euphoric in the most traitorous of ways. Her smile bright as the morning sun, but her eyes carried a slightly unhinged guise. It seemed as if her pupil was fighting with her iris for space in both sclerae.

"How was your time with your friend?"

"It was good," Peter answered, not wanting to look into his mother's unbalanced eyes, which reminded him of the past he was trying so diligently to forget. He passed her and went into the kitchen to get the snack. He opened the small refrigerator, and as he reached to get something to eat, he noticed that everything was strangely in the same position as the previous day. Nothing had been touched. He grabbed his snack and walked as casually as possible to his room, picking up his backpack on the way. He went into his tiny room and closed the door behind him.

Her touch startled him. Adela ran her hands through the thick brunette curls that roofed her son's head. Peter felt an irregularity in the touch. It was much more aggressive than warranted. Peter turned to face his mother.

"Do you remember the everyday acting sessions of your youth?"

"Yes," Peter replied hesitantly. He knew his time of peace had come to an end.

"Well, the more advanced the actor, the more challenging the roles become."

"What do you mean?" Peter inquired. Adela's tempestuous gaze held on to her son's locks.

****

Peter could feel the stares of his fellow classmates as they examined his bald head. For the past month, his mother had been cutting off his hair in series. Sitting in the cold classroom and feeling the irregular breeze move upon his hairless head reminded Peter of the subtle flow of deception his actions had induced. Peter felt a small hand tighten on his shoulder. He turned around and looked into the eyes of his childhood friend. Elizabeth looked at him with great concern in her eyes.

"Peter, what's going on with you?" Elizabeth stole a glimpse at her friend's head, then quickly shifted her attention again to Peter's eyes. "Are you ill?" she inquired.

Peter looked at his friend. He didn't want to lie to her. He didn't want to tell her the rehearsed tale. He didn't want her to know that his appearance was due to duress, starvation, and long nights of listening to his stomach growl at him with detest, all so that he would appear ill. All so that his frame would twin his deceptive bald head.

Elizabeth had been such a wonderful friend to him, but as he looked at her, the words of his mother echoed in his mind. Peter stared at the ground. He felt like he was truly going to be sick, not due to illness, but due to the burden of his heart and the badgering of his conscience. Peter focused on a tiny red speck on the ground. He found solace in the speck. He and the speck had something in common. They both had been trampled upon.

"Peter," Elizabeth said with worry as she gently shook the shoulder of her friend.

Peter came back to reality and looked at his friend once again. He heard himself say, "I have cancer."

Peter watched as the force of the lie compelled Elizabeth to subconsciously release the petite yellow pencil she had once firmly gripped. Peter watched as a small river formed itself in the eyes of Elizabeth and released like a fountain upon her face. Peter looked away. He couldn't watch her cry. He couldn't watch her weep for something he wasn't truly afflicted with. Peter glimpsed back to see the oasis of tears that had formed itself on Elizabeth's wooden desk. Elizabeth's crying caught the attention of the teacher's aide.

"Elizabeth, what is the matter?" the teacher's aide asked compassionately.

Elizabeth tried to swiftly wipe her face so as not to embarrass her friend. "I'm quite alright," Elizabeth's breaking voice tried to project. Elizabeth stole a glimpse at Peter, which was not missed by the teacher's aide.

The rest of the class period seemed like an eternity to Peter as he listened to his friend sniffle behind him for the duration of the class. Each sniffle stung like a wasp.

The bell eventually rang, and Peter slowly packed his bag. He had to play the part of the sick teenager. By the time all his books were safely in his bag, he realized that he was alone with the teacher's aide.

"Peter, is everything alright?" the teacher's aide meticulously asked.

Peter found the red speck on the ground and fastened his attention on it.

"I have cancer," he lied. The hug came so fast that her arms were a blur, then, all of a sudden, Peter was engulfed in an embrace.

Ms. Anderson pulled away from him and said, "Whatever you need. We are here to help with anything at all."

He didn't want to. He didn't want to say it, but visions of red streaks came to the forefront of his mind. He could see his mother's deranged eyes. He could feel the collision of the pail and his forehead. He could see the streaks of red. His own blood painting a single hue portrait on his face. He had to say it. He didn't have a choice.

"We are struggling financially, and the medical bills are piling up for my treatments." Peter lifted his head and looked into the eyes of his teacher with the perfect amount of sorrow, "It's just my mum and me."

Peter compelled tears to form in his eyes and sucked in what was left of his cheeks and said, "It's mighty difficult for us, but we'll make it." Peter's coerced tears slid deceitfully down his face. Peter watched as his play pulled upon the heartstrings of his teacher.

"Wait right here," she said as she walked over to her purse. She pulled out fifty pounds and handed it to Peter. "I know this is small, but I want to help."

"Thank you," Peter mouthed as he wiped the counterfeit tears from his wet face. The tips of the currency gently brushed his face.

Ms. Anderson gently held Peter's shoulder with her right hand. "It's going to be alright," she consoled.

****

"Grandpa, what a travesty!" Halia exclaims. "So, in essence, Peter's mum is having him pretend to be terminally ill?" Halia projects.

"Precisely," Farook answers without hesitation. Olathe shakes her head with pity and shame as one living vicariously through a tale.

"Everything alright, Oly?" Farook inquires of his youngest grandchild.

Olathe looks up at her grandfather. "It's just so sad, Grandpa. So sad. To live like that. It must be especially difficult for Peter. His mother is the only person he can really have a close relationship with because of the abundance of secrets that has to stay between them." Olathe proceeds to shake her head again in order to finalize, with gestures, her pity for Peter and his situation.

"Grandpa, how long does the scam continue?" Perri inquires. Farook gazes at the radiant morning sky and begins his guised autobiography o'er.

****

They stared at the currency that covered their tiny wooden living room table. Five hundred pounds laid bare. Peter glanced at his mother. She was smiling. Each corner of her lips reached for her ears, and for the first time in Peter's life, he was repulsed by his mother. He examined his meager frame and wondered if other children around the world had mothers who starved them so that they could look the part in an everyday acting course. He stared at himself in a full-body mirror that hung on the wall. Why did he have to do this? He wondered. *All this for money?* he questioned within himself.

Peter turned again to his mother. "Mum, I'm hungry. Can I please have dinner tonight?"

Adela glared at her son from over her shoulder. Compassion blew across her face, but for a moment, then her attention shifted back to the pounds. The breeze of compassion departed. She packed up the money, and as if it were the money she was answering instead of her son, she said, "Peter, you know you have a week left of your special diet. You have to play the part, honey."

Tears formed in Peter's eyes. He looked at himself again in the mirror. He turned to the side, and to him, he nearly disappeared from visual grasp.

Tears continued to tarry down his face. He knew he had to stop crying because he was robbing his body of its final fluids. But the tears continued to flow.

Peter turned to his mother. "Look at me!" he yelled through spittle and tears. He held the shoulders of his mother. "Mum, look at me! It's me, Peter. Your son! Mum, I'm famished!"

Adela looked at her son. She knew what she was doing was wrong. A growing boy needed nutrients, proteins, and vitamins. She had barely been feeding him for over a month. She felt shame, but she had learned to suppress shame and anything connected to her conscience. She was doing this for him, she tried to convince herself. So they could have a new life. A better life.

"One more week, Peter," Adela said as she moved away from the grasp of her son and made her way to the kitchen.

She heard as Peter took a seat at the kitchen table. In the kitchen, she heated her dinner and placed a few saltine crackers and a glass of water together for Peter. She walked into their small dining room and gave Peter his crackers and water. Peter looked up at his mother. The look he gave her bore a hole through her copious façade. He turned his attention back to the crackers and slowly picked one up and placed it on his thin lips. Peter licked the salt off the cracker and closed his eyes. He then began to nibble the cracker. Adela turned away from him and headed back to the kitchen. She listened as he munched. Each munch irked her heart. She got her food and went back to the dining room to have dinner with her son. By the time she reached the table, he was finishing the water.

"Mum, I'm tired. I'm going to take a bath and head to bed," Peter said as he wearily got up from the table.

"Alright," Adela answered. She watched as he walked away and vanished behind the wall. She heard the water filling the tub. She contemplated giving him a little more food, but that would go against her plan.

I'm doing this all for him, she tried to convince herself. She engaged in blaring boisterous battles of the mind as she ate in exterior silence. She finished her food and drank her juice. She brought her plate and glass to the kitchen and washed them as her mind brawls raged on. She dried the plates and glass and headed to the living room. She buried herself in the soft settee and turned on the television. She enjoyed the distraction television brought. Television allowed her to concentrate on fiction and temporarily escape reality. She immersed herself in an episode of her favorite sitcom. As one episode ended and the other began, she realized that she hadn't heard Peter come out of the bathroom.

"Peter, honey, are you alright?" Only silence responded to her.

Adela took the short trip to the bathroom and knocked on the door. "Peter, everything alright in there?" No response. "Peter, honey!" Adela tried the bathroom doorknob. The door was locked.

Adela became frantic, and her maternal instincts returned. She walked down the hall, a couple of meters away from the door, then ran wildly towards the bathroom door. The door flew open and shook on its hinges. Adela's heart collapsed as she beheld her son's body, limp under the bath water. She frantically pulled him out and started to administer cardiopulmonary resuscitation. He wasn't responding. She, through tears, aggressively compressed his chest and administered rescue breaths. This went on for what seemed to be an eternity for Adela. Peter finally came to and started coughing up the water that had inhabited his lungs. Adela wrapped him in a towel and held him. He continued coughing as he rested on his mother's chest.

****

Peter sat in silence as he watched the fundraiser, on behalf of his fake illness, begin. His mother had even decked a bit of her shadowy-hued makeup around his eyes so he looked the part to the utmost. Adela sat beside her son and smiled her cheesy smile at everyone who came to greet her.

Peter watched as his principal stood behind the podium and addressed the crowd of approximately four hundred people, "We are gathered here tonight, as a municipal, to reach out a helping hand to one of our own. Peter is a brilliant student with vast potential, and we are here to do our best to make sure that that potential becomes a vibrant reality and...."

Peter zoned the principal out. The racket caused by the overuse of his mind canceled out any external sounds. Peter watched as the effects of the principal's speech began to move the people. Peter examined as the facial expressions of the crowd changed from indifference to sympathy. Many individuals who had shown up were not completely aware of the reason for the meeting, but the sudden realization moved the tide of their hearts to Peter's shore. Peter watched as a sea of eyes eyeballed him with pity. Peter heard when the principal began to speak about the expense on his mother for his chemotherapy sessions and how they were in debt because of his medical bills. Peter's perpetual migraine, induced by his badgered conscience, began to throb erratically. He felt so weak and powerless in this game his mother had him playing. He began to weep silently as the throbbing followed a faint staccato beat along the side of his head. The fundraiser continued, and Peter sat miserably in his seat as he watched the processions and collections continue for his mother's twisted way of making money. He sat and reflected on his childhood for the remainder of the meeting. He reasoned within himself and came to the conclusion that he would have much preferred standing on the median of a major avenue, begging for money, than sitting in an assembly, scrawny and deceitful. Then he reckoned that both were quite distasteful. He just wanted a normal life.

The assembly ended, and persons left one by one. Some greeted Peter and Adela before departing. Adela played her part as the heartbroken mum and thanked the people for their financial support. She was never short of feigned tears. Peter watched his mother as she watched the collectors as they went into the backroom to count the money. Peter felt as if he was going to vomit up the nonexistent contents in his desolate stomach. He dry heaved at the sight of greed that had consumed his mother.

Adela waited patiently for the lucre. The school had promised to give her the money immediately after the assembly. She estimated that the night's event would leave her with at least fifty thousand pounds. The principal came out with an envelope within a few minutes and handed it to Adela. She smiled and thanked him. Peter thanked him as well, and they left.

The car ride home was gruesome for Peter as he watched the smirk on his mother's face. She drove home with the envelope securely in her lap. She caressed the envelope with as much affection as she would a newborn.

The moment they reached the apartment complex and were safely inside, Adela broke the seal on the envelope and swiftly counted the pounds. She smiled as she did so, but her smile suddenly fell and morphed into a frown upon her face.

"There are fourteen thousand pounds in here," Adela stated with a blend of disappointment and abhorrence. Peter just stared at his mother.

"Isn't that a good thing, Mother?" Peter asked. He gave his mother a weak smile.

"That is a lot less than…" Adela spontaneously left the living room and went into the kitchen mid-sentence. Peter was left in the living room staring out into the sudden isolation. As he turned to go to his room, he realized that his mother had left the envelope on the living room table. Peter looked to see if his mother was coming back into the living room. When he heard no footsteps, he took a hundred pounds from the envelope. He eyeballed the money. *This is what all the fuss is about. A piece of colored paper with no intrinsic value*, he stated from the fortress of his mind as he glared at the pieces of currency. *This colored paper could easily be transformed into confetti*, he reckoned. He placed the two bills into his pocket and headed for his room. Peter got ready for bed and then crawled onto his small mattress as sleep drew him ashore.

The pain hit him suddenly and crawled down his back like a hasty reptile. His skin burned as a hot liquid bit at his flesh. His eyes flashed open, and he thrashed violently in response to the unforeseen pain. He then turned to see his mother pouring boiling hot water upon him. He looked at her face, and he realized that her eyes were transfixed on the water as it left the kettle and collided with his skin. Tears rolled down from Peter's eyes and upon his reddened cheeks as he pushed his mother's hand aside and yelled.

"Mother! You're hurting me!"

Peter watched as his dazed mother shifted her attention from the water she was pouring upon the floor to look at her son. Peter saw virtually no iris, just pupil, as he stared at his mother. The way she looked terrified him. She looked so disheveled and unkempt. Nothing like the radiant lady he had known for as long as he could remember.

Feelings of shame knocked on Adela's heart door, even mid-trip, as the look her son was giving her infiltrated her mental distortion. She casually rested the kettle on the floor beneath her, apologized, and walked out of the room.

Peter looked at the door, peered at the kettle, and then touched his back. His hand returned to him with a piece of flesh. He got up from the bed as pain pierced his back. He examined his hind portions through the small mirror in his room. His posterior was raw and red and his flesh mostly filleted.

Peter collapsed onto the floor in front of the mirror and wept bitterly. He looked up at the mirror to behold a tired and battered face. He hated the face he saw. The face was weak. The face was vulnerable.

It happened quickly. His fist angrily collided with the mirror, and he felt warm sticky liquid ooze from his exposed hand as the mirror spit shattered glass about him. He looked at his broken reflection through the damaged mirror. He still hated the fragments of himself that he saw.

He looked like a teenager, but he felt like the six-year-old boy who walked the streets begging for money.

He continued to kneel for a little while with his bloody hands on his lap. He knew he needed ointment and bandages, but he was numb. Pain strikingly numb.

Peter returned to bed and cried soft sobs on his pillow as he waited for sleep to consume his fatigued body.

****

Peter awoke the next morning to the unusual smell of bacon. Everything within him shook with hunger. As he rose from his bed, a sharp pain voyaged down his back, and he remembered the sore events from the prior night.

He examined his small bedroom. Bloody sheets with sprinkles of filleted flesh. Shattered glass and drops of blood. The round outline on the floor where the kettle once sat.

The kettle was gone.

Peter quickly readied himself and wrapped his bruised hands. He packed his backpack and went to the kitchen. There his mother was, well-dressed and prim.

"Good morning, love," Adela said casually as she placed the food on the table.

After Peter finished lusting after the eggs, bacon, fried bread, and beans, he noticed that his mother's eyes were sane and green, and her pupils were in their rightful place at the center of her eyes and not invasively expanded.

"I get to eat this morning?" Peter asked over the rumbling of his stomach.

"Yes, of course! This is all for you, love." Adela smiled at her son.

Peter gave her the best smile he could muster and sat at the table. They ate in silence.

"Mother, what happened last night?" Peter subconsciously asked as he wildly ate his first true meal in weeks.

Adela looked at her son and replied, "We attended the assembly. Did we not?"

Had she really forgotten? Peter inquired within himself. "No, afterward. Here at home. In my room last night."

"Peter, honey, what are you talking about?"

Peter, against his stomach's will, placed his fork down on the neatly folded paper napkin. Peter stared into his mother's eyes as he felt unwelcomed tears rolling down his face. "Mother…you burned me with scorching hot water."

Adela stared at her son in disbelief. "Peter, I'm your mother…I would never do such a thing."

Peter shook his head. She truly did not remember. Peter took off his shirt and showed his mother his back. Through his tears and with a stifled voice, he muttered, "Mum, you did this to me last night! I woke up to you pouring boiling water down my back and whispering that the money wasn't sufficient!"

Adela escorted Peter to the bathroom and rubbed ointment on his back. Peter watched his mother through the bathroom mirror as she cried. Peter turned around to face her. "Mum, I mean you no disrespect, but I do believe you need help. Sorry to be so blunt, but you were high last night. High to the point of not remembering what you did to me. You have to stop before you kill me." Adela's crying turned into violent weeping that rocked the entirety of their small home. Adela collapsed on the bathroom floor and continued to weep.

"Peter, I'm so sorry…. I'm a terrible mother…. I'm going to do better…. I promise you." Adela said through tears as she looked up at her son from her crumbled position on the bathroom floor. Peter knelt down and painfully held his mother as she cried. He gently kissed her forehead, even though his back was burning beyond belief. Peter felt as if someone had lit a dozen serpents on fire and dropped them on his back to do a torturous dance on his strewn flesh.

Adela then realized, as her son cradled her, that his hands were wrapped with bandages. "What happened to your hands?" Adela asked as she reached for her son's dressed hands. "Did I do this?" She looked worriedly into Peter's eyes.

"No, I smashed the mirror in my room after you burned me last night," Peter said tellingly.

Adela's crying escalated once again. "I'm really sorry, Peter. This is something that will never happen again," Adela said through phlegm-filled sniffles.

"I hope not, Mum. I truly hope not. I really want you to get some help," Peter reminded.

Adela buried herself in the crook of Peter's arm. Peter flinched when she did so.

"I will," Adela reassured. Peter kissed her once more on the forehead.

"I have to go to school now," Peter said, to which his mother nodded. Peter got his shirt and backpack from the dining room and grabbed a few pieces of bread before heading out the door.

Every step Peter took was painful, but the ointment was trying its best to dull some of the pain. Peter nibbled the fried bread. As he walked, the contents of his stomach wanted to make a reappearance, but he suppressed all compulsions to vomit.

Peter reached the school building and walked up the steps with added energy. Each class period went by with ease because he could now process information with his brain rather than being distracted by the barrenness of his stomach.

The last bell rang. The day had gone by quickly for Peter.

As he approached the double doors to exit the school, he heard a voice call his name. "Peter, may I speak with you for a moment?" Peter turned to face the voice and realized that it was his assistant principal, Mrs. DeLudge.

"Yes, Mrs. DeLudge."

"You look much better today, Peter," Mrs. DeLudge said with a smile.

"Thank you," Peter replied.

"How are you and mum holding up?" she genuinely asked.

"We are doing better. We really appreciate the financial support from the school. It means a lot, and it is helping me tremendously."

Mrs. DeLudge smiled. "May I ask which hospital you go to for your treatments?"

Peter stared wordlessly at his superior. His mother had forgotten to run through the backstory of his faux life and illness. He had to answer quickly, or else it would look suspicious.

"Birmingham Children's Hospital," Peter heard himself say. "Birmingham…is where I go for my treatments."

Mrs. DeLudge nodded slightly. "That's quite a travel."

"Well, thanks to the generosity of the school and the community, I can now receive the best care possible," Peter said, trying his best to appeal to her emotions.

Mrs. DeLudge eyeballed Peter, nodded once more, and said her adieus. As Peter turned to leave, he questioned if he had said the correct things to his assistant principal. Anxiety ate at him during his short walk home. Once he reached the apartment complex and was safe inside, he sprinted to the telephone and called his mother.

"Hello, Peter, please make it quick," Adela answered. Peter could hear the diner commotions in the background.

"Mum, Mrs. DeLudge inquired of me today regarding the hospital in which I receive my treatments."

Adela moved into the diner's east storage room and allowed silence to gobble the racket of the congested restaurant.

"What did you say to her?" Adela asked with caution.

"I told her I was receiving treatments at Birmingham Children's Hospital," Peter retorted with apprehension. There was a deafening silence, and Peter's anxiety levels surmounted all-natural degrees.

"That's good. That was a good choice," Adela said. Peter released a sigh of relief. "Sorry for not giving you a backstory, my love, but Birmingham Children's Hospital is a wonderful choice. It is two hours away, and they probably have an overwhelming number of Peters on record as cancer patients. I'm proud of you, son, for thinking on your feet. I must go, though. See you at home later."

Adela hung up the phone and returned to the bustle of the congested restaurant. Peter hung up the phone and sat on the green living room couch. His mother had complimented him, and he should be glad, but he deemed the compliment fictional due to the life of lies to which it was directed. That sort of compliment was not of any merit.

****

"This is such a mesmerizing tale, Grandpa," Olathe states as she stares into her grandfather's warm eyes.

"What do you think of the young man Peter and his predicament?" Farook asks his grandchildren meticulously.

"It is quite melancholy for him to be in that situation, Grandpa, but at some point, he's going to have to take a stand for himself and get help for his mother because she most definitely needs it," Halia retorts.

"It's a wild thing to ponder upon the effects of drugs. Adela couldn't even recall what she had done to her son," Perri follows. Olathe sits and shakes her head. Farook gently smiles at her.

"Does the scheme get uncovered, Grandpa?" Perri inquires.

****

Peter walked down the school hallway with added strength. His mother was giving him one full meal a day to slowly bring back Peter's appearance for the grand recovery in two months. Peter walked into his last class of the day. As he went to take his seat, his teacher stopped him and told him that the vice principal would like to speak with him immediately after the last bell. Peter pondered upon the unusual request for his presence from the vice principal. Peter spent the entire class period working out different scenarios in his mind as to the events of the future meeting. The last bell rang, and Peter slowly packed up his belongings and headed for the vice principal's office. He stood in front of the heavy door for a while until he mustered up the courage to knock.

"Come in," the voice of Mrs. DeLudge replied in response. Peter awkwardly walked into the office. Sensing Peter's unease, Mrs. DeLudge asked Peter to have a seat in one of the oak chairs that faced her desk. Peter gawkily sat down.

"Pleasant afternoon to you, Mrs. DeLudge," Peter greeted.

"A pleasant afternoon to you as well, Mr. Davies." Mrs. DeLudge paused to gather her thoughts, then said, "Peter, my husband and I have been deeply moved by your condition and the financial state of your family. We really do desire to help monetarily." Peter's inner man breathed a sigh of relief. "We thought the best way to do so was to surprise you and your mum by paying for your upcoming treatments," Mrs. DeLudge continued. "That was the reason why I inquired of you last week for the name of the hospital in which you receive your treatments."

Mrs. DeLudge sighed and slightly shifted her position in her chair. "Peter, my husband is a pediatric oncologist at the Birmingham Children's Hospital. You are not on file at that hospital."

Mrs. DeLudge's office began to move as Peter's mind willed it. Peter tried to think of something quickly in the spinning room so as not to appear to be concocting a reply.

Peter cleared his throat. "My mother is the one that spoke to my doctors."

With hands clasped upon the heavy oak desk, Mrs. DeLudge asked, "Peter, what is the name of your doctor?"

Peter felt like his air passages were closing, and the room's spinning changed from a slight swirl to a violent whirlwind. Peter swallowed very noisily and said, "I, umm, I have had a few doctors. I recently changed hospitals, so I only remember Dr. Bridges, who treated me last. I don't remember the name of my current doctor because we've only seen him once."

Mrs. DeLudge stared at Peter. Peter wondered how she could properly see him through all the tension in the room. Peter felt exposed. He knew Mrs. DeLudge was unto what he and his mother had fabricated. Sweat started to form on the roof of Peter's head, and he prayed it wouldn't take a stroll down his breaking façade of a face.

"Well, Peter, would you please give my regards to your mother?"

"Yes, Mrs. DeLudge. I will," Peter said with added coy.

Mrs. DeLudge stared at Peter again with that same intimidating look that made Peter want to empty all his guilt out onto his pants.

"Have a good evening, Mrs. DeLudge," Peter said before turning to leave the overbearing office.

"Good evening, Peter," Mrs. DeLudge retorted. Peter could feel her stare piercing his back as he closed the door behind him.

****

Peter keyed open the apartment door. He heard shuffling in the living room. He walked into the room and found his mother there cleaning.

"Mum, why are you home?"

"It's Thursday, Peter. I'm always off on Thursdays. You know that." Adela turned to face her son. "Also, when you haven't seen an individual in a couple of hours, you should greet them properly," Adela scolded. "I taught you better than that."

"I apologize, Mum. I'm a little discombobulated because of the meeting I had with Mrs. DeLudge after school today."

"Why did you have a meeting with Mrs. DeLudge?" Adela asked nonchalantly as she returned to cleaning. "I keep telling you to make sure you get to class on time."

"Mum, she was asking about the hospital in which I receive my treatments."

Adela freed her hands from the cleaning agents, took off her gloves, and turned to give her son her undivided attention.

Peter continued, "Her husband is a doctor at Birmingham Children's Hospital."

Adela's hand twitched.

"She went on to state that there isn't a record of me at the hospital." Peter tried to read the expression on his mother's face, but he wasn't picking anything up.

"Did she tell you why she was trying to search for you at the hospital?" Adela asked.

"She said that she and her husband wanted to pay for our upcoming medical bills." Peter took in a deep breath, "She said they wanted to help." Adela muttered something under her breath. "This isn't good, Mum. I reckon she does not believe I'm ill."

Adela stared at the ground for quite some time before looking up at her son. Peter stared into her familiar green eyes, waiting for words of guidance. *Only true things last,* Peter thought. While his mother stared into space, an eerie relief covered him, and he suddenly felt liberated in knowing that someone else knew. *Maybe it would all end now,* he thought. How audacious the thought.

"Peter, we have to leave," Adela said sternly.

"Where are we going to go?" Peter questioned.

"The United States," Adela said before going into her room. She returned from the room with two passports in hand. "I had these made in case something like this were to have occurred."

Peter stood in shock. "Mother, the United States of America?"

"What I want you to do is to go to school tomorrow, Peter, so as not to look overly suspicious. I'll pick you up from school with everything packed in the car, and we leave. We pack tonight."

Adela stuffed the passports in the pocket of her skirt. She began to pack things into the cardboard boxes she stored in one of the lower kitchen cabinets. Peter could not believe what was happening. In a moment, his life had changed. In a twinkling, he was saying goodbye to the house, the city, the country in which he was born and raised. Peter thought it sickening how a lie that his mother concocted, and he went along with, had him leaving all he's ever known to go to another country. To live another life. Peter came to and began to pack the contents of his fourteen years into cardboard boxes.

****

Friday was a blur for Peter as he went through the secretly sentimental day. Saying goodbye without uttering words. He hugged his friend Elizabeth. He wanted so badly to confide in her, to run away with her, but that simply wasn't an option.

"You want to hang out this weekend, Peter?" Elizabeth asked with sparkling eyes.

"I cannot," he said with a faint smile. "But most definitely next weekend," he falsely reassured.

He watched as Elizabeth walked down the school steps and onto the sidewalk. He watched her until her white and yellow sundress became a mere smudge in his visibility.

As he cried in his heart, he felt eyes upon him. He looked over towards the east wing of the school to behold Mrs. DeLudge and two men he didn't recognize eyeballing him. He tried his best to pretend as if he hadn't seen them. He causally walked down the sidewalk and turned out of the visual range of Mrs. DeLudge and company. His mum was there in their little red car. He got in the car, and he and his mother drove away from their condemnation.

****

They reached the airport at seven thirty in the evening. Peter took notice that his mother had only saved the most valuable of their possessions. They only had four suitcases between them. His mother handed him his passport, but he noticed that it was not his rightful UK passport but an American one.

"Mum," Peter said questioningly. "Where'd you get this?" he asked as he lifted the United States passport in the air for her to behold.

"Peter," his mother whispered, even though they were parked and safely in the vehicle, "we simply cannot use our passports in the predicament that we are in." Adela opened the passport. "Your name is now James Phetterson, my love. You are fourteen years of age, and you are a carefree American boy that was in England on vacation visiting his father." Peter examined the passport.

"The young man in this passport photo has blonde hair, Mum," Peter pointed out.

Adela reached into the backseat and pulled out a blonde wig and glue. Adela began to veil her son's head with the wig. She had a blonde wig for herself as well and began to cover her brunette locks with the false blonde mane.

"So, what's your name going to be, Mum?" Peter inquired.

Adela gave Peter a faint smile, then placed her passport next to her face. "My name is Abigail Phetterson. Do I look like the woman in the picture?"

"Exactly like her," Peter whispered.

"From now on, you have to speak in the American tongue, Peter."

"I don't know how," Peter confessed.

"Remember the American cartoons you used to watch on Saturday mornings?" Adela asked, to which Peter nodded. "Well, you have to speak like that from now on, my love." Peter looked down at his lap. "Peter, I'm sorry about all of this. I promise that when we get to New York, things will be different. Things will be better." Peter looked at his mother and tried to find reassurance in her eyes. The search bore no fruit. Peter had heard that line preached every Sunday morning. He was accustomed to the promises of a better life. A normal life. He had yet to see those promises fulfilled. He didn't trust his mother.

Just as Peter opened his mouth to speak, a stranger walked up to the vehicle and knocked on the car window.

"It's time, Peter. Get the bags, please," Adela said, then got out of the vehicle. Peter unloaded the red car. He watched as his mother spoke to the hooded stranger who gave her an envelope and took her car keys.

"Is everything out of the car, James?" Adela asked her son, who did not respond. "James?" Adela beckoned with a little more volume and force.

Peter stared at his mother for a while before realizing that she was calling him by his alias in a foreign twang. *She must have been practic-*

ing for a while because she sounds American, he thought.

"Yes, mother, everything is out of the vehicle," Peter said as American as he knew how.

"Good," Adela responded. She nodded at the hooded stranger, who, in response, got into their vehicle and drove off.

"Mum, where's he going with the car?"

"He just bought it, Peter. Our life here is finished." Peter watched as his mother took her bags and walked towards the exit of the car park. He caught up to her, and they walked together in sync. Two blonde criminals.

CHAPTER 4

Peter ferociously chomped on gum in an effort to combat the air pressure. After six hours in the air, he was ready again to place his feet on the earth's surface. His mum had slept for most of the flight, but he was quite jittery and perturbed about this unknown place he was about to call home. Several times he looked at his mother's sleeping body and didn't recognize the person. Her wig looked way too comfortable on her head. He wondered if his life in this new place was going to do just that, steal his identity. Peter's stream of consciousness flowed with an amalgam of anxiety and worry. This everyday acting had consumed the very core of his being. It had stolen his name. It had stolen his home. It had stolen his one true friend, Elizabeth. It had stolen everything. He tugged at his wig, but it seemed to be fastened and protected from removal with epoxy resin.

Peter reasoned within himself concerning yesterday's events and their eerie coordination. He thought about the way his mother had fake passports prepared, expensive blonde wigs ready, and a hooded stranger at hand to buy their vehicle.

As his mind continued to ponder sequences simultaneously, a glimmer through the airplane window caught his eye. He stared out into the cloudy abyss until the fluff cleared, and he beheld the sea of skyscrapers. The buildings sparkled in the pre-dawn sky. It was absolutely memorizing to Peter as he gave his mind a break from excessive isometrics.

"Isn't it great to be back home, James?" Peter turned to see his weary, American accented mother smiling at him. Peter tried but could not return the smile. An undesired resentment was slowly germinating in his heart for his mother. He didn't want to begrudge her, but something was telling him that that was exactly what he should do. Peter returned his eyes to the Manhattan sky. The seatbelt signs flashed, the plane descended, and Peter experienced, with first-time-flyer enamor, as the airplane's wheels touched American soil.

A concerto of overhead compartment doors preluded the stream of persons as they departed from the jet. Peter followed suit after his mother, who seemed to have already adapted to the bustle of city life.

They caught a taxi after smoothly going through customs. Adela gave the taxi driver an address. The driver drove violently and without caution. The taxi eventually stopped in front of a towering condominium. Adela paid and thanked the driver as they exited the vehicle. Adela's accent still sounded foreign to Peter. They took the bags out of the trunk and stood on the sidewalk, gawking in awe at the height of the building. They barely heard the taxi as it sped off into the traffic at high speeds.

"Is this really where we will be living, Mum?" Peter inquired.

"Yes, this is our home James," Adela said.

Two men in uniform came for their bags and escorted them into the building. Peter's gawking intensified as he entered the elegant edifice. The lobby was posh and eerily clean. Peter felt like his shoes may have been the carriers of the first speaks of dirt to ever enter the building.

The men in uniform escorted Peter and Adela to the front desk of the condominium's lobby. After the men placed the bags on the ground next to them, Peter noticed that they lingered. Adela swiftly enclosed a few bills in each of their hands. They thanked her and returned to their post at the front door. This was a strange change of pace for Peter.

Adela spoke to the lady at the desk while Peter looked around in awe. Maybe his mother was right. Maybe she really did have plans for them to live a better life.

"Welcome home, Mrs. Phetterson," the lady at the front desk said as she handed two sets of keys to Adela.

"Thank you," Adela replied in her American tongue.

They received baggage assistance once again, but this time to the east elevator. Akin to aforetime, Adela tipped the men in uniform. Again, Peter was sucked into the vacuum of bewildered awe. Adela handed Peter his own set of keys. Peter examined the beauty of the elevator. Smooth classical music serenaded them. The large doors of the spacious elevator opened on the ninth floor, and Peter stared out into a stylish hallway that held only four doors that were uniquely spaced.

"We live in 903, honey," Adela said to Peter, still sounding quite American. They walked down the hall until they found the door with a beautiful gold plaque with an engraved 903. Adela opened the door with ease. Their mouths caressed the floor as they beheld their new abode.

Glass, marble, spiral staircases, art pieces, and a pool seen through the impeccable glass windows. "Mother," Peter called as he placed the bags in the condo and closed the front door, all without ceasing to gawk, "how are we able to afford such an abode?"

"Ten years of saving," Adela replied as she ogled the place with a proud grin.

Peter and Adela toured the condo. The abode was decked with a high ceiling, a beautiful living room, and an electric fireplace. They walked up the two wooden steps into the kitchen paved with marble, glossy and opaque. The kitchen had a modern touch of glass architecture that acted as a translucent wall to separate the kitchen from the living room.

They went through every room. The guest room and bathroom downstairs. The grand dining room with a similar mesmerizing glass barricade as the kitchen. They looked out through the series of glass windows that gave them the illusion of being outside. They opened the glass door and stepped out onto the pool area, decked with a tall decorative railing. After moments of admiring the designs and paintings in and around the pool, they went back inside and unhurriedly journeyed up the elegant glass spiral staircase. They treasured every step and made sure their eyes feasted on all the possible pictorial banquets at their disposal. They slowly journeyed to the second floor of their condo, and their rubberneck staring reached a whole new altitude. Everything in the condo reeked of glamor and a life they had never known. Peter took in a deep breath and inhaled posh and exhaled admiration. He had never before occupied such a grand dwelling place. The only place he could think of that was of the same caliber as the condo was the grand home he had been to those many years ago. The home with the radiant field of pink flowers that was branded into his memory forever. His personal place of tarnish.

Together, they examined the three rooms upstairs. Each room bigger than the last. The bathrooms looked more like little playing fields.

"Choose your room, honey," Adela said as she gently nudged Peter with a smile. He couldn't help but smile back at her. The fascination had blinded his bitter heart. He looked in all three rooms a second time. He chose the middle room. The room had a beautiful view of the city from its tall windows.

"I'm going to run out and grab toiletries. Would you unpack our belongings, please, Peter?" Adela requested as she journeyed downstairs.

"Sure," Peter said as he followed behind her.

Adela grabbed her purse from the sofa and headed for the door. She placed her hand meaningfully on the doorknob. She lingered in that position for a moment, then turned around to face her son.

She placed her hand gently on her teenage son's face in the same gentle manner that one would caress the face of an infant.

"Peter, I love you," she said. "All of this," she gestured at the condo.

"Everything I've put you through," she reached for his face once again. "Just know that it was for you to enjoy this kind of life. A life of luxury. You deserve it, my son. I love you. This is your home now."

Peter stared into the comforting green eyes of his mother. She was his one and only friend. "I love you too," he replied genuinely.

She smiled and went through the door. Peter picked up the bags and brought them upstairs. He unpacked all of his mother's things first, and then he unpacked all of his belongings.

He sat on his bed and gazed at the New York skyline. He watched as invisible hands mixed yellow and orange, with dabs of pink intertwined, in the great art piece known as the sky.

As the sun made its slow descent out of visual range, Peter thought of England. He thought of Liverpool. He thought of Elizabeth. He thought of her returning to school the following term and finding him absent indefinitely. He thought of the begging he did as a child. His mind ran to the period of phone scheming. He pondered upon the fabricated terminal illness. He thought about how he still had the performance garb upon the bald skin of his head. He peeled off his wig as his thoughts drifted to the city. The grand condominium. The beautiful skyline. As the sun's descent made its grand finale, Peter decided to let go of his past life with its hardships and beauties. He let it vanish with the sun.

"This is home now," he said as American as he knew how.

****

"What a great leap that had to be taken for a lie, Grandpa," Perri states.

"Well, my son, that's what lies do. They bury and entangle. The deeper and more complex the lie, the further one has to go to get out of the grasps of it," Farook adds.

"But does a person truly get out of the grasp of it?" Halia questions.

"The only escape is to tell the truth. Truth is emancipation," Farook states.

"Grandpa, have you ever been to the States?" Olathe inquires of her grandfather.

"Only once," Farook answers meticulously.

"Did you enjoy yourself, Grandpa?" Olathe questions with bright eyes that gleam as she looks up at her grandfather.

"Yes, I did," Farook answers. He is glad that they are not asking where in the States he sojourned. "I learned a lot on my visit," Farook scrupulously adds so as not to reveal the length of his stay.

"Adela had quite a bounty saved in order to afford such a home, Grandpa," Perri states, to which Farook nods.

"Quite a bounty," Halia reiterates. "I know for sure that it is extremely expensive to live in New York City."

"It is," Olathe states matter-of-factly. Farook, Perri, and Halia laugh.

"Have you been there, Oly?" Perri questions with amusement in his eyes.

"No, but the way Grandpa describes it, it's easy to assume that it must be a place for affluent residents," Olathe retorts with animation.

"Wonderful word usage, Oly," Halia states as she smiles at her sister.

"Thank you, Halia," Olathe says through brilliant beaming.

"So, Grandpa, what is the city life like for them?" Halia inquires.

****

Adela sat squeamishly in one of the narrow seats that lined the accounting firm's lobby. She looked the part for her interview in her freshly ironed dress suit. She had gotten a chance the day prior to properly dye her hair the blonde hue needed for her new identification. No more wigs. She looked around the lobby, twiddled her thumbs, fixed her stray blonde lock, and then repeated the process.

"Abigail Phetterson, they are ready for you now," she heard the receptionist say. It took her a moment to respond to her alias. She had had Peter calling her Abigail so she could get accustomed to the pseudonym, but it hadn't quite yet registered. There was a delay to her response, but not long enough to cause any suspicion, Adela reasoned within herself.

Adela got up from her seat and walked down the long and unassuming hallway.

"It's the second door on the right, Mrs. Phetterson," the receptionist called after her. She nodded and entered the room. She suddenly found herself in the presence of three suits accompanied by three uppity-looking men. She sat in the seat across from them, twiddled her thumbs, fixed her stray blonde lock, and sat up confidently. She was ready to answer whatever questions they threw at her.

****

"How was the interview, Mum?" Peter asked as he ate cereal in the kitchen.

"I believe it went well," Adela said in her neo-western dialect. "Peter, you must start speaking in the American tongue. Don't call me mum. Call me mom."

Peter stared at her for a moment, then said, "Alright. How was the interview...Mom?" Peter struggled to project.

"That's better. But instead of alright, say okay."

"Okay. How was the interview, Mom?" Peter said as red, white, and blue as he could utter.

"It went well. They asked me a platoon of questions about my experience in the field, education history, and a few other things. They said they would get back to me soon," Adela said as she relieved herself of her heels.

"That sounds good, Mom." Peter decided not to inquire about his mother's forged documentation that gave her entrance to the interview.

"Are you looking forward to school, honey?" Adela questioned as she sat at the table with her son.

"To be honest, I'm frightened. Things just seem so different here. So fast-paced. I feel like I won't gain acceptance," Peter responded into his cereal.

Adela lifted her son's head. The action reminded her of the time he was six years old in the field of pink tulips. "You are going to be alright. You are an excellent young man. You'll make friends with ease."

Peter gave his mother a halfhearted smile. Her words provided him little reassurance. Deep down inside, he knew her words were unsound.

****

The summer went by like a brisk breeze. Adela had gotten a call back two weeks after the interview, and she was given a full-time accounting position at the firm. Adela's new position kept her extremely busy and away from her son most days of the week. Peter spent his solitary summer days wandering the New York streets. He watched street performers. He went to art shows. He spent an apt amount of time in the public library. He tried his best to keep himself occupied. As the time neared for Peter to begin high school, anxiety bit at his mind like a treacherous and worrisome reptile. In the nights preluding his first day of school, sleep departed from him, and anxiety was soon accompanied by insomnia.

Peter lay in his grand bed, looking out upon the darkened New York skyline. Under his draping comforter, he searched the depths of his being for an answer to the sudden dual companionship of anxiety and insomnia. After the exploration, he came to the conclusion that he was afraid. He was afraid of having to act again. He was afraid of accidentally introducing himself as Peter and not James. His mind was being tormented by the memories of sporadic physical abuse by his sole protector. He was afraid of his mother.

The revelation made him jump out of bed a few hours before he was to leave for school. He hadn't slept at all. He journeyed downstairs for a drink of water. He was afraid of his mother.

After he finished his drink, he went back upstairs and tried again the fall into the sweet arms of slumber. He did fall, only to be awakened two hours later by his mother. She had his uniform prepared. He wearily went through the morning motions, extremely fatigued. He ate, bathed, brushed his teeth, got dressed in his freshly starched pants, placed his hefty backpack on his tired back, said goodbye to his mother, and then ventured down the hall to the elevator.

His walk to school was short. He and his mother had visited the school twice prior. He had headphones on, listening to a dialect coach and trying his best to mimic. He didn't seem crazed because he just appeared to be mouthing along to a good song. He went over his name, address, and forged backstory in his mind. Instead of worrying about making friends, he was worried about remembering his name. Contrary to the past, Adela had actually gone over a highly detailed backstory with Peter about almost all the false details of his fictitious American life.

He reached the school and walked circumspectly up the polished steps. He went straight to the front office. He received a student aid escort and a key to his new locker. After he successfully opened his locker, the student aid bided him farewell and left him with his class schedule. He revised his class schedule repeatedly as he placed some of the contents of his burdensome backpack into his assigned locker. He looked around at the hallway full of students. He observed that there wasn't much diversity at the school, just a sea of unassuming faces.

He saw her hair first, and then he saw the rest of her. She stared back at him, then began to walk over until she stood only half an arm's length away. Peter had never seen someone with such strikingly red hair in all of his days.

"If you keep staring like that, you're going to bore a hole right through me," the girl said as she stretched out her hand for a handshake. "I'm Marie. And yes, this is my real hair color."

Peter smiled at her wit. "I'm James. James Phetterson."

"Are you new here?" Marie inquired.

"I'm new to the school, but not the area. I was a homeschooler," Peter responded.

"Homeschool," Marie repeated as she shook her head. "You must be a strong person because I would have died multiple deaths if I had to spend all day gaping into my parents' pale faces."

Peter smiled at her, and she returned the smile. She shifted her attention to Peter's hair. "Dude, what's with your haircut? It looks like someone tried to cut your hair with a chainsaw."

Peter touched his freshly dyed natural hair. "I wanted to try something new."

"Well, it didn't work, but don't worry, I'll help you with your appearance."

Peter stared at her.

"Don't worry, I won't dye your hair red," Marie said to reassure. Peter laughed as Marie snatched his class schedule from his hands. She went into her backpack and got hers.

"We have one class together. That's cool. Do you know where all your classes are?" Marie asked.

"No idea," Peter coolly responded.

"Well, not to worry. We have a few minutes before the first bell, so

I'll show you around." She began to walk swiftly away, and Peter haggardly followed suit. Within ten minutes, she had dragged him past the doors of all his classes for the semester. "See you in fifth period, blonde Chainsaw," Marie said as the first-period bell rang tenaciously.

Peter waved goodbye to her. He liked his new nickname. He reasoned that he had just made a friend.

He walked to his first class and sat in the mid-section of the classroom. He bypassed the awkward new student introduction because it was the beginning of a new school year, and everyone in the class was a freshman, so everyone was, in a sense, new.

The classes went by slowly and cyclically to Peter as he introduced himself time and time again as James Phetterson, an all-American boy. It was a relief to him when the lunch bell rang. He followed the flow of students to the cafeteria. He waited in line to receive his mush of a meal, then found a seat in an isolated corner of the cafeteria, almost under a towering set of belchers.

"Chainsaw, there you are!" he heard the recently familiar voice beckon. He turned to see Marie and her unusually red mane approaching him.

"I'm telling you, only my house has food worse than this," she said as she took a seat across from Peter. Peter watched as she melodramatically waved the spoon across her face in scorn and pretended as if she was going to hurl. Peter smiled as she hesitantly ate a spoonful of cafeteria mush and feigned nausea once again. He came to the conclusion that he really liked having her around. He had met her only a few hours prior to them sitting across from one another in the cafeteria, but she had made him smile and laugh more than he ever remembered doing. He savored having the fallow ground of his soul plowed by joy and his face fertilized with a smile.

"How's your day going?" Peter asked his friend.

"Good, the same ole same ole. To be frank, I think school should stop at eighth grade," Marie said as she raked through her food with her plastic fork. "I deem high school to be completely unnecessary."

"Why is that?" Peter asked.

"Because high school is a repeat of middle school, except with more exams. High school is a continuation of studies that we won't ever really use as adults," Marie stated matter-of-factly. Peter just stared at her. She was truly an interesting character. She was so outspoken and loud. She was the complete antithesis of Elizabeth. He missed Elizabeth.

"Are you okay?" Marie asked, observing the sudden change in Peter's facial expression. "I'm sorry if I offended you. I didn't know you were such a fan of high school," Marie slapped her forehead with her hand in realization. "I totally forgot you were a homeschooler, so this is like paradise for you. I have a big mouth. I'm so sorry. I would be happy to be here too if I were you."

Peter smiled at Marie, who returned the smile bashfully. "I wasn't at all offended by your comment. I just recollected something as you spoke," Peter responded.

"Okay," Marie said as she tilted her head slightly to the left. "You speak sort of funny, you know that?" the comment caught Peter off guard, and he stared at her, wondering if she knew. *But how could she know?* he reasoned.

"But that's okay with me," Marie said through a mouthful of mush. "I can deal with your weird homeschool speech." Peter breathed a sigh of relief.

"I'm going to get a soda to wash down the dog food," Marie said as she rose from the table and headed for the soda machine. Peter shifted his attention back to his own mush and smiled. He felt a little hand gently touch his shoulder. He turned to see a petite blonde girl with large brown eyes staring at him with concern.

"Hey, I don't mean to be intrusive, but I just want to let you know that Marie is bad news. She's dangerous. She may not look like it or sound like it, but she is. She'll befriend you first. She'll make you feel like the most important person in her life. You'll get to the point of trusting her, and then she becomes extremely controlling," the girl said without even taking a breath. "I just wanted to warn you," she concluded, then left.

Peter stared into his mush as he processed what was just said to him. He raised his head and looked over where Marie was. She turned to look at him. It was like she sensed his stare. She smiled at him. He returned the smile. She was alright. She was a good person, he concluded.

****

The rest of the day went well for Peter as he enjoyed the company of Marie in his fifth-period class. The class commenced right after lunch. Marie distracted him with little paper notes throughout the entire class period, but he didn't mind. Each time her hand released a note upon his desk, he felt himself getting more and more jovial. In just a few hours, she was breaking down all of his walls. He loved having a friend or something close to a friendship.

The school day ended, and Marie was escorted into a luxurious vehicle by a well-suited man. Peter walked back to the condo with zest in his footsteps. He concluded that he had just had one of the best days of his life.

He smiled, going into the building. He grinned at the doormen. He whistled as he went into the elevator. He beamed as he pressed the fancy button for the ninth floor. The door opened, and he walked down the hallway with ease. He smiled as he opened the door.

Peter's smile fell and morphed itself into a frown. His cultivated face had receded back to its fallow state. Peter stared at them. His mother and a grandiose man. The man's arm draped casually around his mother's shoulder.

"Livingston, this is my son James," Adela introduced. Adela sensed the awkward turn the atmosphere had made. "James, this is my friend

Livingston." Peter gaped at the man as he unlatched his hold around Adela's shoulder and stood up to greet Peter. Peter looked up at the man, who was at least six feet and five inches tall.

"Hello James, it's great to finally meet you. Your mom speaks highly of you," the man Livingston said as he shook the life out of Peter's hand. Peter looked over at his mother, who was beaming at the stranger ever so lovingly. They had only been in New York for three months. Peter thought it strange that his mother would be looking at anyone in that fashion.

"Well, James, I have to run. I hope to take you and your mother out for dinner this weekend. On me." Livingston beamed at Peter, and Peter continued to look stoically at him. Livingston turned and kissed Adela on the cheek before passing the silent and indifferent Peter. The tall man exited the condo.

A minute after the door closed, Adela turned to face her son. "Well, that wasn't very nice, Peter," she admonished. "The man shook your hand and properly greeted you, and you just stared at him with complete indifference."

"Who is he?" Peter asked, without truly addressing his mother's statement.

"He's a business associate, Peter," Adela answered, doing her best to dodge her son's questioning glare.

"You've been working at the firm for two months now. How is it that you have become so close with a business associate already?" Peter interrogated.

"Well, I've known him for a little longer than two months," Adela gingerly answered.

Peter narrowed his eyes. "How long have you known him, Mum?"

"Two years, Peter."

"Two years," Peter repeated, flabbergasted. He evaluated the situation. "How can that be?"

"He was a vital instrument in our move, Peter. He helped us get the passports and this condo." Peter took a minute to process the information he was receiving. In just a moment, he came to the realization that someone else was in on their secret.

"How much does he know?" Peter slowly asked, eyes permanently narrowed.

"A lot. I left out a few details, of course." Peter stared vacantly at his mother. "Peter, don't eyeball me like that. He's trustworthy. You know I wouldn't let him into our lives if I didn't know that for sure." Peter placed his backpack on the living room floor and journeyed to the kitchen to scavenge for something to fill his barren stomach. His mother was truly an anomaly, he reasoned. She was the enigma he could not thoroughly decipher. How is it, he thought, that she could have had someone in on their lives and excursions without making him aware of it. Adela eventually joined Peter in the kitchen.

"I love you, Peter. Always remember that everything I do is for you," Adela said, trying her best to console her son. Peter looked into those eyes that for so long had reminded him of a luxurious field. He continued to look into her eyes. To him, it seemed like the field had overgrown grass and weeds that had begun to choke the life out of the pure garden.

****

"Skip class with me," Marie prompted.

Peter looked at his friend of three days. "Where would we go?" he questioned.

"Wherever we want to go. I can call my driver to come and get us."

Peter debated the offer. A part of him wanted to go, but another part knew that it was a bad idea. He stared into his third-day cafeteria mush and tried to think of a response to give to his friend.

"How about we hang out after school instead?" Peter asked, trying to offer a more compromising alternative.

Marie smiled, "Well, it's not as fun, but it will do." Peter returned the smile. They finished lunch and journeyed to their fifth-period class. Again, like the preceding two days, Peter was distracted by notes from his friend throughout the class period.

The rest of the school day went by like a blur as Peter prepared himself for his first after-school powwow as James Phetterson.

"Get in the car, Chainsaw," Marie insisted from the backseat of the Bentley Continental flying spur. The car was black and sleek. Peter took a moment to look around at the city. He turned his head to the east as he felt little eyes trying to pry him open. He saw her. The girl from the cafeteria who warned him to stay away from Marie. She stared at him while standing under an oak tree. A few people surrounded her in conversation. She shook her head at Peter in disapproval. Peter shifted his attention back to the city. Peter then looked at Marie's driver, who seemed to be getting a little agitated. Peter placed his attention back on Marie, who was still beckoning for him to get inside the vehicle.

He jumped in. The driver closed the door, then circled around the vehicle to return to his designated seat. Peter watched as Marie wined down the expensive windows and theatrically breathed in. He noticed that everything she did and said was dramatic. *She was quite the character*, he said within himself.

"Ah, don't you just love New York, James?" Marie said, her eyes closed and head tilted back upon the car seat.

"It is quite delightful," Peter responded.

Marie turned and gave Peter a strange look, her red mane making an outlandish nimbus around her head. "There you go again with your foreign speech. You homeschoolers have weird lingo. This is probably the first excursion of your life, you weirdo." Peter felt concurrently esteemed and insulted. He had to work on speaking with the vernacular of the youth of his new reality.

They mingled for half an hour as Peter took in the New York décor. He loved the diversity that New York had to offer. In half an hour alone, he had seen so many breathtaking places that were so different but so extraordinary in their own unique way. The pages of New York took on another chapter as the houses in Peter's vision fattened. He stared, in awe, at grand home after grand home for fifteen minutes.

"Your first time in these parts?" Marie asked as she watched Peter gawk.

"Yes," Peter said as he tried to swallow the awe.

"What does your mom do?" Marie asked.

"She's an accountant," Peter responded.

"Cool, I think my mom is too. Either that or a vet. I get the two confused sometimes." Peter laughed at her organic comedy. Peter's laughing stopped abruptly as the driver halted in front of two elegant gates that carried a look of shimmering brass. The gates opened after a few short moments. Peter ogled at the beautiful canopy of trees that seemed to span for eternity alongside the elegant driveway.

Marie placed her hand below Peter's chin, then gently pushed up to close his mouth. "You really don't get out much, do you, Chainsaw?"

Peter tried to find words as the grand abode came into view. "I've only been to one place in my life that looked akin to this," Peter confessed. The driver drove them all the way up to the front door, passing the large fountain that acted as a centerpiece for the vast yard.

"Thanks again, Henry," Marie said to the driver as she and Peter exited the vehicle.

"My pleasure, Ms. Kensington," Peter heard the driver say before Marie slammed the car door shut. They walked the short steps to the front door. Marie opened the door, and Peter's mouth caressed the floor.

Everything in the grand home sparkled.

"Marie, what kind of work does your family do?" Peter inquired.

"My dad owns all of the world's soda companies or something along those lines. We are rich in the leading cause of diabetes. We're practically saints," Marie said sarcastically. Peter chuckled. "Good ole one percent," Marie continued. "Tax evasions and all."

"It seems as if you despise your wealth," Peter conversed as he feasted his eyes upon polished things.

"It seems as if you despise your wealth," Marie jeered. "Who are you? Shakespeare?" Marie laughed. "You are a funny and strange dude, my friend, you know that?" Marie asked, to which Peter laughed. "But no, it's not that I hate being rich. It has its perks," Marie said with a half-smile. Only one corner of her mouth lifted in assurance of her words.

"I've come to the conclusion that once someone attains what they deem to be success, they lose themselves. My parents have done just that. My mom with her accounting or pet care…but my dad especially. I never see him," Marie's voice faltered a little. "I've basically raised myself, James. With the exception of my nannies, but nannies don't count because they are paid to pretend to care about you."

Peter broke his visual feast to look at his friend, whose pain and heartache could clearly be seen on her face. He walked over to her and hugged her. At first, she was startled, but then she followed through with the embrace. As they separated from the hug, Peter witnessed as the spring from his friend's eyes exploded, and tears fell upon her face. At that moment, Peter realized that everyone has things they are going through. Peter, for so long, had felt isolated on the isle of burden-bearing. He grasped, at that moment, that everyone went through the worrisome task of bearing burdens. He reckoned that the weight of each person's burden was not dependent upon their situation but rather upon the perspective in which they chose to see their predicament.

"I'm sorry for being such a buzzkill," Marie said as she wiped her tears. "Let's do something fun."

"May I call my mother first?" Peter asked. "Just to let her know where I am and that I'm okay."

"Yes, you may," Marie said in her best rendition of Peter's double-dialectic voice. Peter smiled as she pointed him to the nearest landline.

"Mom, it's me. Sorry to bother you at work. I just wanted to let you know that I'm at a friend's house in Cold Spring Hills," Peter said into the phone.

"Do you want to watch a movie?" Marie mouthed, to which Peter nodded.

"Okay, James, but I want to see you back home by nine," his mother hurriedly replied. They said their goodbyes, and Peter hung up the phone.

Marie escorted him upstairs and had him wait by the east stairs while she went into her room to change into casual clothes. "You can come now," Marie said, to which Peter followed the voice. Peter found himself standing in the doorway of a bedroom the size of a meek house.

"This is where we'll be watching the film?" Peter inquired.

"James, I'm liberal, but not that liberal," Marie retorted as she reached for a container from underneath her bed. The size of the bed looked like that of two kings, a queen, and a prince. "No, we are going to watch the movie in the theater." Peter decided not to comment on the fact that they had a movie theater in their home. He reasoned that he had uttered enough praise for the day. He followed the red mane around corners, past numerous doors and art pieces, and finally through two large beige doors. They entered the grand home theater. Peter thought his vision must have been deceiving him. He felt he might overdose on elegance.

Peter cumbersomely took a seat in one of the luxuriously soft theater chairs. Marie went into a room in the theater's northwest wing. Suddenly, the wall adjacent to him came alive, and pictures ran across the screen. The lights were suddenly dimmed, and the only illumination came from the twinkling lights on the ceiling that gave the illusion of a radiant night sky sprinkled with glistening stars. Peter never dreamed of being in such an elegant place.

Marie immerged from the room and took her seat next to Peter. She opened her tin. Peter didn't think much of it until he heard the flicker of the lighter. The smell pouched him like a heavyweight. He had never smelled anything so potent. He turned his attention back to the screen. They sat in silence for a little while.

"Want a draw?" he heard her ask. He turned and looked at her. She looked different. She was clothed in a false elation.

"No, thanks," Peter responded quickly. He yielded his attention back to the movie.

After a few moments, Marie leaned in closer to Peter and whiffed the joint across his face. The potent odor tickled his nasal passages. "James, it's just an herb," Marie tempted.

"I don't use drugs," Peter responded.

She continued to swing the joint across Peter's face.

"James, stop being a baby. You're going to have to man up and experience life at some point," Marie pestered as she continued to swing the joint in front of her friend's face. "James, just…"

Peter sternly grabbed her arm. "I said I don't use drugs, Marie. Stop pestering me." Marie stared at him for a moment. Her facial expression changed from surprise to fright, then finally to laughter as Peter let go of his grip on her arm.

"Okay, James, whatever you say, but just know I have a vast supply just in case you want to light up with me one day." Peter stared at her as she started to engage in inappropriate laughter. The rest of the movie was an eerie and uncomfortable experience for Peter as Marie used one joint to light the other. She wasn't lying about just how vast her supply really was, he thought.

Marie and Peter said their awkward goodbyes. Peter got into the vehicle and was driven home by Henry. The New York appeal, with its hues and lights, was far less alluring to Peter as he journeyed home. His psyche painted pictorials of Marie. Stroke stroke, of her eerie laughter. Stroke stroke, hues of smoke. Pictorials on repeat. Pictorials irreversible. He reflected on his discomfort in that situation. The complexity and deception of drugs frightened him to the utmost degree. His mind fluttered to his mother. He reflected on how drugs allowed his mother to harm him and not even remember a tittle of the moment the succeeding day.

"We have reached your abode, Mr. Phetterson," Henry said, snapping Peter out of his cluttered trance. Peter journeyed out of the playfield of his mind and looked up at the tall condominium. He thanked Henry and exited the vehicle. As Henry sped off and Peter entered the building, his thoughts again wandered to Marie. As he keyed open the door to the condo, his ears were greeted with conversation. Peter walked up the short stairs into the dining room area to behold his mother and Livingston causally conversing.

"Hi, James, how was your time with your friend?" Adela asked her son.

"It was good," Peter fibbed.

"Good evening, James," Livingston greeted.

"Good evening," Peter said hesitantly. It was the first acknowledgment Peter had ever given Livingston.

"I want to bring you and your mother out for dinner this Saturday, if that's alright with you?" Livingston questioningly proposed.

"Sure," Peter responded quickly. "Please excuse me," Peter said, then journeyed to the kitchen to grab a snack. Peter took his food upstairs to his room to battle with concentrating on homework.

****

An awkward aura sat in the midst of Peter and Marie for the next few days. They didn't talk about the events that took place in the movie theater, but instead, they entertained lighthearted chatter that contained little depth. In the span of a breath, the first week of school in America was finished for Peter, and the weekend had come. He turned down the request for company by Marie because he had promised his mother to accompany her and Livingston to dinner.

Peter stood mesmerized as he gazed at the Saturday evening sky. He took in the mixture of colors being rendered for his visual gratification. His trance was broken as he heard the ring of the doorbell. He opened the door to reveal Livingston.

"James, son, you're looking sharp," Livingston complimented. Peter noted that that was the first time a man had called him son. He liked the ring to it. He liked how easy it was for Livingston to say it. In the depths of his being, he wanted him to say it again.

"Thank you," Peter responded. He wanted to call him dad. He had the urge to act for the first time in his life. It was a fictitious scene that he wanted so desperately to be reality.

"So, where's your mom?" Livingston questioned as he stepped into the condo.

"She's still getting ready," Peter replied.

"Women, it seems like we are constantly waiting for them, but it's worth the wait," Livingston said with a smile, to which Peter returned. Livingston had called Peter son; at that point, Peter would have smiled at anything. Livingston took a seat on the living room sofa. He was so grand that his legs seemed to span for miles beyond the bounds of the settee.

"How old are you, James?" Livingston inquired.

"Fifteen," Peter replied.

"Alright, so that would make you about high school age now, correct?"

"Yes," Peter responded.

"You liking high school?"

"It's alright."

"You made any friends?"

"Just one. Her name is Marie."

Livingston smiled at Peter. "Making friends with the girls first. Are you sure you're not my kid?" Peter smiled at the comment that serenaded his ears.

Livingston took out a flask from his jacket, opened it, and took a swing. He wiped his mouth off with his expensive-looking sleeve, then fixed his flawlessly cropped brown mane. He looked at Peter, then held the flask out to him. "You want some, son?" Peter's ears chimed at the sound of the s-word. Twice in one night, he had been called "son" by a man.

"What is it?" Peter inquired.

"Liquor," Livingston responded.

"I'm fifteen," stammered out of Peter's mouth as he looked at Livingston in disbelief.

"Son, I had my first drink when I was twelve years old. It's the first step to becoming a man. You must learn how to hold your liquor." That sounded like a lie to Peter, but he was in the presence of a man who was calling him son. He reached out and took the flask. As the flagon approached his lips, he got a whiff of the potent smell. He placed it gingerly on his lips, paused for a moment to consider the decision he was about to make, then took a quick gulp of the foreign juice. His throat burned. He felt like he had just swigged gasoline. He looked at Livingston, whose eyes were being entertained by laughter.

"I'm proud of you, son," Livingston said. That was the fourth time that night that Livingston had called him son, Peter noted. Peter was infatuated with the sound.

CHAPTER 5

The children sit, wholly mesmerized by the tale. Farook and the children nibble on chocolate chip cookies and sip on skim milk. They are all deep in thought, soaking in the arresting tale.

Olathe turns to her grandfather, shifts her position on the soft Tabriz carpet, and glides her tongue across her front teeth as to restore her white pearls.

She breaks the thunderous silence. "Grandpa, are you really telling us that an adult has given a teenager alcohol to consume?" Olathe inquires with her hand over her heart in surprise.

Farook chews and swallows his chocolate-infested baked treat. "Yes, my dear, that is exactly the case."

"It seems like the majority of the people in Peter's life are drug users, Grandpa," Perri interjects in between gulps of his skimmed milk.

"Practically all of them are," Halia adds.

Olathe looks at her grandfather with excessively curious eyes. "Have you ever used any sort of drugs, Grandpa?" Olathe inquires with a sly and curious expression.

Farook tries to appear as deep in thought as possible. He tries his best to look as if he has to search the deep ocean of his memories to find the response when he knows it lies flaunt on the shore of his mind. Farook places his right hand meticulously on his chin as one in thought.

"Yes, yes, I have. It was a very long time ago. My short drug usage taught me that not everything in life is expedient."

Perri projects confusion upon his face. "What do you mean by that, Grandpa?" he inquires.

Farook shifts his position on his lazy boy recliner. He commences, "Our society reasons that young people have to experience things in order to make the decision as to whether those things are good or bad. I think that is foolishness. You guys don't have to use drugs to know that it is dangerous. You can just trust the word of an individual who has been through it. I want to tell you three that you do not have to learn from your own mistakes; learn from mine. It's much easier for you that way."

The three children nod at their grandfather's profound statement in sync.

"Thanks for telling us that, Grandpa. I've never seen life from that perspective before. It is extremely enlightening," Halia commends.

"Agreed," Perri follows.

Olathe forms an x with her arms and looks her grandfather square in the face. With avid animation, she proclaims, "As of this day, I know for sure that drugs are not for me, and I have never even used drugs," little Olathe says matter-of-factly.

Farook, Perri, and Halia shake the house with laughter. Halia clutches her side as the pain that joy brings exercises her diaphragm. Eventually, the laughter ceases, and Halia says, "Olathe, as of this day, I know for sure that you are called to be a comedian and actress, and I've never even seen you on the big screen."

"Thanks, sis," Olathe says in between giggles.

"What happens next, Grandpa?" Perri inquires from the edge of the Tabriz carpet.

Sheneen Monique Soares

****

Livingston charmed Peter and Adela with ease. Fancy dinners, football games, and spontaneous gifts. Peter began to spend most of his free time with Livingston. They played sports, watched sports, and secretly drank more and more liquor.

On one of their many formal dinner excursions, Peter noticed a large bruise on his mother's arm that was peeking out from under her sleeve. When Livingston excused himself from the table, Peter took the opportunity to question his mother about the bruise. She claimed that she had fallen at work. As the weeks progressed, Peter observed more and more bruises on his mother's skin. Peter asked about every new bruise he saw. Adela kept making up new elucidations as to how she received the bruises.

Coming home from school one day, Peter heard Livingston yelling profanities upstairs. Peter quietly closed the door behind him. He smoothly walked up the stairs, Livingston's voice amplifying with every step. Peter reached the top of the stairs, and he was sure his eyes deceived him. Peter beheld a drunken Livingston swaying with an invisible wind as his hand tried to keep its grasp on an uninhabited liquor bottle. Peter felt frozen in space. Frozen in time. As the violent drunken wind rocked Livingston, Peter beheld his mother weeping on her knees, blood running from her forehead. The love Peter had for his mother began to thaw his frozen posture.

It happened quickly. Too quickly. Peter watched with terror as Livingston raised the glass bottle above his head. Peter heard the crash. He heard his mother's scream. Peter watched as a rivulet of blood flowed down his mother's face. Peter grabbed Livingston and pushed him forcefully against the wall. Livingston laughed vulgarly at Peter. Peter reached for his mother, but before he got the chance, he was tackled to the ground. Peter swayed to and fro as Livingston's fist repeatedly collided with his face. Through blurred vision, Peter beheld his mother as she dropped her expensive vase upon Livingston's head. Livingston fell next to Peter. Adela cradled her son as he went in and out of consciousness.

Peter woke up in the hospital. He became fanatic as he recalled the events that had so recently taken place. He called loudly for his mother. The doctors examined him and then allowed him to join his mother in her hospital room. Peter walked into the hospital room to behold a battered version of his mother. She had bruises on almost every area of her skin. Adela's bloated eyes slowly opened. She saw her son and tried to turn her head comfortably in her neck brace. A tear fell from her mangled face.

"Peter, I'm so sorry. I am so sorry. I keep putting you through things like this. I'm so sorry," Adela said slowly as she wept uncomfortably.

Peter held Adela's hand. "Mom, it's not your fault," he whispered.

Adela wept bitterly. She felt as if she had failed as a mother. She felt like a failed person. She pressed the morphine button and allowed the drugs to numb the physical pain. She wished the hospital carried morphine for heartaches. She wanted to run away from herself. She thought that she was so sure about her ability to discern the character of others, but she had failed. She had placed her only child in danger.

The doctor opened the door and announced that they both would be released that night. After hours of sitting in the hospital room with Peter sleeping on and off and Adela pumping morphine into her weak body, they were allowed to leave. Peter rolled Adela out in a wheelchair. They were picked up by a taxi.

When they reached home, Peter let his mother rest while he cleaned up the broken glass in the upstairs hallway. Peter's mind was congested. He felt as if he had been sadistically pushed into a nightmare that almost cost him his life.

He went to bed exceedingly depressed. He woke up tremendously despondent and indifferent towards life and living. He went through the motions of getting dressed for school. He ate. He checked on his mother. At school, a few people asked him about his bruises. Marie pestered him, but he didn't feel like telling her about the events that had transpired. Marie knew there was something exceedingly wrong. An atmosphere of dejection lingered between them at lunch, in between classes, and in fifth period. Marie noticed that Peter no longer responded to her notes in fifth period. He just appeared to be haunted under a stormy cloud. Marie didn't know what to do to get him out from under it. She tried everything, but nothing seemed to be working as she watched her friend travel deeper and deeper into depression and despondency.

Peter wanted to talk to Marie. He wanted to confide in her, but he didn't know who to trust anymore. Everyone in his life had proven themselves to be monsters in angel veneers, and that scared him to the utmost degree.

For two weeks, Peter kept quiet at school. At home, he helped his mother in whatever way he could as she healed. Adela's bruised skin was coming back to. In a week, she was able to remove the bulky neck brace and move her neck quite comfortably on her own.

"Are you going to press charges?" Peter asked one day after school as he and his mother sat at the dinner table.

Adela looked deep into her plate as if searching for the answer to her son's query amidst the chicken and broccoli.

"I can't," Adela answered almost inaudibly into her food.

Anger slithered into Peter's heart, and rage took hold of the reins of his thoughts. *Why was she behaving like a fool?* he questioned within. *Why did she lie about the bruises? Why did she lie to me?*

"Peter," Adela continued as she watched her son's temper rise. "I fabricated everything. If I go back and retract my statement, it wouldn't look good in court. Plus, we have to lay low here. You know our predicament."

Peter turned to his mother with his face bright red like a ripe tomato. "So, you're telling me that a man can just come into our lives and beat on us like punching bags because we are liars! I hate this, Mum! I'm tired of you pulling me into these insipid situations! You are supposed to protect me! You are supposed to love me! But instead, you treat me like your own personal experiment! I'm not an experiment!"

"Peter, calm down," Adela said through tears.

"Don't tell me what to do!" Peter yelled. He released his fork, and it went flying at the glass door. He looked at his mother, who jumped in surprise when the fork collided with the glass. In his rage, he wanted to slap her. Tears formed in his eyes as he repented from thinking along those lines. *What is happening to me?* he thought.

He quickly dashed up the stairs. He went into his room and wept bitterly. He flooded the pillows with his tears. He didn't understand his emotions. He wanted to help his mother. He wanted her to get a fair trial for what had been done to her. He wanted Livingston imprisoned. He wanted all these things and more, but he soon came to the realization that he and his mother were helpless due to their criminal lifestyle and their avid avoidance of the justice system. His thoughts became cumbersome. He felt numb.

Peter searched the New York skyline. He was looking for a ray of encouragement. He remembered that he had two bottles of vodka underneath his bed. He debated drinking it. Liquor was the infamous character in their recent horrid days. The liquor seemed to call him. He recalled how carefree it made him feel. He recalled the first drink on the sofa those months ago. He reminisced upon the adult parties Livingston had taken him to.

He thought about how helpless he and his mother were because they could not report the crime for fear of the justice system. Fear of being caught. Fear of their lies finally apprehending them.

What do I have to lose? he reasoned within himself. He reached underneath his bed and felt for the familiar glass bottle. He pulled out the long glass decanter, unscrewed the cap, and then began to chug the contents. His throat burned as he downed the liquor. It wasn't wise to drink so fast, but he didn't care. His head began to throb, but he didn't care. His room began to spin, but he found false freedom in it.

He stared at the bottle as he drank; he was hoping to find happiness at the bottom. He took the last gulp and rested the bottle next to him. He started to laugh inappropriately as the spirits whispered jokes. In a twinkling, he was unconscious.

He woke up late that night. He reached for the second bottle of vodka from underneath his bed. He downed half of it, looked at the New York sky as it spun, then downed the other half. In a twinkling, he was unconscious o'er.

He woke up to voices. He realized that he was lying in contents that once inhabited his stomach. He took a shower without the lights on in the bathroom. He took two pain pills for his migraine, as Livingston taught him, then got dressed for school.

As he picked up his backpack and walked down the stairs, he recognized the voice. Livingston. He ran down the stairs and started throwing wild punches at Livingston. One of the punches collided with Livingston's jaw. Livingston held Peter's arms as he thrashed erratically.

"James, I know you are upset, as you should be, but I just wanted to let you and your mother know that I wasn't in my right mind the other night. I'm incredibly sorry. I love you both, and you know I wouldn't do anything to hurt you sober-mindedly."

"Get out!" Peter yelled. Sprays of spittle accompanied Peter's words and landed on Livingston's jaw. Livingston let go of Peter, who looked like a madman with his haggard eyes and thrashing arms. Livingston peered at Adela with remorse-filled eyes. Peter could not decipher if the remorse was genuine or deceitful; too much liquor still remained in his system. Livingston eventually let himself out.

"How could you let him in the house?" Peter loudly questioned.

"Peter, calm down. He's truly sorry," Adela reasoned in vain.

Peter could not believe his ears. He paced around the room as the residual spirits in his bloodstream told him to. He couldn't believe what he had just heard come out of his mother's mouth. *Is she truly stu-*

pid? he questioned within himself. *Has she truthfully lost her mind?* he thought.

How could she choose this man over you? the spirits chimed in. Anger boiled within Peter. He reached for the nearest vase and threw it across the room, just a foot away from his mother. Adela looked at her son in astonishment. The look she gave him made him laugh incongruously.

"You think that Livingston is the only one that can throw things at you?" Peter jeered in between laughs.

"Peter, that's not you talking...."

"It is me talking," the spirits yelled through Peter in avid defense. "It took me almost sixteen years to finally come to the realization as to how stupid you really are." Adela stared at her unrecognizable son. What had she done? What had she created?

Peter snatched his backpack and headed out the door. He reached school a couple of minutes before the bell. He surveyed the hallway for the red mane. He found her, then casually leaned against her locker.

"Chainsaw, you look terrible today," Marie commented as she organized her books for the day's classes.

"I feel terrible," Peter casually responded.

As he spoke, Marie got a whiff of her friend's breath and abruptly stopped what she was doing. She quickly retrieved the books she needed, then swiftly closed her locker. She took a few steps toward Peter so that there was only a pint-sized gap left between them. Her lips curled up into a dubious smile.

"Chainsaw, have you been drinking?" Peter smiled in response. "Chainsaw, I knew you and I were going to be great friends. I knew you were fun," Marie beamed.

"Let's skip today at lunch. Let's go somewhere," Peter offered with a sly smile.

Marie laughed vivaciously. "You are speaking my language, Chainsaw. I'll call Henry right now." Peter watched as she speed-dialed her driver and changed the time arrangements for the day.

"So, what's the plan for today, boss?" Marie asked after completing her call.

"We can go to your house again and watch a movie."

"The new and improved Chainsaw," Marie said as she threw her arm around Peter's broad shoulders. "I much prefer this version of you."

****

Perri, Halia, and Olathe look up at their grandfather in disbelief. "What is happening to Peter?" Perri rhetorically questions.

Olathe places her delicate hands over her pretty oval face that sports a worrisome expression. "Is it ever going to get better for Peter?" she deafeningly whispers.

"This story is making me appreciate mum and dad all the much more," Halia utters.

"Agreed," Perri follows.

"I'm seriously going to write a speech for mum and dad regarding their excellence," Olathe says as she unmasks her face. "I'm going to thank them for not giving me drugs."

Farook, Halia, and Perri giggle at Olathe's abrasively sincere comment.

"This story is changing my life, Grandpa," Perri shares. "I know it is impossible, but I feel like I know Peter." Farook is taken aback by the comment. "At school, I see some of my peers acting out, and I hear of them engaging in illicit activities," Perri continues. "It's so easy to judge them and talk about their poor lifestyle choices with my friends, but I never consider why they may be acting out. Instead of constantly judging, I could reach out and be a catalyst of change in their life."

Perri looks at his grandfather for a response. Farook looks at his grandson, and then he looks at his granddaughters. He tries his best to render a casual face, but Perri's comment is rattling his heart to the paramount of degrees. *My life is positively impacting them*, he says within himself as tears fall from his heart.

"Grandpa, are you alright?" Perri asks after a few moments of silence goes by.

"I am extremely well, just here pondering upon your wonderful statement."

"Peter's life has a lot of ups and downs, but if he comes to, he can really make a powerful impact in the lives of many," Halia says to which Farook responds with a smile.

"So, what happens next for Peter?" Olathe questions with her hands resting elegantly under her chin.

****

Marie scanned the hallways like a detective. The coast was clear. Marie and Peter ran to the exit as if they were being chased by an angry mob. They didn't stop running until they were safely inside the vehicle. Once the door closed, Henry continued the dash on wheels. Marie and Peter laughed adrenaline-filled laughs as the city blurred in response to the speed of the vehicle. Peter relaxed into the leather seats. Feeling highly liberated, he propped his feet up, taking off his shoes and socks even.

"Do you have any liquor?" Peter heard himself ask as he felt the spirits escaping through his pores.

"Slow down, Chainsaw," Marie said animatedly. "Let me see what we have." She opened the mini-fridge and pulled out a bottle of rum and shot glasses. She poured a shot for herself and a shot for Peter. Peter drank the liquor and noticed that it hardly carried any effect on him.

"Another one," Peter demanded as Marie generously poured.

Peter had three more shots before settling into the leather seats once again. He was astonished that his body was still holding up after so much alcohol. He smelled like a bar, and he looked like a train wreck. The ride to Marie's home seemed shorter as Peter and Marie chatted nonsense.

After the car came to a stop, Marie staggered out of the vehicle and attempted to open the front door of her home. She drunkenly keys open the door after multiple sloppy attempts. The door flung open. Marie and Peter danced and sang around the house. They eventually made it to Marie's room. Marie changed and retrieved her infamous tin from beneath her bed. Peter watched as she dropped the tin and ran to the nearest bathroom to vomit up the poison her body rejected. Within a few minutes, she resurfaced, smiling from ear to ear. "We said we were going to watch a movie, right?" she asked.

"Right," Peter replied as he picked up her tin and lighter for her. They took the journey to the home theater. Peter sat more comfortably in the theater seats. Marie ventured into the northwest room of the theater to activate the screen. Images began to move.

Marie eventually immerged from the room. She gleamed at Peter as she approached him. Peter kept his eyes on the screen. It seemed so much more entertaining to him. The movie hadn't even begun. Peter was mesmerized. He felt as Marie took the tin and lighter out of his hands, but he didn't shift his attention from the screen. The previews were captivating to him in his illusive state. Peter smelt the smell he smelled all those months ago. He looked over at his friend. She smiled at him as the lit joint illuminated her face. She looked beautiful. He watched his arm as it reached over and took the spliff from between her lips. There was a war going on inside of him. His detest for drugs was fighting with the liquor in his system. They were fighting for his will.

After a few moments of staring at the joint, Peter took a draw and coughed. It wasn't what he expected as he searched for nirvana within the tightly coiled white paper containing green herbs. It took a little while, but feelings of elation chipped in. He and Marie laughed at the sad scenes. They danced on the chairs as the people in the movie broke out a catchy ballad. They ran around the theater. They danced in front of the large screen. Colors, pictures, movement. They eventually became fatigued and sat for the remainder of the movie. They smoked more of the contents from Marie's tin box.

"This movie is really long," Peter commented. He could hardly see Marie through the cloud of smoke that sat in the atmosphere between them.

"You know, you look like the main character," Marie stated.

"William?"

"Yup, you look like William." They laughed inappropriate and unwarranted laughs. "I'm going to call you William from now on," Marie said in between chuckles.

"I'm really hungry," Peter stated. Marie paused the movie, and they ventured to the kitchen. They ate chocolate mousse and laughed at the name of the food. They ate a pot full of spaghetti. They boiled eggs and ate those. They munched on potato chips. They placed their heads under the soda fountain and downed the carbonated drink. They then filled two glasses to the brim with liquor and returned to the theater.

"You're the best friend I've ever had," Peter incoherently uttered.

"Right back at you, William," Marie said with a smile as she lit another joint.

****

They woke up late in the afternoon the next day. It was a Friday, and they had missed school. They laughed as they got up from the movie theater ground. They freshened up in separate bathrooms and jumped into the vehicle waiting in the front for them. Henry whisked them away to the city.

"I'm going shopping today. I know it's not a boy thing, but would you like to join me?" Marie asked as Peter rubbed his throbbing temple.

"Do you have any painkillers?" Peter asked, unintentionally evading his friend's inquiry. Marie handed him three painkillers from her purse and a bottle of water from the car's mini-fridge. Peter took the pills and downed the water. He closed his eyes and waited for the pain to subside, not solitarily the pulsating pain from his temple, but the pain in his heart that he was trying to dash away from but could not seem to evade. *What's the point of these temporary escapes when sobriety is inevitable?* He questioned within himself. He opened his eyes as his migraine receded morsel by morsel.

"I'm going shopping today. Do you want to join me?" Marie repeated.

Peter rubbed his temple as it continued to throb erratically. "I probably should get home. My mom is probably worried," Peter painfully responded.

"Alright," Marie said with lingering disappointment. Peter smiled at her, then lifted her drooped head with his left hand. He leaned over and kissed her on the cheek. Her face lit up like the morning sky. The car stopped, and Peter got out of the vehicle that parked parallel to the condo he called home. He lingered at the car door and stared into the vehicle at his redheaded friend.

"See you soon," Peter said.

"Get out of here, Chainsaw," Marie said with a smile. Peter closed the door and watched as the vehicle drove swiftly away. Deeper into the arms of the city.

Peter entered the condominium, took the east elevator to the ninth floor, and then keyed open the door. His mother stood at arm's length with wet eyes and a militia of boxes around her.

"Where have you been?" Adela asked sternly.

"Look who's a mother again," Peter whispered as he rubbed what remained of the migraine pestering his inner temples.

"Peter, look at me! Where have you been?" Peter looked at his mother with a confused expression. He wondered why she was getting so worked up about him not being home for a night.

"Mom, calm down. I just spent the night at Marie's." Peter noticed several letters with magazine word cutouts clenched tightly within his mother's hands. "What are those?" he questioned. Peter began to take notice of the boxes. He looked within them. She had most of their things packed. Deja vu settled in, and Peter felt as if his world was spinning. His mother couldn't possibly be doing this to him again.

"Mom, what's going on?" Peter nervously inquired.

"We have to move again, Peter," she said sternly.

"What?" Peter said loudly as his nostrils flared.

"Yes, we have to leave again," Adela repeated. "We've been getting threats from someone. I think it's Livingston. Threats to expose us. Threats to kill us."

CHAPTER 6

Peter woke with a start as the noise of the alarm clock punched its torturous nails into his already throbbing temples. Peter found himself in a sea of beer cans. He pushed three empty cans off the cluttered bed. The cans collided with other vacant cans that decorated his small apartment room floor.

It was the start of his senior year. The first day. He wondered why he even bothered with school, considering that he was either drunk or high for most of it. He laid there in bed and considered these things as the alarm clock continued to pester his migraine. He smacked the alarm clock and watched as it flew into the sea of cans. Stone-cold.

Then he remembered; there was just something about school that enthralled him. Even though he was under the influence for most classes, he loved school. His favorite subject was mathematics. He loved how the formulas and equations exercised his brain and ridded his attention from his life. He found freedom in focusing solely on deciphering the math problem.

The end of freshman year, sophomore year, and junior year had been rough for him socially as he made the decision to become an isolationist. He hadn't mingled in anything as common as friends in over two years. The isolation helped him to keep school purely academic. Lone ranger was his best costume. He just didn't trust people. As he laid there in bed, his mind fluttered to Livingston, the thief. Turns out that it was Livingston who was sending the threats, and they could do nothing to fight back. Livingston had drained their accounts clean. They could do nothing about it because of the illegitimate nature at which the funds were attained. If it weren't for the modest amount of cash Adela had hidden, they would have been completely destitute.

They had moved to Brighton, New York. Adela found a job at a diner as they went back to meager livings. Adela didn't want to draw attention to herself by applying for another high-end job. Peter spent his days doing homework, reading books at the public library, and drinking absurd amounts of liquor. He scored a job at a gas station so that he could finance his habit. The strange thing to Peter was that he didn't like drinking at all. He actually hated the taste of the liquid poison, but the ale gave him a temporary escape from reality. It gave him a false jovial personality that masked the depression that he was trying so desperately to escape from.

He lay there in bed. Surveying his life. He felt like the chapters of his life were written by a sick, sadistic dictator who didn't care much about his misery. Whenever he saw the religious kids at school inviting people to their Christian club meetings, he would spit on their banners and rip up their flyers in front of them. They would give him fake smiles and tell him that they still loved him. He would scornfully laugh at them until one would get annoyed enough to ask him to leave.

Peter felt like he was losing himself. In the two years of living in Brighton, he hadn't had a conversation with anyone other than his mother, and she was always at work. He felt desperately alone. When the loneliness became overbearing, he would drink, which was often. A coworker would sometimes sell him weed that he illegally grew in his backyard. When Peter smoked, his mind always drifted to Marie. In those moments of false elation, he wondered how Marie was. What was she doing? Did she miss him? Did she wonder why he left so abruptly? Did she wonder why he didn't say goodbye? Why he hasn't called.

Every time Peter would raid the fridge after a hit, he would think of that last day he spent with Marie. The time in the movie theater. The goodbye kiss he left on her cheek before departing from the vehicle. Peter would find himself crying sometimes, but then his crying would morph into laughter as he remembered her jokes. And that hair. Red like a bright tomato. He'd never seen hair like that before, and he hadn't found hair like that in Brighton.

Peter eventually got out of bed. Freeing his mind from avid pestering. He took a bath and brushed his teeth. He flossed, then gargled with generic mouthwash. Gas station liquor still lingered on his breath. He killed a couple of cockroaches that hung from the bathroom ceiling next to the third path of mold. He got dressed, ate some cereal in the tiny lonesome kitchen, and then headed out the door.

He waited at the bus stop. He leaned against the bus stop post. The bus eventually arrived, and he dropped his two quarters in, per routine, and sat next to his bus companion. She was a round lady with beautiful dark skin and kind eyes. Even though they had never spoken a word to one another, they had an unspoken rite of sitting next to each other every day on the bus. She made him feel safe and protected like a real mother should. She occasionally gave him packs of chewing gum from her bulky purse. He spontaneously would give her cans of soda from his backpack. All without saying a word.

She got off at her usual stop across from the large supermarket. Peter assumed that that's where she worked. She never left without smiling at him, and he always returned the smile. The next stop was his, and he jumped out of the bus and walked across the street to his school. For the entire day, there was constant talk of college. It seemed as if all of his senior year was going to be dedicated to the enigma that was higher education.

Two months later, Peter sat in the public library. He contemplated applying for college. He was third in his class, and he had a good chance of getting into a respectable school. He sat in front of the bulky computer and typed in his information. *William McCloud,* he wrote in the line that asked for his first and last name. He hesitated before doing so. This was his second alias. Writing his pseudonym upon an application for an accredited institution irked him. He wanted a drink or a hit, but there was no computer to work from at home. His body was having a hard time functioning without alcohol as he filled out the application.

His mother had made him change his name once again. She changed hers too. She didn't want Livingston to find them. Peter's new alias was *William McCloud*. He had gotten the chance to choose the name, and he chose it based on the movie he and Marie had watched those two years ago. Adela's new alias was Alice. Peter established that his mother wanted to keep her aliases within the first letter of the alphabet. They had allowed their congenital brown-hued mane to grow out naturally again. No more box blondes were they. Peter enjoyed the simplicity of letting his brunette locks grow out with their natural curl instead of dyeing and straightening them.

He focused on the applications once again. Filling out the applications was a tedious job for him. He had to discern, for even the most rudimentary of inquiries, which to lie about and which to answer in partial truths. He spent three consecutive weekends filling out college applications. He applied to five schools.

He waited for responses from the schools. Once the first of March came around, Peter took the little key that hung in the kitchen and went to the mailbox every day in search of academically padded envelopes. He returned with bills and brochures.

One day he opened the front door to their apartment, beer in hand, to find his mother sitting around their extremely small dining room table. The dining room basically served as a small attachment to the kitchen.

"Mom, what are you doing home?" Peter questioned.

"Is that any way to greet your mother?" Adela scolded.

"Sorry, Mom," Peter apologized. He reached over and planted a kiss on his mother's forehead. As Peter pulled back, he realized that his mother was beaming. "Why are you looking at me like that?" Peter inquired with a smile.

"Look what came in the mail today," Adela said as she ran her fingers across three grand envelopes. Peter looked down at the envelopes. His heart suddenly filled with bliss. It was then that Adela noticed the beer dangling in Peter's right hand.

"Peter, what are you doing? It's three in the afternoon! Why would you be drinking at this hour?" Adela said with concern. Peter stared at her. She really cared. He wanted to joke about being a full-blown alcoholic, but he knew that wouldn't leave a comedic mark on her.

"I'm sorry, Mom. Just felt like having one after school today," Peter said with a casual shrug.

Adela looked up at her son. "Well, stop feeling like it! Please, Peter, I don't want to lose you." The words seeped into Peter's bones and marrow. *I don't want to lose you*, bounced around in his mind. *Someone cares*, he stated within herself. *She actually cares.*

Peter smiled and reassured his mother that he would stop drinking after school, even though he knew that when she returned to her regular shifts, he would binge. Peter placed the can on the dining room table and reached for the first envelope. He got in. Peter opened the second. A similar message of congratulations. He opened the third. He got into them all. He placed his hands behind his head in a commingling of joy and awe. He had done it. He had achieved something. Adela smiled and hugged her son. Then something hit Peter. Financial aid. He went through the three packages again. The first college offered half tuition. The second offered a skimpy scholarship. The third offered a grant that covered almost thirty percent of the tuition.

Peter's face fell. "We can't afford it. Plus, I would have to get money for books." Peter crumbled onto the dining room chair with a defeatist mentality. He chugged the rest of the contents from his canister.

"Honey, you still have two schools left to hear from. There is no doubt in my mind that you'll get into all of them. Don't count yourself out yet," Adela said as she gently touched her son's face. "Alright?" Peter nodded in response and allowed the liquor and his mother to act as solace.

Two weeks later, they sat at the same small table with two dense envelopes in front of them. Peter sat across from his mother with a beer in arm's reach. He opened the first envelope. Acceptance. Thirty percent tuition. He noisily exhaled and opened the second envelope. That was his last hope. He opened it. Acceptance. Sixty percent tuition.

"That's wonderful," Adela said with a reassuring smile.

Peter stared out of the small apartment window as he drank the remainder of his canister's contents. "But we still can't afford it," he said into the distance. He noticed a young lady walking by. The book she was engrossed in looked interesting to Peter. Peter wondered if he could find that book in the public library. He deemed the public library the closest he was ever going to get to higher education.

"We'll make it work, Peter," Adela said, whispering his birth name in secrecy.

"How?" Peter threw back at her.

"You, maybe, could join a work-study program," Adela suggested.

"Mom, I've looked up everything. Work-study. On-campus jobs. It just won't work. Even if I go on the tuition payment plan, I'll still be short a couple hundred per month," Peter sighed in frustration. "It was stupid to even apply." Peter got up and staggered to his room.

"Peter!" Adela yelled through tears. "We're going to make this work! You're going to college! You hear me!"

Peter laughed inappropriately. "Mother, don't make me any promises. Everything that comes out of your mouth is a lie." Peter stared at his mother, who was obviously hurt by his statement. "Mom, I'm sorry. I didn't...." Adela raised her hand in his direction to stop him from continuing to speak.

"You're going to college, you hear me? If that is the last thing I do," Adela said softly, feeling guilty for her son's predicament. Feeling guilt for everything. Peter watched as a tear fell from Adela's left eye. Peter refused to stay for the rain. He found refuge from the storm in his room. He hated when that happened. He hated when his heart would speak before his mind got the chance to process the words. He didn't mean to hurt his mother, but that was the way he felt. She had used him his entire life and made vain promises that had not yet come to fruition. *You're going to college.* Her words rang in his mind, but how could those words be true when all their money was gone. Her diner job and his gas station gig barely covered their rent and bills every month, much less college.

He wanted so badly to go to college. He wanted a place of escape. Something to keep his mind off his life. Something to keep his mind off alcohol, which had taken up all the thoughts in his cranium. He had to go. Maybe he would like himself there, but he doubted his ability to go. He reasoned that he was going to have to settle with the accomplishment of getting accepted into all five schools. He pulled off his socks and lay in bed until sleep consumed him.

He woke with a start as a gentle hand caressed his curls and forehead. He sluggishly opened his eyes to behold his mother. Adela's eyes looked like a dark forest with green trimming.

"Mom, what are you doing?" Peter asked as he gently pushed his mother's hand away from his forehead. She smiled. Her smile was grave and hollow, and it sent a frigid chill down Peter's spine. The predicament brought him back to the dark days in Liverpool. Everyday acting sessions. False diseases. Scam calling. He knew that look. The high had placed an idea in her mind to muse.

"Follow me," she said as she walked out of the room. Peter lazily got out of bed and followed his mother to their small dining room. He watched her as she opened one of the large cabinet doors and reached deep inside. She pulled out a black handgun.

Peter's eyes widened. All fatigue left him at that moment. He was wide awake. "Mom, what are you doing with a gun?"

Adela smiled her uncanny smile. "Wait right here," she said. She went into her room and came back with a long-mouthed shotgun. Peter didn't know what was going on. His mind scrambled.

"Mom, what are you doing with these guns?" Peter inquired nervously.

"You're going to college," Adela simply and casually replied.

"What am I going to do? Shoot everyone in the financial aid office?" Peter sarcastically inquired.

"No, Peter," Adela whispered, then laughed a peculiar laugh. "You're going to pay for the school of your choice per year, and you are going to get an education."

"And just how am I going to do that?"

"We're going to rob the gas station," Adela said as unnerving intimidation dripped from her frightening grin.

****

Olathe's expression is timeless as she squeezes her face in shock and horror. Halia looks equally as mortified as her sister.

"Rob a gas station?" Halia says in disbelief. "When are they going to stop their madness?"

"It's hard to stop madness when you're mad," Perri casually states.

"Grandpa, I truly would never imagine you telling us a story like this one. It's so climactic in every way. I can almost always guess the next events in a story, but this one has thrown me for a loop," Halia says to her grandfather.

"Adela and Peter are so diverse in their criminality, Grandpa," Perri states.

"Indeed, my son," Farook agrees.

"Rob a gas station...," Halia mouths almost inaudibly and to herself mostly.

Olathe is still squeezing her face in unbelief. "Rob a gas station.... Do they actually go through with it?" she questions.

****

Peter shelved his last box of noodles at the gas station. Jamal, his weed dealer and fellow sales associate, was also on duty. Elsa, who was supposed to be working but idled on her cell phone, sat quietly in a corner of the store.

Peter examined the large clock on the east wing wall of the convenience store. Eight twenty. Ten minutes until his shift ended. Ten minutes. He made small talk with Jamal. Jamal had become a good acquaintance. Peter discreetly bought a small Ziploc of weed from Jamal. *I'm going to need it later*, Peter reasoned within himself. He looked at the clock. Eight twenty-eight. Two minutes. Peter placed ten dollars on pump two for a stocky man with a truly creative haircut. The man thanked him.

Eight thirty.

"Alright, man, see you tomorrow," Peter said to Jamal. Jamal responded with a nod. Peter picked up his backpack and headed out the door.

He breathed in the almost fresh air. It was time. He zip-lined to a park south of the convenience store. He locked himself in one of the filthy, roach-infested stalls. He started the transformation process. He unzipped his backpack, revealing two large pillows. He pulled them out swiftly and shaped the stiff pillows meticulously into the form of a vast belly. He changed his pants into oversized sweats. He placed the pillows against his abdomen to allude fat. He drew the sweat strings tightly and tied them snugly against the pillows. He grabbed the large, crumbled long sleeve white tee from the bottom of his backpack. He pulled it over his head and made sure the pillows were in place. He changed into sneakers that gave him an inch or two in height. He pulled on black mitts. He grabbed the black ski mask from his backpack and placed it over his head. He stuffed his clothes into the backpack. He unzipped the side of the bag and retrieved the dark-hued burlap sack. He was ready. His phone vibrated. His mother had texted. *Ready?* it read. *Yes*, he quickly replied.

He then took out the last thing he needed. The guns. He holstered one around his waist and pulled out the black handgun. He left his backpack behind the garbage can where Adela could easily grab it before get-away. He stuffed a few clumps of horrid-colored toilet paper into his ski mask to keep the illusion of a rounder man.

He stood there in the stall for a while. He decided not to mentally debate what he was about to do. He left the stall. Peter took a minute to examine himself through the graffiti-covered public bathroom mirrors. He was unrecognizable, even to himself. He exited the bathroom and walked into the darkness.

Eight forty-eight.

Peter swiftly walked to the rear of the convenience store. He laid his back against the dirty place. *Am I about to do this?* he questioned himself. College. Another kind of life. He was ready.

Peering from behind the curve, Peter observed that the pumps were clear. He knew he didn't have much time; it was a gas station, after all. He walked around to the entrance of the store. He promptly opened the door to the convenience store and held the gun in front of him. The door chimed behind him, alerting the presence of another being, but Elsa and Jamal were far from alert.

Elsa casually looked up from her phone. Peter watched as her teal-colored gum fell from her mouth in slow motion. The gum landed amongst the small clutters of dirt that lined the convenience store floor. Elsa slowly stood up with her hands dangling in the air. Her palms facing Peter in surrender. No resistance. Elsa was far from the cash register, so Peter approached Jamal, who was only a couple of feet in front of him. He kept his eyes on Elsa, who appeared to have transformed into a frightened statue.

Jamal still hadn't turned to see who had entered the store. He was busy reorganizing a shelf with his back turned to the door. His back turned to Peter. Peter stood behind Jamal.

"Can I help—" Jamal didn't get the chance to finish the customary inquiry as the gun rested on the back of his head. Jamal slowly turned around, and the fear in his eyes stunned Peter for a moment. As Jamal turned, he rotated his ocular into the barrel of the gun. Peter flung the burlap sack at Jamal, who scrambled to catch it.

"Put the money in there, and there'll be no trouble," Peter said in the thick Italian accent he had been endlessly practicing. It sounded strange to him, but he knew it would sound authentic to anybody else.

Jamal walked sort of out-of-bodily to the cash register. Peter looked over at Elsa. She was as still as a statue. Jamal opened the register and filled the bag with cash. Jamal idly handed the sack to Peter. Peter grabbed it and dashed out of the store. Peter quickly spotted the black, unmarked vehicle. He jumped in hastily. They sped off.

Peter watched through the rear-view mirror as a vehicle slowly pulled into the gas station. In just a moment, that same vehicle was but a speck in the rear-view mirror. They had done it.

Peter took off his ski mask. The soiled-looking toilet paper fell onto his lap. He looked at the burlap sack, which was slightly ajar, flaunting its contents. He shifted his attention to his mother as she unmasked her face. She sped cautiously down the highway.

"Are you proud of me?" Peter questioned without contemplating.

"Yes," Adela said, smiling more at the stacks of cash than at her son. "Now more than ever."

CHAPTER 7

Peter passed by two police officers. The officers sat in their vehicles right in front of the gas station and convenience store. Their presence served as a deterrence to future delinquency. Peter approached the convenience store for his shift. He waved at the officers. They waved back. Peter walked into the store to behold a very nervous and high Jamal.

"Man, did you hear what happened?" Jamal asked Peter with crazed crimson eyes.

"What happened, man?" Peter questioned, playing oblivious as best as he knew how.

"We were robbed yesterday, man!" Jamal said, a little more loudly than he may have intended.

"What? When? Did you get a good look at the guy?" Peter questioned, playing his role.

"Yesterday. About fifteen or so minutes after you left. He was a six-footer. Kind of a rounder guy. He had a thick Italian accent," Elsa answered for Jamal as Jamal stared out into his own personal, herb-created abyss.

"That's crazy. Did you report it?" Peter inquired.

"Yeah," Jamal responded, still in his dazed state.

Peter gave Elsa a look as if to ask, *What's up with him?* Elsa beckoned for Peter to join her at the east wing of the store, next to the refrigerators.

"Jamal is really shaken up about this," Elsa began to share in a whispered tone. "A robber shot and killed his dad five years ago. The experience last night sent him into a strange state." Peter thought about the information she was disclosing to him about his acquaintance. "He didn't properly grieve, you know. I think this experience just reminded him of all of that." Elsa sighed and touched her multi-colored locks.

"Wow…," Peter muttered as he thought of his unredeemable and selfish actions. Peter looked at Jamal. Eyes red as ever and not making an ounce of effort to conceal it. Peter walked over to Jamal.

"Why don't you head home, man. I'll cover your shift tonight," Peter offered to an incoherent Jamal.

"Alright," Jamal said, still mentally absent. Jamal grabbed his things and headed out of the convenience store. Peter watched as Jamal listlessly walked home. Peter watched until Jamal faded from visual range.

"That was really nice of you," Elsa said with a smile as she refilled the cigarette display behind the store counter.

"It's the least I can do," Peter said behind a well-refined poker face.

****

"I don't believe Peter's completely off the deep end," Halia states.

"Why do you say that?" Perri asks his sister. "He just robbed a convenience store."

"The thing is, someone that is completely off the deep end wouldn't even consider what Elsa said. He wouldn't have cared about Jamal's mental state," Halia reasons.

"True," Perri agrees.

"I think Peter just needs a hug, Grandpa," Olathe states with her grand brown eyes anticipating a response from her grandfather.

"I reason the same thing, my precious girl," Farook beamingly responds to his granddaughter's statement.

"So did they retrieve enough money for Peter to go to college?" Halia questions, engrossed to the utmost.

****

The money they had stolen from the local convenience store was only sufficient to pay for one semester of college. Peter chose a college fairly close to home so he could commute on a daily basis. They couldn't quite afford the on-campus housing that was being offered in the packages from the more prestigious schools. Peter didn't really care about prestige; he cared about being in a place all day that allowed him sweet release from his claustrophobic apartment room that smelled of alcohol and dead dreams.

College made him feel alive and alert. Defying society's norm, being in a higher-level institution became a catalyst for change in Peter's drinking habits. He found himself drinking less and less as he spent whole days on campus and evenings in the school library completing copious amounts of homework. He was taking the maximum number of credits possible. He hadn't yet declared a major, but he knew it would be something that was greatly intertwined with mathematics.

His social anxiety receded in college. He engaged in small talk here and there with classmates and library mates. He even joined several study groups. He occasionally popped up at social gatherings with them outside of school.

His first semester was bliss. That was until the money ran out and the deadline for the next semester's payment approached like an infamously unwelcomed guest. His mind was cluttered with thoughts of the hundreds of dollars needed to pick up where his scholarship had left him financially stranded. He thought about it all of finals week.

"How were the exams?" Adela questioned her son as he wearily walked through the apartment door one Thursday evening.

"Tiresome," Peter said as he closed the door behind him. "The one today was outlandishly lengthy. I got the results of the exam I took last week. I passed it. For the other three I took this week, I feel confident. I should get the results for those next week," Peter said with a feeble smile as he unburdened his back from its academic freight.

"You really love it, don't you?" Adela questioned as she sipped mint tea. It had become their nightly ritual. Beef jerky and mint tea.

Peter poured himself a cup and took a seat across from his mother around their small dining room table. He reached for the jerky and chewed on the dry meat for a while as he thought about school, then it registered that his mother had asked him a question.

"School?" Peter inquired, to which Adela nodded. "Yes, I do love it." Adela smiled as she excused herself from the dining room table and journeyed two feet into the wee kitchen to wash her mug.

"There's only one problem, Mom," Peter said as he finished the jerky and sipped his tea.

"What's that?" Adela insouciantly questioned as she placed her floral teacup in its little place on the drying rack.

Peter pulled out the bill that he had retrieved from the mailbox and slid it across the table in the direction of his mother. "The payment for next semester is due next Friday. That's the last day of extensions. Do you have any ideas yet as to how we can get the money?"

Adela, who leaned against the kitchen counter, shrugged her right shoulder and trailed with her eyes to the infamous third cupboard.

Peter's eyes widened like a fresh new blossom. "Are you suggesting we…again?"

Adela laughed inconspicuously. "Peter, we can do this. Look how easy it was last time?" Adela said. It frightened Peter as to how *blasé* she appeared—as if speaking of riding a bike instead of engaging in lawlessness. Peter felt uneasy, irritated, and thirsty for something that had a little more zest than your common cup of mint tea.

"Mom, let's explore our options, please," Peter said, irritation dripping from his every word. Peter thought of Jamal. He didn't want to be selfish again. Peter didn't want to brand moments into the lives of individuals that would bring about nightmares and pain pill abuse. "We must be able to think of something else."

"Like what?" Adela asked imperturbably. Peter glared at his mother. *Who is this woman?* he asked himself. She had become so unmoved by unruliness. Had her conscience been seared? Peter searched her eyes to see if maybe she was under the influence of something, but he saw nothing but the healthy green garden he did not inherit.

They stared at each other for a while. Peter was bewildered. Adela patiently awaiting a response. Adela realized that her son was planning to stare at her indefinitely with a deep but emotionless stare. "Let me know when you think of something," Adela said, then exited the miniature kitchen. She journeyed to the pea-green settee in front of a television set that nestled in a box-like room. The minuscule space was under the impression that it was a living room.

Peter stared at his mother as she causally skipped through television channels. Was he going to end up like that? Lawless and unrepentant? He had to suppress malice at that moment. He had to suppress it with much force. He continued to stare at her for a while, but then he found himself in his room. He reached under his bed for his emergency liquor, if liquor could ever be deemed an emergency for the sober public. He drank the contents of all six canisters.

He lay in bed, thinking of the possibilities. He first went through a mental list of legal endeavors, but as he itemized cognitively, robbery kept popping up like an unctuous fiend. Robbery was truly fast and easy, that is, if everything went as planned. He foolishly let the thought of robbery be entertained in his mind. He mentally clicked on it, even though he knew the mental pop-up would lead to a misleading site promising a quick fix. Could he do it again? He and Adela had been quite the planners and executors of the crime. They were careful and timely. *I could do this again*, Peter reasoned.

He sat up in the bed and began to think of a place they could easily rob. It had to be out of town. Police officers had been patrolling the local area with more fervency than before. His mother could get a ditch vehicle again. They could change off in a public restroom after the execution, then take public transportation back home. It was a plan.

****

Peter questioned his capability to hold the gun. His palms perfused with sweat. Adela, noticing Peter's mini dilemma, reached into the back seat and then handed him the mitts he thought he had forgotten at home.

"Are you ready?" Adela questioned her son. Her face barely visible from underneath her cumbersome blonde wig.

"As I'll ever be," Peter uttered as he placed the ski mask over his head. He felt the spirits roaming around in his system. He had indulged in one beer with the intent of keeping his nerves under subjection. It was working. It took all the willpower he had not to drink the entire pack, but he couldn't be incoherent to rob a store.

He adjusted the pillows that were across his abdomen. His mother had even decked him with colored contact lenses to throw law enforcement off during identification questioning. His eyes were now deceivingly green like hers.

Peter placed his hand over the old car door handle. His mother spontaneously leaned over and planted a kiss right on his ski mask, in his cheek vicinity. He turned his head to her. "I love you," she said with a smile.

"If this is love, please don't show me hate," Peter said, almost inaudibly, as he opened the car door. He wasn't sure if his mother heard his words; if she did, she would probably be hurt by them, but at that moment, Peter did not care.

He took a moment to take in the unfamiliar town. He and his mother had been on stakeout for the past couple of days, and they knew that the local police didn't do their runs in the area until ten o'clock. It was eight fifty-five. *I can do this*, he said within himself as he dashed into the store.

It happened fast. He ran in with the gun pointed. Two customers shirked in fear and dropped to the ground as commanded. He pushed the idle cashier in the temple with the mouth of the gun, ordering him to fill the burlap sack. Peter grabbed the hefty sack and bolted through the doors as adrenaline consumed his being. He jumped into the car, and his blonde mother bolted through traffic.

Then they saw the flashing lights.

****

Halia clasps her hand over her mouth. "Is it really happening?" she inquires. "Are they really going to get caught?"

"Oh, my goodness," Olathe states with animation and anticipation as she lifts her hands up to create a barricade for her face. "I have to know what happens next!"

"Grandpa, don't leave us at a cliffhanger. Please continue," Perri pleads, completely engrossed.

Farook smiles at his grandchildren, then takes a long drink of his milk and stares out the grand window. The children give each other puzzled looks.

"Grandpa!" they say in unison. Farook pretends as if he is surprised by the call of his grandchildren; he even jumps a little in a beautiful theatrical finish. He smiles at them, and they smile back. Olathe falls into a bowl of giggles.

"Alright, where was I…." Farook gets comfortable in his chair as the children look up at him with ardent anticipation.

****

Red and blue lights trailed them. A high-speed chase. If there was one thing Peter knew his mother knew how to do well, it was driving. She weaved through traffic like a pro, fitting their tiny getaway car into the smallest of spaces. They were a few vehicles ahead of the three police cars that chased them. She pressed the accelerator. Nighty five miles an hour. A hundred miles an hour. A hundred and ten miles an hour.

They took a sharp right turn down a dark street, and Peter grabbed the door of the vehicle for dear life.

"Peter, I'm going to slow down this vehicle to forty-five miles an hour, then we jump out!" Adela yelled.

"Then we do what?" Peter yelled back; he was sure his ears deceived him.

"Then we jump out," Adela said as she slowed the car and placed her backpack on her back. Peter did the same.

"Three," Adela said, beginning the countdown. *What if I die?* Peter questioned within himself.

"Two," Adela said as the car slowed to fifty miles an hour, rapidly approaching a dead end. *Death is upon me*, Peter thought.

"One," Adela said, slowing the car to forty-five miles an hour and preparing for the jump. *I'm pretty much dead*, Peter reasoned as he grabbed the car handle and propelled himself out of the vehicle. He landed in a roll. The backpack did help to cushion his fall, especially with those pillows lining the pack. It was also a good thing that the road was fenced by grass. They both fell onto the soft green carpet on either side of the road. They got up quickly and sprinted for the rows of trees to the west of them. As soon as they were safely hidden, the car exploded. Peter had never heard a sound so deafening in all of his days. Even though they were a reasonable distance away, they still fell backway.

Peter caught a glimpse of his mother's face amidst the illumination brought forth by the flames that engulfed their once gateway car.

"Perfect," she mouthed. Peter and Adela got up swiftly as they saw the red and blue lights cautiously approaching the burning vehicle.

"They must think we're dead. Engulfed in flames. That will buy us some time," Adela said with a smile as she took off her wig and stuffed it deep beneath a bush. Peter quickly took out and threw away the colored eye contacts. They both took off their mitts and stuffed them deep into Peter's backpack. Adela quickly placed her hair into a neat bun on top of her head. Peter pulled on his sweater. Adela took the burlap sack and a pillow from Peter's backpack. She stuffed the lucre-filled sack into the pillowcase behind the pillow. She then swiftly placed the pillow against her stomach and speedily pulled her blouse over it. She looked six months pregnant.

They walked along the green path until they found a sidewalk and continued west. A platoon of law enforcement vehicles blazed by them. Adela walked confidently as the red and blue lights reflected upon her face. Peter nervously clutched onto his backpack. Peter and Adela eventually found a bus stop. Adela sat next to a lively elder. It was a surprise to both Peter and Adela that the elderly lady was at the bus stop so late at night. Peter leaned against the bus stop post.

"How far along are you?" the elderly lady asked Adela with a smile.

Adela gleamed and caressed her stuffed child. "Six months," she answered with a smile.

A gleeful and vivacious laugh slipped through the crevice upon the old lady's face. "That's delightful," she said with a smile. The elderly lady turned and gave Peter a coy look. Adela discerned her thoughts.

"That's my firstborn," Adela said with a smile.

"Oh, how wonderful!" More glee. "But you had them so far apart," the lady said with concern. "Who did he have to play with growing up?" the lady questioned.

"He and his father are very close," Adela brilliantly lied on impulse. She had become a sharp professional at formulating faux life stories. Peter wanted to retch as he watched the drama continue to unfold. *Close with my father, aye?* Peter repeated in his mind. When he caught the lady looking at him, he turned his smolder into a smile that she so graciously returned.

A young man in a tie-dye shirt and khaki shorts approached the bus stop. He had a skateboard dangling from his left arm, and he used his right hand to unplug an earbud that blared violent melodies, loud and clear.

"Does anyone know what's going on?" the young guy questioned. "The entire walk here, I've seen a flow of police cars and fire trucks going east."

"I have no idea," Adela retorted as ignorantly as possible while she caressed her covered pillow. She could never pass for a woman that recently jumped out of a moving vehicle going forty-five miles an hour. "I guess we will find out tomorrow on the news," Adela said. They all beheld as a newscast truck passed by them, headed east.

The bus then materialized from the dark western abyss. They all got on. Peter even helped his pregnant mother on the bus. Peter forked up some quarters, then sat in the seat next to his mother.

The bus doors closed, and they slowly drove off. Everyone looked out the east windows to behold the illuminated street. They could still see the small fire caused by the gateway vehicle. In no time, the scene was out of view, and the commotion on the bus came to an end. Adela smiled at her son, caressing her belly.

They were the last two to leave the bus at ten thirty. Peter helped Adela out of the bus, and they hurried to the apartment. Adela didn't want any of her neighbors seeing her in her unctuously swollen state.

Once safely inside, Adela hugged her son, and they spewed adrenaline-injected laughs. Peter even patted her fake belly before she changed. Adela was on such an adrenaline high that she allowed Peter to drink in front of her as she counted the money.

"One thousand, five fifty-five," Adela said with a ravishing smile.

"Let's drink to that," Peter said with a smile as Adela popped open a can of beer.

"You know, Peter, I still don't approve of you drinking so much," Adela said as she chugged a beer and opened another.

Peter laughed in his heart. "Ah, Mum, just let it be," Peter said as he drank. He realized he had just spoken in his native accent. He remembered Liverpool and compared the level of deviance. *Liverpool, you've never seen anything like this*, he thought as he chugged his liquid escape.

****

The money they had stolen sufficed for the following semester. Both Adela and Peter would stick their hand in it to take out small amounts for various things and for various reasons.

Peter even felt a wee bit more social that spring semester as he joined his study group friends in more social gatherings.

One day as he placed his hand in the sack, he came up with a mere sixty dollars. "Mom," he called. Adela came out of her room and joined Peter in their small living room.

"What happened to the money?" Peter asked as he showed Adela the desolate sack. "Is this really all that's left?" he asked as he showed her the sixty dollars.

"Life happened, son. We are going to have to budget our spoil next time," Adela stated.

"Next time?" Peter questioned wearily.

"Peter, you have three years of college left after this semester is over," Adela said matter-of-factly. For some reason, Peter had come to the conclusion that their robbery days were behind them. Peter reasoned that jumping from a vehicle would be the sign that they needed to lay low for a while. Adela noticed the frightened expression on her son's face and decided to offer an alternative. "Have you heard of those credit card information scanners that persons are placing at gas pumps and ATMs in order to confiscate people's card information?" Adela questioned, to which Peter shook his head. "Well, it is extremely simple. You'll just attach the readers at each pump when you go to work early Saturday morning. I will attach two to the ATMs near the diner," Adela said as she got comfortable on the settee that embodied the hue of pea soup.

"Where would we get those readers?" Peter asked as he took a seat on the ground next to the entertainment center.

"I have about a dozen in my room. I tried two. They work," Adela responded with her eyes closed and her legs propped up on the pea soup. Peter stared at his mother. She always seemed to be fourteen steps ahead of him. It was unnerving.

Minutes later, Adela jumped from the settee with a start, then swiftly got dressed for work. She came back out of her room to find Peter in the same position next to the entertainment center. He was deeply immersed in thought.

"Meet me at the diner tonight. My shift ends at ten o'clock. We'll head over to the ATM, and I'll show you how to set up the readers."

"Okay," Peter hollowly responded. The minute Adela left, Peter found his stash and drank until he blacked out. He woke up and vomited. He looked at the clock. Nine forty-five. He washed his face, gargled mouthwash, and headed out the door. He walked the couple blocks to the diner. He was about to open the diner door when his mother spotted him and instructed, with gestures, for him to remain on the outside. Peter obeyed and sat down on the sidewalk. He was extremely nauseous, and the walk didn't help with nausea. He reasoned that he had probably overdone it with the drinking. He heard the door chime open, and he beheld his mother, who looked at him with worried eyes.

"William!" Adela shrieked. Peter pondered for a moment on why his mother would be calling him William; then, he remembered that they were in a public place.

"Alice!" Peter squealed, trying his best to reinvent his mother's momentary reaction. He smiled at her, but she was not amused.

"Why do you look like the inside of a bar?" Adela questioned her son. Peter laughed.

"The inside of a bar is an aesthetically pleasing place," Peter said as his mother helped him up from off the ground.

"I'm going to need you to stop drinking," Adela said sternly. Peter laughed all the more.

"Let's just do what we have to do, Mom," Peter said with a crooked, drunken smile. They crossed the street and headed to the bank that was closed, but the brilliantly lit ATM stood ready to be used. Peter watched as his mother carefully aligned the skimmer. It really was quick, and it looked like nothing had been tampered with. *Brilliant, this is a great alternative to pushing guns in people's faces*, Peter thought.

The next day, Peter woke up early for work. It was Saturday, and his manager had recently granted him more hours on the weekends. He readied himself, grabbed a bagel, and headed out the door. When he got to the gas station, his manager had just opened the store. The manager only stayed for a handful of hours, then gave Peter the keys for closing. When his manager's car was but a speck in his visual range, Peter pulled six readers from his backpack and quickly went around to each pump, installing them hastily because he knew at any minute Jamal would show up for his midday shift. He finished swiftly and returned to the store. Jamal showed up within a minute of Peter's return back into the convenience store.

"What's up, man?" Jamal greeted as he threw his belongings behind the counter.

"Nothing much," Peter responded.

"You still lighting up with me tonight?" Jamal questioned. Peter had forgotten the plans they had made to smoke, but he was glad that it was brought back to his remembrance.

"Sure thing, man," Peter said with a smile. *A smoke would be nice,* Peter thought.

Jamal got a few boxes and began to unpack some things. Peter stood idly at the cash register. Waiting for a customer.

She came into the store with a petite blonde girl. She was gorgeous. The two went around the store picking up snacks; then, they approached Peter. His palms began to sweat. His heartbeat accelerated to the rate of that of a young athlete, which he was not. She took off her sunglasses and looked at him with a questioning glare.

"Chainsaw?" the red mane spoke.

CHAPTER 8

"Marie is back!" Olathe squeals.

"I wouldn't deem that a thing to rejoice over," Perri says to his sister.

"Perri's right, Olathe. Marie is quite a dubious person," Halia follows.

"Dubious, but not unredeemable. Plus, it has been over four years since they've seen each other. Who knows what kind of person Marie has become?" Olathe reasons.

"I hope your discernment is correct," Perri states.

"Is it, Grandpa?" Halia asks her grandfather. Farook tries to keep his composure as he commences the salient tale once again.

****

They stared at each other for a while as they stood outside the small convenience store. Jamal and Joan, Marie's friend, mingled on the inside.

"Your hair is brown," Marie stated as she recalled the straight blonde hair her friend once had. "And curly," she added.

"And yours is still flaming red," Peter said with a smile as he reached out and swiped a red lock out of Marie's face. Marie smiled at his touch but then swiftly returned to her staid and questioning posture.

"What happened, James?" Marie asked with penetrating eyes.

"People here call me William. Or Will for short," Peter corrected. Marie looked baffled.

"Alright," she said as she shook her head. "What happened, Will? Why did you just…leave?" Marie began to find it difficult to speak as tears tried to choke her. "I waited for so long for you to come back…. I thought you would at least call me." A tear stole away from Marie's eyes and took a stroll down her face. Peter ended the stroll abruptly by wiping the tear and drawing Marie in for a hug. Marie stiffened at first, but then she surrendered to the embrace that she had longed for.

"I didn't mean to hurt you. My life is just so…complicated," Peter said, still embracing his friend. They eventually broke the hug. "I didn't want to get you involved in what was happening. You didn't deserve that," Peter meticulously explained.

"It was so bad that you couldn't have even called me?" Marie asked, still hurt and bitter and looking for a more elaborate elucidation.

"You have no idea how bad Marie. No idea," Peter said as he leaned against the convenience store window.

"Enlighten me," Marie stated. Peter looked at her. Her blue eyes and red hair contrasted so strangely, but it worked on her. She was beautiful. She stood like an army sergeant over him, lingering for a riposte. The sun made a cool aura around her frame and gave her red hair the illusion of fire.

"So, umm. What are you doing in these parts? Lost your way on the journey to the Hamptons?" Peter asked, trying to lighten the atmosphere and change the conversation topic from off of him.

"James Will Chainsaw, you are going to answer my questions," Marie said with her finger pointed at him as to warn him that she knew he was trying to distract her, and she was not buying it. She placed her hands back on her waist. "No, I didn't get lost. I'm volunteering here all of spring break. I joined my university's community service center."

"Can you take a break and have some fun with me tonight?" Peter asked with a smile. Marie tried not to, but her face cracked, revealing a timid smile. She nodded.

Peter went through the rest of the workday in a trance as he anticipated the events to take place later on. He had invited Marie to hang out with him and Jamal in the evening. He had given her the address and time. She agreed and told him that she would meet him there right after she and the university volunteer team finished serving at the homeless shelter. Peter and Jamal had planned to smoke that night. Peter didn't know if Marie still smoked, but he would find out that night. If not, he reasoned, they would do something else.

"You ready, man?" Jamal inquired of Peter as Elsa entered for the seven o'clock shift.

"Yeah," Peter replied as he walked out of the convenience store with Jamal. "Can we stop by my place real quick? I think I want to change."

"Sure thing, man…. So, who's the girl? I know you're not changing for me," Jamal said with a nudge. Peter blushed. Peter wished that his skin had a greater abundance of melanin, akin to Jamal's, in order to conceal his nervous system's response to his thoughts and feelings. Jamal smiled at his reddened friend. "So, you like her?"

"Umm…I just…It's complicated," Peter stammered. Jamal smiled and shook his head. They reached the apartment complex. They ran up the stairs and entered the apartment on the southwest wing of the compound. Jamal sat quietly in the claustrophobic living room as Peter searched for something to wear. His room was a mess, and he stumbled over liquor bottles repeatedly. He retrieved a crisp button-down purple shirt from the hole in the room called his closet. He then searched for and found his best pair of dark-hued jeans. He debated as to whether or not the clothes reeked of formality; they were going to smoke after all.

He ended the mental debate and changed quickly into the getup.

Jamal laughed aloud as Peter exited his room and entered the small living area. "What is this? Are we going to prom or something? Are you wearing cologne as well?"

Peter blushed again because he actually had on a spritz of the cologne his mother had brought him for his sixteenth birthday. Jamal laughed, got up, and smelled Peter, then laughed all the more.

"Man, you are wearing cologne!" Jamal's laughter rocked the apartment building. Peter smiled and gave Jamal an affable nudge towards the open door. When Jamal was safely outside, Peter ran to the stash of cash in the hideaway behind the entertainment center. He quickly opened the hidden compartment and took out a few bills. *Just in case*, he thought. He closed the compartment and quietly moved the entertainment center back over the hiding place. He locked the apartment door. He and Jamal continued their journey.

As they approached Jamal's house, Peter spotted the Red Mane. Even in the darkness, her hair was electrified by the intensity of its hue. She turned as she heard footsteps approaching her.

"Way to keep a girl waiting, guys," she said with her arms waving in the air. Her exceedingly loose-fitting sweater gave the illusion of dark wings as she raised her arms. She looked like a terrifying yet beautiful bird.

"We apologize. Your boy here had to change," Jamal said with a smile as he pointed at Peter. Peter gave him a grave look. "Oh, was I not supposed to say that? I apologize," Jamal winked at Peter, who gave him another tempestuous glance.

"You look nice," Marie commented, to which Peter casually nodded. "I much prefer your hair like this over the straight blonde hairstyle."

"You were blonde, man?" Jamal questioned as he swung the door to the house open. Jamal looked back at Peter with a baffled expression emitting upon his face. Peter casually shrugged his shoulders as if the topic was of no merit for further discussion. They walked into the house. It was a spacious one-story home.

"It's just you who lives here, J?" Peter questioned as he looked around.

"Just me. And my cats. And my weed," Jamal smiled as he parted the curtains to reveal a meshed area that housed copious amounts of cannabis.

A red and beige cat immerged from a dark area of the house and ran across Peter's foot.

"This is absolutely stunning," Marie said with a smile.

"So, you still smoke?" Peter questioned.

"Among other things," Marie answered elatedly. Jamal closed the curtains and went into a room. A large black and gray cat ran out of the room and ran across Peter's foot. Jamal then returned with three small and husky-hued plastic bags.

"My treat for tonight," Jamal said as he handed them a bag each and kept one bag for himself.

They settled in on the spacious settee. They opened their miniature bags. Marie took a whiff of the contents in her bag and smiled. "Good ole Mary Jane," she said as she swiftly grabbed one of the many lighters in her vicinity that littered the vast living room. She lit the cannabis.

The lighting in the living area was extremely dim due to Jamal's specific light settings on his dimmer switch. Marie smiled at Peter as the lit joint illuminated her face. She looked beautiful to him. He watched as his arm reached over and took the cannabis from between her lips and placed it on his. He wanted her to remember. She froze, and they stared at each other. Visions of their time in the movie theater swam around in each of their minds. Vivid and clear. Distant and near. It was like they were sharing a long-overdue conversation, using their eyes as the medium. Intimate and public concurrently.

"I'm feeling extremely third-wheelish," Jamal said after staring at Peter and Marie, who were staring at each other. His words broke their glare. Peter knew she remembered. Marie smiled at Jamal, then took her joint from between Peter's lips and engaged it with hers once again.

"Get your own, Chainsaw," Marie said with a smile.

"Why do you keep calling him Chainsaw?" Jamal queried. Marie laughed. She crossed her legs on the sofa as if getting comfortable in order to tell a lengthy tale.

"When we were freshmen in high school…Jame…Will used to sport straight blonde hair that looked like it had been trimmed with a chainsaw," Marie laughed in remembrance. "He frightened me with that hair, but he had a pleasant face, so I befriended him." Jamal joined in on the laughter. Peter leaned down deep into the couch. Maybe the couch would swallow him, he thought. He thought strange things when he was high.

Five cats ran out from the east hallway and joined them in the smoke-infested living room. Marie laughed exorbitantly. "What are you doing with so many cats, man?" Marie questioned in between squeals of laughter. Her laughter frightened the cats. The felines slowly backed away from her, which made her laugh even more. Her eyes were sprinting towards the hue of her hair as she continued to smoke. "Let's call you…Cat Man," Marie said with a brilliant smile. "Cat Man and Chainsaw. My two friends…. You know, it's my birthday today!" Marie spontaneously squealed.

"Are you serious?" Peter questioned.

"Yeah, it is your birthday because you got free weed," Jamal spewed.

"No, it's my actual birthday!" Marie said in between unprovoked bursts of laughter. Jamal and Peter began to playfully sing the birthday song in multiple and differing keys. Marie made several poses as if dancing to the tune, with the joint still lying on her lips. Peter scooted over to her and placed his arm around her shoulder. She fit perfectly in the crook of his arm, he thought.

"Let's celebrate!" Jamal exclaimed. "They have a twenty-four-hour diner just around the corner."

"Let's do it, Cat Man!" Marie bellowed. Jamal turned off the lights in the house, turned on the outside ones, then they departed.

The diner was just a stone's throw away, and they were in the restaurant ordering absurd amounts of food in no time. They laughed and ate like pigs. Chainsaw, Cat Man, and the Red Mane.

Peter and Marie made plans to spend more time together the next day. Marie didn't volunteer on Sunday. Most people in the area were religious, and they packed the churches. Marie and her group planned to resume their work on Monday, the official commencement of spring break. They reconvened at the same diner they had committed gluttony in the night before. Marie sat across from Peter, sipping her coffee, eyeballing him.

"So…are you ready to open up to me yet?" Marie asked as she used her pinky to stir her dark caffeinated drink. Peter found himself staring at her again. Could he trust her? His mind fluttered to his mother. *She had tried that with Livingston and looked how that turned out well*, he reasoned within.

Peter leaned into the diner table, looking Marie straight in the eyes. "It's not that I don't want to open up to you, Marie. I do, but I cannot. In moments like these, you're going to have to trust me. As your friend, I'm asking for you to trust me."

Marie continued to stir conspicuously as she eyeballed Peter. "It's pretty bad then, huh." Peter irritably tried to ignore her persistence. Marie raised her eyebrows at Peter's display of faux indifference. "I figured as much," she continued. "The hole you're in must be pretty deep if you had to change locations, your name, and your physical appearance," Marie continued to pester him, hoping for a crack in his poker face, but she didn't even witness the slightest of cavities. Marie felt her temper rising. "Well, James Will, if you are not going to talk to me, I have no business here. I have better things to do."

Marie crossly rummaged through her large handbag, pulled out the two dollars needed for her coffee, slammed the currency onto the table, and then proceeded to slide out of the diner booth. She sluggardly headed for the door. Peter knew it would be the right choice to have her walk through that door. To have her walk out of his life indefinitely. But he didn't want that. Last time they had been pulled apart involuntarily. This time he had a choice.

"Marie, wait." Peter didn't know what to say as she slowly spun around. Aggravation galloped upon her face. "Stay with me, please," he said, as sentimental as he knew how.

Irritation melted from her face as she gawked at Peter's mawkish expression. Marie tried to decipher the authenticity or inauthenticity of Peter's mien. She wasn't too sure of its genuineness, but it won her over, and she took her seat at the table once again.

"I'm going to get it out of you, Chainsaw," Marie said as she picked up the menu. Peter smiled at his redheaded friend.

****

Peter returned to the apartment in the evening to find his mother at the dining room table. Her head was down. Her hands curtained her pate. Her brown hair swept the table as she leisurely swung her head back and forth. Worry overtook Peter.

"Mom, is everything okay?" Peter asked as he quickly closed the apartment door behind him. No response. Back and forth. Back and forth. Back and forth went her head. The troubling head motion continued for a few more moments.

"Just dandy!" she yelled out of the indigo as her head violently flew up, leaving a line of mucus on the table where her hair once swept. She had been crying. Her eyes appeared slightly unhinged, but she mostly just looked like a weeping woman.

"What's the matter, Mom?" Peter inquired as he took a seat next to his mother. He gingerly placed his left hand on her back. Adela swung her head vertically a few times. Peter was certain at one point that it was going to fly off. Then she looked at him. Sitting so close to her, he realized that her pupils were indeed dilated. He immediately felt uncomfortable. The hand on his mother's back parted and returned to its home on his lap. Something about his mother being in that state brought out the little boy in him. The little boy who held his forehead as it bled. The little boy who slept with a burned back. The little boy who faked cancer. Peter reflexively reached for the scar on his forehead that was discreetly hidden by his matted curls. He remembered the pail. He remembered how his forehead bled all night. He remembered how he almost passed out. But above all else, he remembered those eyes. The same eyes he beheld now. Broken and battered eyes. She still stared at him as if she was trying to look into his soul. The drugs had stolen the garden and unbridled the dark forest. He looked down at his hands that sat idly in the safety of his lap. He couldn't look at her anymore in the state she was in.

"I lost my job," she said robotically. The news forcefully lifted Peter's head.

Despite his dread of her eyes, he looked at her. "How could this have happened?"

Adela laughed at a nonexistent joke, then swatted at an imaginary fly. "I have no idea. My manager said something about reports of irregular behavior." Peter wondered what his mother had done in her incoherent state. His mind took a vacation for a few seconds, then a legion of thoughts appeared all at once. What were they going to do? He questioned within himself. How were they going to pay the bills?

Adela interrupted Peter's train of thought. "Peter, I'm going to have to go into the stash until I can find another job. We have to pay the bills."

"What we have left would only last about a week," Peter responded.

"We are going to have to do it again, Peter, but bigger this time." Peter knew what she was suggesting. It had to be the drugs talking.

"Mom, you must be...joking," Peter said, his voice frightened him as it took on a higher octave. "We almost died last time. The car was engulfed in flames. Do you not remember the flames? The high-speed chase? Don't you remember how we had to jump out of the car, almost breaking our shoulders and necks in the process? Don't tell me that is something you would want to do again?" Peter was enraged. Adela was jovial.

She smiled at her son; her smile dipped in eerie. "We would be extra careful this time. I've been planning this one for months. It's bigger. It's better. More money. I put a lot of time and brainpower into this one. It's a guaranteed success," she ended with the same eerie smile.

Peter closed his eyes, wishing he were in another place. In another family. Eating dinner and talking about sports, maybe. A suburban home with a white picket fence. He opened his eyes again. He was in the same apartment.

"What about the card readers?" Peter questioned as it came to mind. A sound of annoyance came out of Adela's mouth. She fanned her hand in the air.

"That was a terrible idea. The people kept getting their banks to refund the money. They couldn't trace it back to us, though, just back to the location. They took the skimmer from the ATM we placed at the bank. We only got about a hundred dollars from that, and a hundred dollars can't do jack." Adela laughed, then kept repeating the word jack.

Peter closed his eyes again, wishing himself away. He opened his eyes o'er. He was still there. "So, what's the plan?" Peter heard himself ask. Adela smiled. She wiped off the body fluids, which had masked her face, onto the sleeve of her blouse. She sprinted into her room like an excited adolescent. Peter reasoned that the neighbors downstairs must be exceedingly exasperated with them.

Adela came back from her room with a blueprint of a bank in the next town.

"This plan is bulletproof," she said in an unnerving tone that complimented her haunting eyes.

****

"Will Chainsaw!" Marie exclaimed as she entered the bare convenience store. Peter smiled at the appearance of his friend. "Are you off soon?"

Peter examined the clock. "I'll be off in ten minutes," he said with a smile. The ten minutes went by quickly as Marie and Peter chatted in between customers. They left the convenience store and walked together, on the frigid night, back to Peter's apartment.

"Well, this is a downgrade compared to where you used to live," Marie said as they entered the apartment complex. Peter smiled at how direct and unfiltered Marie truly was. He sometimes wished he shared the same frankness. So many times, he wanted to speak out. So many times, he wanted to state his opinion. To debate with his mother. But he stayed quiet. He sometimes felt like he was paying for his silence with the lifestyle he was living.

"Were you born frank?" Peter questioned with a friendly nudge.

"Were you born secretive?" Marie retorted. Peter chuckled as they walked up the long stairs to his apartment door. He opened the door to the apartment.

"Just get in," he said with a smile. They walked in, and Peter journeyed to his room. As he was about to close the door, he realized that Marie was following him. "What are you doing?" he questioned.

"I'm entering your habitation," she said with a dubious smile. He wasn't going to change with her in the room, so he waited as she took her time eyeballing every inch of his room. She examined the collage of liquor bottles that graced the floor. "Quite the drinker, I see," she said with a smile. "You have any more?" Peter smiled and instinctively reached under the bed for a lukewarm beer. Even though he was sure his mother was using illicit drugs, he knew she still didn't like the idea of her son abusing substances, so Peter was never allowed to place the alcohol in the standing fridge. His drinking remained a divulged clandestine.

Marie chugged the beer, threw the can on the ground, and then beckoned for another. Peter gave her another; she chugged that one too, then stared at him. "No worries, I won't ask you for another. Beer must be really expensive for you anyway." Peter laughed at her comment that carried a whiff of insult, but he didn't care.

After she went into his closet, examining every piece of garment he owned, she returned to the living room, giving Peter an opportunity to change his clothes. Peter hurriedly pulled on casual clothes and joined her in the living room. She was looking through their small movie collection.

"What are you guys? Amish? Just looking at these movies, I feel the need to repent. I don't like repentance or feeling the need to partake in it," Marie said. Peter suddenly felt ashamed of his mother's movie collection.

"I have two movies in my room," Peter said as he went for the movies and returned.

Marie snatched them, then smoldered at Peter. "Peter, these movies are for teenage boys ages thirteen to sixteen. You are a grown man now. In college and the such. What are you doing with these?"

Marie observed that Peter looked like a fish out of the water, dazed and mentally flopping. "No worries," Marie said as she reached into her grand purse and pulled out a laptop. "You have a friend in me," she said with a smile.

Peter rummaged the kitchen for snacks and found half of a microwave pizza and a bag of cheese and sodium-infested chips. He heated the pizza, went and got two warm beers from his room and poured the warm liquor into plastic cups, then joined Marie on the ground near the couch. She had the movie ready and streaming.

"I found an age-appropriate film for us," Marie said with a smile, then focused her attention on the screen. Peter took a moment to look at her. She had her hair in one braid that formed a rocky road down the dome of her head and stopped at the nape of her neck. She wore small pearl earrings. Peter assumed that the earrings were probably worth more than his apartment. She decked herself in the same bird alluding sweater over a soft white cotton blouse. Everything looked normal until he beheld her pants. She decked her lower body in safari print pants that contrasted dramatically with her tame festooned upper body.

He must have been looking at her for too long. He realized that a little too late. "Chainsaw, I am not the movie. Pay attention," Marie said without taking her eyes off the screen.

Thoughts swam through Peter's mind as they watched. He reasoned that he would actually prefer to talk to his long-lost friend instead of staring at a screen together. He broke the cinematic monologue. "Why do you like movies so much?"

"That's easy. It gives me a temporary escape…. Like drugs, but sometimes even more potent. It sucks me into another world. Another reality. When I feel like I may be overdoing it with my usage, I just watch a platoon of movies to get my mind off things," Marie retorted.

Marie looked at him, "So question for question?" she asked with a chary smile. Peter gave her an uncertain look. "Why did you leave Manhattan?" Peter shook his head in response. "That's not how the game works, Chainsaw!" she said a little more strongly than she should have. Her temper sometimes got the best of her. She smiled at him, trying to play it off casually. "Back to the movie then," she said, turning back to the screen.

Peter's eyes lingered on her face for a while. He had taken notice of her episodic upsurges that seemed to spring from thin air. The slightest thing enraged her. He noted how she always seemed to play coy after each outburst. *Do I really know Marie?* he questioned within himself. They had spoken frequently in Manhattan and for the past few days, but Peter wondered if he actually knew Marie. Other than their rare moments of disclosure, they spent a lot of time talking about nothing. Just empty conversation without merit. As he thought about these things, Marie turned to him and smiled. She placed her head on his shoulder. He forgot everything he was deliberating in the confines of his mind. *Marie is a great person*, Peter concluded as Marie nestled into him.

They continued watching the movie. Marie's head continued to rest on Peter's shoulder, and he thought of nothing else. He wondered if he smelt alright.

Halfway through the movie, Adela opened the apartment door. Peter noticed that her eyes were sober and green, as they should be for someone who was interviewing for jobs.

Marie lifted her head off of Peter's shoulder and stood. "It's wonderful to finally meet you," Marie greeted. Adela smiled and shook Marie's hand, making all the customary first-time greeting rounds. Adela grabbed something from the fridge and excused herself from the living room. Peter and Marie resumed the movie and finished it, curled up like cats until it ended. Marie kissed Peter on the cheek goodbye and headed out the door.

"Is the coast clear?" Adela's room door questioned. Peter smiled and reassured her of the vacant state of the coast. Adela walked out of the room with a wide smile on her face. Peter knew what was coming. "So, my son, why is it you never told me you had a girlfriend?" Adela asked. Peter could feel his face redden.

"Because I don't," Peter replied. Adela glared at him doubtfully.

"So you cuddle with all your friends?" Adela rhetorically asked.

"Mom!" Peter exclaimed with a smile that he could not control.

"Peter, you have no need whatsoever to be embarrassed or defensive. You're twenty years of age; if you want to date, the decision is up to you," Adela said, then she realized Peter didn't want to continue talking about the matter. "Alright then, are you ready for Saturday?"

Saturday. It was the day they planned to commit one final act of robbery. It had frightened Peter as to the specificity and the detailed planning that his mother had done. She had everything coordinated. The location. The disguises. The getaway. Everything had been planned before Peter was even made aware of it. They were going to rob the grand bank in the next town. They had the guns. They had the disguises, and every night, they went over the plan, the methods in which they were going to move in and out.

Peter felt as indifference began to creep in. Indifference frightened him a lot more than melancholy loneliness. Indifference clothed itself in numbness, and Peter much preferred to feel something rather than nothing at all. He didn't want to get to the place where he simply didn't care about breaking the law. He didn't want to get to that place of indifference, but he felt it apprehending him like a sneaky apparition.

He let the ghoul speak. "As ready as I'll ever be," he heard himself say as they went over Saturday's plans once again.

****

The stubborn knocking startled Peter awake. Peter staggered to the front door. He opened it, and there stood Marie. She smiled at him.

"Were you sleeping?" she asked, to which Peter wearily nodded. "Well, stop it because we are going out tonight." It was Tuesday, and Peter had gotten the opportunity to get in more hours of work at the store. He had been awake since five that morning, and his body was extremely fatigued. He had settled into bed at around seven-thirty. He checked the clock; it was nine thirty.

"Where are we going to go so late?" Peter asked drowsily.

Marie laughed, then looked again at Peter with amusement in her eyes. "Oh, you were serious. It's obvious you don't get out much,

Chainsaw. Well, change out of those pajamas, and let's go." He was exhausted, but he obeyed. His mother had been absent sporadically, and that night she wasn't home.

He went into the room and drew on clothes as swiftly as possible in his fatigued state. They left the apartment and got into what Peter assumed was Marie's vehicle. She drove like a maniac. Wildly and without caution. Running red lights. Driving thirty-five miles over the speed limit. Peter was surprised that they were never stopped by the police. He was also surprised that they safely reached their destination. They drove up to a large warehouse. It was ten thirty when they arrived.

"Why are we at a warehouse?" Peter questioned.

"You'll see," Marie said with a mischievous grin as she exited the vehicle. Peter slowly followed suit. Marie reached for his hand as they walked towards the large warehouse. Peter noticed that there were quite a lot of vehicles surrounding the warehouse. As they got closer and closer to the warehouse, the boisterous thuds of reveling crashed against Peter's ears. The thumping of the bass began to beat through his frame.

They opened the large warehouse doors. Peter witnessed the repetitive flicker of dancing and lights. He felt like he was trapped in a movie. Everyone was dancing to the wild beat that had reached a tempo of hypnosis. There was a strange air in the place as everyone seemed to be much more friendly than humanly possible. People were smiling at each other, giving off a false aura of euphoria. It was strange, but it enticed Peter.

They danced for an hour, then Peter became fatigued and made his way to one of the couches that lined the back of the warehouse. There was something wrong. Many whom he had seen dancing when he walked in were still on the dance floor. He reasoned that everyone must have some sort of supernatural stamina, or they were on something; given the atmosphere, Peter concluded the latter. He had to catch his breath. He looked into one of the large coolers that surrounded the couches. He desired to grab a beer, but he decided against it and grabbed a water bottle instead.

He saw her flashing hair in the moving strobe lights as she approached him. Marie sat beside Peter, then leaned in so that he could hear her over the music.

"Tired?" she questioned loudly in his ear. Peter nodded. "Take this," she yelled, dropping something into his hand.

He looked at her, clenching whatever it was that she had given him. She was sweating exorbitantly, and her eyes were unbalanced in appearance. It was clear that something foreign had recently entered her bloodstream. Peter continued to look at her. He was unsure about revealing whatever it was that was in his hand, but Marie smiled a magnificent smile, and he caved. He opened his hand and in it was a tiny blue pill. The pill was round and had a smiley face on it. It reminded him of some of the candies they sold at the convenience store, but he knew that the contents were at enmity.

Anxiety and fear poked needles into his back. Just one drink at fifteen had turned him into an alcoholic; now, he was presented with this blue smiley face that seemed to grimace at him. He felt a warm hand on his face. He looked up at Marie, who was still displaying a grin that had a masked angelic look, but her eyes looked devilish and droopy. "Take it, Chainsaw. It's a great escape," Marie said, close to Peter's ear. Ruse and sultry words grazed Peter's ear. He liked it. He popped the pill and drank the water. He felt nothing for a while.

Then it happened.

Everyone was so beautiful to him. He desired to embrace everyone. He tried to embrace everyone. He hugged strangers as if they were long-lost friends. Then he just wanted to dance. The music sounded so much better to him. He felt like the beat was controlling his being. He and the music had become one. He danced and danced. As the night went on, he took two more of the little pills. More embracing. More dancing. Someone passed him a small gas bottle with a dark substance within. He chugged it and laughed. He watched as Marie replicated in front of him, then again and again. He danced with all four Maries. Someone gave him another pill, and he danced all the more until he felt like his feet weren't touching the floor. He was floating. Then the earth stopped rotating. The music stopped playing, and everyone in the club vanished. He was alone in the warehouse. He witnessed as the walls of the warehouse collapsed and dramatically dissipated. He was suddenly barefooted on the sidewalk of a busy road. Confusion took root in his mind.

Then he saw him. Six-year-old Peter, begging on the median. Peter watched in fear and confusion as cars stopped to give money to the six-year-old version of himself. Peter watched for a while as the little boy's container of money expanded as persons continued to give. The red container continued to expand and expand until it exploded, and money flew every which way. His six-year-old self turned to face him from the median. Peter watched as his attractive baby face reddened and expanded. Horns began to grow out of the child's head. The head of the child continued to grow and alternate between hues. The child's head hovered over Peter, scornfully laughing at him. Peter screamed in torment until the child began to vanish. He watched as the scene became liquid and seeped into a pothole, leaving him standing in darkness.

He was suddenly in his bedroom in Liverpool. He watched in agony as his mother began to pour boiling water unto the bare flesh of his doppelgänger. The water scorched the being's flesh, backpedaled into the kettle, and then burned his flesh once again. It repeated vividly and endlessly until Peter was crouched on the floor in a fetal position, crying and rocking back and forth, wishing himself away.

He watched as the scenery broke and shattered into fine pieces of glass, then he was in the bathroom. He beheld another version of himself lying lifeless under the bathwater. The eyes of the doppelgänger unexpectedly flashed open and looked at him. Peter jumped in fright. He was swiftly transported back to the bedroom. He wasn't watching himself anymore; he was himself. Peter looked across the room into his mother's terrifying red eyes. Foam gushed from her mouth like a fiend. He saw the pail in her hand. She threw it violently at him. The pail collided with his forehead. He timidly reached for the gash. He stared, through blurred vision, at his bloody hands. Blood streamed from his head like a raging current. He tried to stop the blood with both of his hands, but it kept spewing at irregular speeds. Peter looked in the mirror, which was the only thing visible in the room at that point. He was drenched in blood from head to foot. He heard the sound of his mother laughing in the thick darkness behind him. As the life left his body, he crumbled to his knees. Letting the darkness eat away at his flesh.

****

Farook looks into the six wide eyes present before him. Halia, Perri, and Olathe all stare at their grandfather with a mélange of fear and shock.

Halia breaks the silence. "Was Peter hallucinating, Grandpa?" Halia questions still gazed and completely engrossed in the salient tale.

"Yes, Hal, Peter was experiencing highly vivid hallucinations," Farook replies.

"Marie is a mess," Perri whispers.

"I take back what I said about Marie. She needs help," Olathe retracts.

"What did Marie give to him, Grandpa?" Perri questions.

"A drug called ecstasy," Farook retorts.

"That's a really potent drug, Grandpa," Halia states, to which Farook nods.

"The mixture of the ecstasy and alcohol called for those vivid hallucinations," Farook adds.

"Why do people even use drugs, Grandpa?" Perri asks.

"For many reasons, my son," Farook answers. "Some see it as an escape. Others may see it as a way to seek and find acceptance. The reasons vary per person, but drugs are highly destructive regardless of the reasoning behind usage. Drugs steal the identity of the user."

"What do you mean by that, Grandpa?" Halia questions.

"Drugs always take a person further than they are willing to go. Drugs destroy dreams and plans and leave an individual in a place where all thoughts and all plans are in alignment with the will of the drugs. Drugs become a user's universe. Their reason for breathing. Drugs become their identity," Farook retorts.

"You said you've used drugs before, Grandpa, for a short period of time. What did it feel like?" Olathe curiously questions. Farook pretends to be deep in thought, then he answers.

"First, I felt really good. Euphoric even. But it was short-lived and ended in depression. It wasn't worth it," Farook honestly states.

"I think that may be the hook, Grandpa. Drugs make a person feel great, then it makes them feel crummy, but then they want to feel great again, so they abuse it," Halia adds.

"On an endless search for happiness," Olathe interjects.

"I prefer sober happiness. That way, I know it's real and not a fragment of my intoxicated imagination. Lasting and true," Perri states.

"You better keep it that way," Farook warns, to which the children laugh.

"Thanks for being so transparent with us, Grandpa," Perri says with a radiant smile.

"Yes, thank you," Halia adds.

"Grandpa is the man!" Olathe exclaims, to which the family enjoys another round of laughter.

"What happens next, Grandpa?" Halia inquires.

"Did Peter die?" Olathe questions with alarm in her eyes as she encloses her face with her soft and delicate hands.

****

Red and yellow. That's what Peter saw as he surfaced from his own personal pool of delirium. Red, Marie's hair. Yellow, the sunlight that warmly caressed his face as it seeped in from the warehouse's high windows.

"James," Marie said with caution. "Can you hear me?"

Peter slowly opened his eyes. Marie was leaning over him. Her hands delicately placed on his shoulders.

"What happened?" He tried his best to say from an extremely dry throat. As the words escaped from his lips, a throbbing migraine took over as if punishing him for speaking.

Marie released her hands from his shoulders and sat next to his head. "You were dancing for six hours, then you blacked out."

"What time is it? What day is it?" Peter asked, still lying on the ground, afraid of moving a limb.

"It's Wednesday. One fifteen in the afternoon," Marie casually stated.

"What!" Peter exclaimed, turning his head to look at her. A sharp pain ran down his spine. Peter bellowed. He eventually regained his composure and returned to his safe position. "I'm late for work," he muttered.

Marie laughed. *What kind of demented person would be laughing right now?* Peter said within himself.

"That's what you're worried about? Missing work?" Marie inquired.

"I'm not like you. I don't have money running as my bathwater. How come you didn't try to wake me sooner? Were you just going to leave me here? Why didn't you call for help?" Peter said as loudly as he could project.

"I just woke up myself, then I saw you! Don't act stupid!" Marie yelled.

"You're the stupid one, Marie! Why did you bring me to this place! Why did you do this to me?" Peter yelled back, despising the pain he felt.

"I did nothing to you! You made all of the choices on your own! I didn't stuff the pills down your throat! I didn't give you the alcohol to drink! So don't blame me for your stupidity! I gave you one pill, not four! It was your choice! So stop blaming me!" Marie blared in Peter's ear. Peter cringed. Every amplified word that came from Marie's tempestuous mouth aggravated Peter's lingering migraine. "I'm sorry," Marie whispered quickly after her outburst.

Peter tried to stand. Every limb on his body ached, and his head was pounding as if to the same beat that once blared in the now desolate warehouse. Peter staggered as his mind willed everything in the warehouse to spin. He collapsed to his knees. He leaned against the wall for support as he sat down. Marie took a seat next to him. Except for a few stray beer bottles, the place was empty. It was as if they had imagined the rave. Everything was swept bare. The place had been discreetly evacuated. Peter wondered what time everyone left. Peter wondered if any of it was real.

The images of his vivid hallucinations came to mind, and he responded by shutting his eyes with all his might as a form of escape, but he could not escape the secrets of his soul.

Marie shook his shoulder, and he opened his eyes. She handed him a bottle of water which he took and slowly sipped from. They sat on the hard warehouse floor for a while. Marie turned to Peter and asked, "Do you think you're well enough to leave?"

Peter turned and looked at her. "Well, let's see," he said as he tried again to stand. Everything ached, but the dizziness had subsided. "Yeah, we can go," Peter said almost inaudibly. He could hardly hear himself over the pounding that rang throughout his feeble frame. He felt as if he had just been in a boxing match and was brutally defeated. Marie took his arm and placed it around her shoulder for support.

As they walked out of the warehouse, they spotted a form in the distance. As they neared the large doors, they realized that someone was curled up in a fetal position off to the northeast side of the warehouse. As they neared the exit, they realized that it was a young man. He looked around sixteen years old. His face was extremely pale, and a translucent substance trickled from the corner of his mouth and kissed the floor. He was obviously unconscious, but Peter and Marie wordlessly passed by him, leaving the warehouse. They reasoned that he would be fine. He would wake up later, they concluded within themselves. Or someone would find him, they said inwardly, giving themselves an alternate supposition.

As Peter got a whiff of fresh oxygen, he barfed. The contents that remained in his stomach slid down a nearby bush. Marie helped to clean off his mouth with a paper napkin from her purse.

They returned to Marie's vehicle. Peter flopped onto the leather passenger seat. Marie got in the driver's seat, and they quickly hastened away, leaving only dust behind them.

"Hungry?" Marie asked her somnolent friend.

"Yeah, a little," Peter muttered. Marie turned into a drive-through at high speed, causing all fatigue to flee from Peter's feeble body and also causing every inch of his frame to throb in pain.

Marie ordered absurd amounts of junk food. Fries and burgers galore. She also ordered copious cups of coffee. Peter didn't fancy the dark caffeinated liquid, but he sipped it slowly as he tried to digest oil-infested potato wedges.

"Where are we going?" Peter asked in between bites. The open road flying by them at great speeds.

"Let's just stay at my hotel for the night," Marie said as she bit into her burger. "I think your mom would have a panic attack if she saw you like this." Peter didn't try to debate it. He let her carry him away to her hotel. He wondered if he had just been kidnapped. He wondered if his mother would pay the ransom note for him. *She would rob a bank for the money*, Peter thought as he sipped the bitter liquid.

They reached a lofty hotel that oozed posh and privilege. Marie parked at the front entrance of the building. The valet took the keys from Marie and drove the vehicle away to the parking lot.

"Let's go, Chainsaw," Marie said. She noticed that Peter was frozen in admiration. It had been a while since he had been in a place so aristocratic. Again, he felt like he was contaminating the extravagantly spotless dwelling with his mundane presence and shoes.

They journeyed in the elevator to the twenty-fourth floor. "Do all the volunteers stay here?" Peter asked.

"All the ones that can afford it. The rest stay in a motel a few blocks down. The university pays for their stay," Marie answered.

"So, you decided to use that soda money after all," Peter commented with a weary smile.

Marie returned the smile. "Well, being an only child has its perks. Once I turned eighteen, my father made me manager of one of my trust funds."

"One of your trust funds," Peter repeated in disbelief. "How much is in the trust fund that you are now managing?"

"Quarter of a million dollars," Marie stated causally.

"That's a lot of money," Peter said as nonchalantly as possible.

Before the glossy and slightly translucent elevator doors opened, Peter watched as a section of the elevator opened, revealing a keypad. Marie swiftly pounced on an eight-digit pin; afterward, the keypad beeped three times, then disappeared again into the elevator door. The elevator door opened to reveal the penthouse suite. Marie threw her bag on the floor, then journeyed to the bedroom. Peter looked around. He didn't know hotels had accommodations so house-like in nature and aesthetics. There was a kitchen, a living room, two bathrooms, a grand bedroom, a pool, and an entertainment room. Peter took a seat at the dining table and continued eating. Marie emerged from the room wearing a bright yellow sundress. They ate in silence.

"What was that stuff that I took last night?" Peter casually asked after a session of peaceful silence.

"X," Marie replied with a mouthful of burger.

"Ecstasy?" Peter questioned for clarification.

"Yup," Marie responded as she wiped the grease off her chin and downed more coffee.

"It had me seeing all kinds of things," Peter confessed. Marie gave him a half-smile.

"It mixed with alcohol really messed you up. The fat sweaty guy that you were hugging gave the alcohol to you, and you chugged it. That's when you started walking around the warehouse like a stranded puppy. You were screaming sporadically while I tried to trail behind you. Maybe that's when the hallucinations began." Peter nodded as Marie tried to help him piece the night back together.

"What did you see?" Marie gently inquired. Peter intuitively closed his eyes as the mental images resurfaced. The images had escaped again from the deranged and drug-controlled portion of his being. The images had absconded to torment him o'er. A slight whimper released itself from Peter's lips. He felt himself being sucked back into the dark and frightening abyss. Her touch brought him back. Peter cautiously opened his eyes to reveal Marie, who had beheld his frightened expression and was holding his hand in hers.

"You don't have to talk about it," she whispered.

Peter felt weak. Weak and used. He felt as if he didn't know what it meant to be a man. All his life, he had been protected and hushed by women. Wasn't he, by nature, supposed to be the protector? He thought. But there he was, in a grand hotel room, being comforted like a child by a five-foot-five, petite, red-headed woman who took on the similitude of a fairy from one of those girly Saturday morning cartoons. *What is wrong with me?* he thought. The more he thought about his lack of masculinity, the more upset he became. He released his hand from Marie's grasp, which caught her off guard.

"Well, it makes no sense for me to try and volunteer today. By the time I get there, they'll be wrapping up. So, what do you want to do?" Marie questioned her stone-faced friend.

"Let's just stay in. I need to rest and regain my strength for work tomorrow," Peter said.

They journeyed to the couch and stayed there for a while, flipping through channels. They watched a channel until they lost interest and then changed to another. Peter dozed off, then woke up with a splitting pain that ran across the side of his head. He held his head and bawled. He couldn't help it; as the pain rocked his body, his mouth let out a whimper. His racket woke Marie, who was sleeping beside him on the sofa.

"What's wrong?" Marie asked as she reached for Peter, who had his head between his legs and his hands upon his quivering pate.

"My head," Peter eventually mustered the strength to say.

Marie walked into the grand bedroom and came back out with a small plastic bag. She emptied the substance on the table and then began to form lines with a blade. She took a dollar bill from her purse and rolled it up. She drew in a line of the substance into her nostril and shook her head violently as it began to make its way into her bloodstream. Peter watched with terrified and puffy eyes as his friend's pupils expanded and pushed against her ocean blue iris.

Marie walked on her knees over to the sofa where Peter was. She took his face in her hands. "James, you're going to have to take a hit.

It will help. Regular pain relievers will do absolutely nothing for you in this case."

Peter stared into her terrifying eyes with his wet and red ones. Marie wiped the tears off Peter's face. She kissed his forehead, his nose, then planted one right on his lips. She tried to pull him closer to her, but he pushed her away. She laughed uncontrollably, then wiped her nose.

"James, your headache is just going to get worse if you don't take a hit," Marie said as she stared at him. Peter felt an awkward chill pierce through him. He felt the potency of the third presence for the first time. Marie was gone, and he was staring at a wild redhead whose tongue was drenched in the smooth liquid of deception.

He didn't want to do it. He stared at the white powder. Cocaine. He was almost certain that that was what his mother was abusing. That substance had been the cause of so much pain and suicidal thoughts. But there it was. In front of him. Inviting him to sail the shores of the unknown. He decided against it, but then the pain hit his body again, plunging him onto the floor. The pain was increasing. He yelped in torment. The pseudo-Marie laughed at his agony.

"Stop torturing yourself, Chainsaw. Just take a hit." She placed the rolled-up bill in his hand. "It will stop the pain," she whispered in his ear. "Do it!" she suddenly yelled, then pushed him towards the table.

Peter knelt there crying. Tears had escaped involuntarily beforehand because of the pain, but this time he wept purposefully. He felt so beside himself. He felt so helpless. He didn't want to do it, but the pain in his head was telling him otherwise. He had to escape the pain, physical and emotional, as the mental images of his deliria resurfaced.

He felt an ungodly nudge. An ungodly presence. He knew nothing about God. He wasn't even certain that there was a God, but he knew that something that was the antithesis of the goodness of God dwelt in that hotel room. He saw it in Marie's eyes. He saw it in the substance that lined the table in front of him. He had seen it several times in his mother's eyes. He had felt the influence of the third presence when he was in the field of flowers all those years ago. He knew it was there when he stood by the roadside begging. He felt its anger as the pail collided with his head, leaving a permanent scar. He felt its touch as it used his mother to caress and cut his locks those years ago.

At that moment, he had no explanation for it, but he felt the burn of scorching hot water as it collided with his back. He screamed as he looked up at his mother, who had now materialized in the room. "It's not real. It's not real. It's not real," he repeated to reassure himself. He closed his eyes, trying to shut out the deliria, but the darkness crept in and met him behind the curtain of his lids.

He started to see images of his mother as the third presence used her to yell, "Just do it!" Spittle flew from her abnormally widened mouth. He had to escape.

He drew the substance into his right nostril using the rolled dollar bill. He heard laughter in his head. The third presence was laughing.

He opened his eyes. Marie was smiling at him. It took a few moments; then, he started to feel the effects of the third presence. Even in the midst of euphoria, he was not deceived; he knew, just like the lies of alcohol, that it wasn't real. He knew that all the pain was still there, but the third presence had told his brain not to feel it.

He felt deceived and free. Comfortable, yet exceedingly uncomfortable simultaneously. He sat there, pain-free but highly disappointed in himself. He felt like he could do anything, but he didn't want to get up. He felt like he could run for president or become a professional athlete. The sky was the limit for him. He decided to play along with the third presence.

He let the deceiver speak sweet nothings into his ear. *You are matchless*, the presence whispered. *You are a god in your own right*, it sang. Peter knew it wasn't genuine, but he laughed and took another hit when he felt the third presence's voice fading. After the hit, the third presence chortled again and began the vain glory oration in Peter's ear.

They must have fallen asleep because Peter woke up with a start and a raging headache. He took another hit and left the hotel room. He didn't need the code to go downstairs. He beckoned on the outside for a taxi, then sped home. When he got home, he dressed quickly for work and was about to leave the apartment when he realized that it was one in the morning. He set his alarm clock for five and collapsed in his bed. Sleep consumed him.

****

The racket of the alarm clock knocked at Peter's cranium, and he arose. He got his things and went to work, which was only a couple of blocks away. While walking, he thought about the events that had taken place the night before. The burning in his right nostril reminded him of the sin he had committed against himself. It was a strange thing, cocaine. He truly heard it speak lies to his inner being. The potency of the third presence was shocking. It spoke dishonesties to him, but he was beginning to fancy the fabrications. He was beginning to fancy the escape.

He worked as one in a trance as he thought on this neo presence that now stalked him. He needed its lies. Everything in Peter's sober world appeared exuberantly dull. All hope and happiness a sober life could bring evanesced around the lingering presence. Peter knew his life had never been one of continuous laughter and youthful bliss, but it was far better than how the third presence was trying to render it in his mind. It was trying to make him dependent on its own version of happiness. It was trying to make him dependent on the hole of false elucidation that it had plunged him so far into. And strangely, he gravitated towards it.

Peter felt a hand on his shoulder, breaking his stupor.

"Man, I've been calling your name for a while now with no response. Are you alright?" Jamal questioned with concern.

"Yeah, I'm alright, man. Sorry about that," Peter answered.

"Okay, if you say so," Jamal answered, not buying Peter's cool response. "There's someone on the phone for you." Peter walked wearily to the company's phone.

"Hi," he heard as he picked up the phone.

"Hello," he responded.

"I'm sending a driver to pick you up, if that's okay."

"That's okay," he repeated. The voice had a direct link to the door to the third presence that was beckoning to him.

"Your shift ends at five, right?"

"Yes," Peter answered.

"Wonderful, I'll be finished at the shelter by five thirty, so I'll see you back at the hotel at six," she said gleefully.

"Okay," Peter said, thinking of the third presence's key.

"See you later then."

"Bye," Peter said, then hung up the phone. He looked at the clock. It was four in the afternoon. He was two hours away from being in that hotel room again. Two hours away from being in the chasm.

He worked for the next hour without a drop of emotion. Perfectly indifferent. He was trying with all his might to mute his crowded mind. At a quarter to five, he saw a luxury vehicle drive into the lot and park adjacent to the store. He reasoned that it must be the driver Marie had sent for him.

"Hey man, can you cover for me? I think I'm going to leave a couple of minutes early," Peter said to Jamal, who was restocking the snack section.

"Sure thing," Jamal responded.

Peter gathered his few things and left from behind the counter, said goodbye to Jamal, then left the store. The man behind the wheel eyeballed Peter from behind the tinted windows for a while. The driver eventually got out of the vehicle.

"Are you Will?" he questioned.

"Yes," Peter responded. Without another word, the driver went around the vehicle and opened the back door for Peter. Peter got in. The driver closed the door and returned to the front left seat. Peter peered through the tinted windows to behold a perplexed Jamal staring at him from behind the glass barricade of the convenience store. Jamal stared until the car became a smudge. *William is truly a mysterious guy*, Jamal reasoned within himself.

Peter pulled a soda out of the mini-fridge that was surrounded by little twinkling lights. Before he could even finish his drink, they had reached the hotel. The trip seemed much faster to Peter, but that was because he was so preoccupied with the congestion of his cranium.

He saw her next to the valet. Waiting for him. She sported a beautiful white sundress. Her red mane was in one braid that stopped at the nape of her neck. Her little sandals sparkled in the sunlight, and she, without a shadow of a doubt, reflected the image of an animated fairy. Peter smiled as she approached the car before it properly came to a halt and opened the door. She surprised him with a full-blown embrace while he still sat in the idle vehicle.

"I've missed you," she said as the embrace came to an end.

"But we saw each other yesterday," Peter said, with a smile, as he got out of the vehicle and threw his arm around her shoulder. He planted a kiss gently on the top of her head.

"That doesn't mean I can't miss you," Marie said, with her arm around his waist and a beam on her face. They walked into the hotel, clinging to one another. They entered the elevator, and Marie pressed the elegantly lit twenty-four. "How was your day?" she questioned Peter with a smile.

As the elevator moved, zipping them upward, Peter felt the nagging pain return, piercing his temples. "It was okay," he responded with a grin, even though he felt as if a group of individuals was pounding on his temple from the inside of his head. "How was yours?" he questioned.

"I had a really great day today," Marie said with her never-ceasing smile. "We fed the homeless, we worked in the soup kitchen, then we spent a few hours finishing up the last coat of paint on a new house that was built for a family in need." Peter raised his eyebrows; even that simple movement had disbursed jolts of pain throughout his cranium. He flinched but tried his best to keep his composure.

"Wow, you're basically a saint," Peter said, to which Marie laughed.

"Definitely not," Marie said through spurts of laughter. "I do volunteer work because it makes me feel like a good person, and I need that feeling every once in a while to cancel out all my crazy weekend activities." As she finished confessing, the elevator stopped at the twenty-fourth floor, and she keyed in the code for the floor. The elevator doors opened to reveal the room he had been in that morning. It was untouched. Everything still where he left it. He felt the icy fingers of the third presence, and he saw the evidence of its being laid bare upon the living room table. *Weren't maids supposed to clean hotel rooms every day?* Peter questioned within himself. Or maybe Marie had requested to keep her room untouched by foreign hands. The only foreign entity allowed in the room was him. And the third presence. *I guess that's how she wants it in order to hide her stash*, he concluded.

Peter took a seat on the settee. His head was pounding like a drum. The pounding amplified to the point of audibility in his ear. That was definitely the worst case since the warehouse expedition. He covered his ears with his hands and squeezed his eyes shut as involuntary tears fell from him. He could feel Marie's touch on his arm, and he could feel her wiping away his tears, but he could hardly make out her voice over the racket. He wanted a hit, but he didn't know how to pull his arms away from encompassing his head. He started to get flashes of the same vivid hallucinations he had gotten in the warehouse. He screamed as the vivid hallucinations, sprinkled with the worst moments of his past, flashed through his mind. The third presence was offering him an escape. His eyes flashed open like a fiend, and his arms swung from his head, and he reached wildly for the white powder on the table before him.

Marie grabbed his arm. "Talk to me, James," Marie said lovingly. "Talk to me," she repeated. Peter's throat was very dry, and he wanted so badly to let the third presence consume him, but as he turned and looked at Marie, he realized that the pain in his heart and soul was amplified to greater volumes than the aching in his head. He had felt so alone for so long. Without foresight. Living for the day. Living for a brown-colored liquid that could only temporarily take him away from his sorrows. Living for breathing's sake.

"It's okay to talk to me," Marie said as she held his hand with one of hers, then gently brushed a lock of hair out of his eye with the other hand. *She is my friend*, he thought. *She actually cares about me.* Peter stared into Marie's blue eyes. She stared back at him with anticipation.

Before his cluttered mind could approve his words, he heard himself say, "My name is Peter. Peter Davies. I'm originally from Liverpool, England. That's why you thought I spoke strangely. I was trying to mask my accent."

He paused. She didn't say anything, so he continued.

"At the age of six years old, my mother brought me out to a field outside a grand home. It was a field filled with radiant pink flowers. She told me to steal a flower, and I did. That field was my place of tarnish. That's where I lost my innocence. I know it sounds silly, but at that moment, I lost everything, and my will had become my mother's will for me, which was filled with deception and lies." Peter took in a breath. He realized that the feeling of sweet release trumped the third presence's beckoning for his will and attention.

He continued. "In no time, she had me on street corners pretending to be homeless and begging for money. We weren't homeless. She called it everyday acting, which is stupid, but I bought into it. I collected quite a sum from begging, but people eventually gave less and less, so it stopped. Then she started dabbling in telephone scamming. Oddly enough, quite a lot of people bought into it and gave her their credit card details. I helped her for a while. Answering the calls. Writing out the numbers. Authorities started getting suspicious, so it concluded abruptly. I thought my life would be normal at that point. It kind of was for a while, but then she appeared high as a kite in my room one night and shaved my head. She then proceeded to starve me so I could appear sickly."

Peter's voice began to break as he recalled and expounded upon his past. Tears escaped upon his cheek; he wiped them away and continued. "I pretended to have cancer. People donated thousands to help with my medical bills that did not exist. I was ashamed, but I had to keep up the performance for my mother's sake. Eventually, some persons at the school became suspicious of my case and started digging. We had to leave. We then came here. To America. To New York, with fake passports, which is why you knew me as James Phetterson. My mom got a great job at an accounting firm. We were able to live in that luxurious condo in Manhattan because my mom had saved the con-money throughout the years. Then a man named Livingston came into the picture. He was the one that helped us to get the fake passports. My mom had edited pictures of us, and Livingston had gotten the passports put together. That's why I had the straight blonde hair because James Phetterson, my alias, has straight blonde hair."

Marie continued to digest the information that was coming to her at rapid speeds. She hadn't known anything about her friend until now. Peter continued. "Livingston started getting physically abusive. I came in one day from school to witness him beating my mother. I wasn't going to just let the man kill my mom, so I charged at him. He knocked me to the ground and pummeled me. If it wasn't for my mom dropping a vase on his head, I'm sure he would have murdered me. He knocked me unconscious. I woke up in the hospital. That's why I looked the way I did when you saw me at school. After that final time I spent with you in the theater, we started to receive death threats. It was from Livingston. He also drained all our funds. We could do nothing about it because ninety-five percent of the money was illegally attained, so we had no case. Plus, it was impossible for us to get involved with the legal system. We had to leave. I wanted to call you so many times, but I just couldn't. I wasn't allowed to…I just…It was…" Peter began to weep, and Marie held him.

"I'm sorry, Peter," Marie whispered as she held her friend. "It's not your fault. Your mother should not have put you through any of that." Marie reached for something in her back pocket, then presented it to Peter. "Here." It was a rolled-up dollar bill.

They each inhaled two lines, then curled up on the couch together like puppies. The third presence and Marie both told him that everything was going to be alright. Her words echoed into his chest as they both drifted asleep.

Peter woke up to the smell of pancakes and sausage. It delighted him. He was frightened when he opened his eyes and realized that he was in a hotel room and not at home in Liverpool. It took some time for him to register where he was. He was slightly discombobulated.

"Good morning, Peter Davies," Marie said as she entered the living room with two plates in her hands. The sound of his birth name threw him aback. He was apprehensive for a moment; then, he remembered that she knew.

"Good morning," he said with a smile, taking a plate from her and scarfing down the majority of the food that once decorated the plate.

They ate in silence for a while. Along with the food, Marie was trying to digest all that she had heard the night before. She had so many questions, but she was trying to find the most meticulous way to phrase and ask the queries.

As she poured more syrup on her pancake, she decided to break the silence, "So, you told me quite a bounty about your mom, but what about your dad?"

"I don't know who my father is," Peter answered with his mouth full of food.

"Oh," Marie said in response. She let silence reign for a moment, then she asked, "Since you moved to New York, have you guys committed any crimes?" Peter stared at his final pancake, debating whether or not to disclose any more information to Marie. She already knew too much, he reasoned. *Can I tell her about the robberies or the ATM skimming?* he wondered.

"Yeah, some credit card skimming. We did that once we moved from Manhattan," Peter answered. He decided to leave out the information about the robberies.

"So enough about that, what are we doing today? I'm off the entire day," Marie announced with a smile. Peter contemplated his plans for the day. *What day is it?* he wondered.

"What day is it?" Peter asked.

"Friday," Marie answered. *Friday.* Peter repeated in his mind. *Friday!* He then realized that it was mandatory for him to be at home today.

"I have some things to finish at home. Then I have to go to work," Peter replied.

"Alright," Marie said, with the same look of disappointment he had witnessed those years ago. He pulled her into an embrace.

"Today is the last day I'll be in town. I'm leaving quite early in the morning tomorrow," Marie said suggestively.

"Well, you can come say goodbye to me at the store tonight. I'm working a couple of hours from seven to two tomorrow morning." His body wanted to go along with Marie's plans, but something was telling him that it would be a mistake. He had already opened up to her about his past, and he deemed that enough intimacy to last a lifetime. He didn't truly understand why he turned down the offer, but he knew it was the right decision.

"Alright, I'll see you tonight then," Marie said with a forced smile. Peter kissed her atop her head and departed.

The taxi driver drove like a manic, per usual in New York. Peter was home in no time. His mother sat patiently at the small dining table.

"Where have you been?" Adela questioned her son.

Peter hesitated. He wasn't too sure about telling the truth, but he did it anyway. "I was with Marie."

Adela laughed. "The redhead?" she questioned. Peter nodded. Adela's laughing abruptly ended. Terror swam across her face as she stood and looked deep into the brown eyes of her son, trying to read the contents of his soul like a book.

"Peter, is this the same Marie? The redhead from Manhattan? The one you went to high school with? The Cold Spring Hills girl?" Peter looked down at the ground in response. "Peter, look at me!" Adela commanded, to which Peter obeyed. "What do you think you're doing? You're not supposed to be in communication with this girl!" Peter's head fell again, and he began to adamantly examine the cheap vinyl that lined their rented floor.

"What does she know?" Adela asked with anger laced in every word. Peter lifted his head and stared into the green garden of his mother's eyes.

"Nothing, Mom," Peter lied. "She doesn't know anything."

"Peter, you cannot afford to be so reckless!" Adela scolded. Peter laughed within himself. *Are you not the professor of recklessness?* He exclaimed to his mother from the fortress of his mind.

"Have you been in communication with her this entire time?" Adela continued to question.

"No, I have not, Mother. She was here for a volunteer trip, and she saw me in the convenience store. She leaves tomorrow," Peter said. Finally telling the truth about something.

"Well, I'm glad she's leaving. Maybe having a job wasn't a good idea for you," Adela said, deep in thought.

"Mom, you don't even know her!" Peter exclaimed, then wondered why he was so enraged by his mother wanting his one and only friend to leave. Wanting him to live again in isolation. "No offense, but you just don't know her."

"Do you?" Adela questioned forcefully. "Do you really know her, Peter?" Peter let the question float in the air between them without a response. "Well, the good thing is that she is leaving tomorrow. I don't want you having any further communication with her. Am I understood?" Adela said sternly, to which Peter nodded.

"Alright, son, let's get to work," Adela said over a blueprint of the bank two towns over.

****

"Hey there," Peter looked up when he heard the familiar voice. There Marie was, across the counter at the convenience store. His face lit up like the fourth of July. He looked at the large clock that perched on the south wall. It was nine thirty. He was two and a half hours into his shift. Four and a half hours to go.

"Hey there," he repeated with a smile.

"I'm leaving tonight. Everyone else is leaving with the bus in the morning, but I checked out early because I want to get back to get some work done before classes begin again on Monday," Marie said quite matter-of-factly.

"Oh, okay," Peter said, debating what to utter next. "I'll miss you," he said softly. Marie smiled, but tears filled her eyes.

"Can I talk to you outside for a minute?" Marie asked.

"Sure thing," Peter said. Peter asked Elsa to run the counter for a few minutes as he stepped outside to talk to Marie. They felt the cool breeze caress their faces as they opened the convenience store doors. Peter leaned against the west wall of the building. Marie stood in front of him. This reminded them of the conversation they had in the same spot a week earlier.

"This may be a little forward or maybe just crazy, but…." Marie had never looked so nervous. Peter couldn't recall a time in which he'd seen Marie appear nervous. "I think I'm in love with you," Marie blurted.

Peter couldn't believe his ears. He refused to believe his ears. Did Marie just tell him that she loved him? But not just loved, but was in love with him? Could this be real? Or another hallucination? He thought. His mind ran wild. *What is love?* Peter questioned internally.

Marie batted her long eyelashes and tried to transport her blue eyes into Peter's soul as to read the contents thereof. Peter was lost in thought and forgot that Marie must be waiting for a response. He remembered after a few moments and then drew her in for an embrace. They held each other for a while. Marie was greatly anticipating a verbal response, but she settled for a physical one.

"I'll call you," she said as she pulled away.

"Sounds good," Peter replied, completely disregarding the warning of his mother that traveled around in his head.

"Okay," Marie said as she turned to leave. Peter noticed the deflated look that paraded on her face as she prepared to depart. He had to do something. He knew he cared for her. *Maybe one day it could grow into love*, he reasoned internally.

He reached for her arm and gently spun her around to face him. He held her face in his hands and gently planted a kiss on her forehead. As his lips departed from her forehead, he whispered, "I love you too."

Joy radiated in Marie's eyes. Without words, Marie and Peter stood there staring at each other in front of the convenience store, in full *tête-à-tête*.

****

Handfuls Of Yesterday

Peter sat with the mask in his lap. He was the bunny. His mother was the duck. They watched as the officers left for their lunch. They watched until the cruisers turned out of their visual range.

"Are you ready to do this?" Peter heard Adela ask. He turned and looked at her. The only familiar face he has ever known. Begging him, beseeching him to take what wasn't his.

Peter glared at the bank across the street, but all he could see in his mind was the field of pink flowers. His personal place of tarnish. He glared at his now manly hands that sat nervously next to the abnormally large bunny mask that sat way too comfortably on his lap. The bunny seemed to laugh at him. He looked at his mother. His palms began to sweat. He looked again at the mask that paraded an ostentatious smile. Peter felt as if he was going to be sick, but he managed to squeeze out a response, "Yes."

"Okay. Remember, stick to the plan," Adela warned.

Stick to the plan. Stick to the plan. Sick to the plan. Peter rehearsed in his mind. The plan. The intricate plan they had been brewing for weeks. Adela for months. The plan was audacious, but Adela deemed it attainable, and as usual, Peter was going along for the ride.

"Let's do it," Peter said as he watched his mother put on her mask and fasten it around her red wig. Peter did the same. He placed his mask on and fastened it around his straight black wig. They both wore wigs and colored eye contacts to conceal their identity. Peter's brown eyes now appeared blue, and Adela's green eyes now appeared hazel. They even wore garments that contorted their body images. Adela, who was a slender woman, appeared slightly overweight. Peter, who was a well-built young man, looked slim, almost meager. They didn't look like themselves, and that was the objective.

Peter and Adela grabbed their guns and ran swiftly across the street. Peter and Adela knew they had to work fast. The officers had lunch nearby, and if they were alerted, they would be able to respond quickly.

Peter and Adela blasted through the bank doors. A wisp of black and red wigs.

"Everyone, get down!" Peter and Adela yelled. They were stampeded by a parade of screams as customers and tellers alike fell to the ground in fear. Adela and Peter had two guns each, one in each hand pointing in every which direction.

"We leave here with a hundred thousand dollars, and no one gets hurt!" Adela sternly exclaimed.

"You!" Adela yelled. Adela grabbed a petite bank teller from the ground by her hair. Adela flung the teller in Peter's direction. The lady's tag confirmed that she was the bank manager. "You're going to give him fifty thousand dollars." The woman hurriedly obeyed. "Hurry! You have two minutes to get fifty thousand into his hands."

"And you!" Adela grabbed a scrawny young teller who didn't look more than eighteen years of age. "You're going to get me my fifty. You have two minutes." The young man scurried off, following the lead of the bank manager.

"Everyone stay on the ground!" Peter yelled when he detected the slightest of movements.

Peter and Adela saw him. A middle-aged man who wore a shirt that signified that he worked for the bank. The man got up and dashed for the alerting system. In the blink of an eye, Adela lifted her gun and pulled the trigger.

CHAPTER 9

Peter watched in disbelief as gunpowder escaped from the muzzle of the revolver that his mother held in her right hand. Peter witnessed as the man fell to the ground in the distance. Everything seemed to be going in slow motion, like an ostentatious tale.

Adela turned and looked at Peter. Her arm still in the air. Still in shooting position. Still holding the revolver. Her fake hazel eyes revealed that she, too, was taken aback by her actions. Peter saw surprise in her eyes, but not guilt, which was more frightening to him than the actual act that she had so recently committed.

The gunshot had caused the manager and the teller to return with haste. They handed them the sacks filled with currency.

Adela and Peter bolted through the bank doors and ran wildly to the nearby alley. They found the trapdoor that they had sought out a week back and quickly changed once inside. They threw the wigs in one of the dark corners of the area. They pummeled the masks to the best of their ability and left them on the mucky ground. They continued to change clothes and took out their colored eye contacts.

Peter and Adela causally walked out of the small compartment, securely closed the trapdoor behind them, and then leisurely strolled to a home they knew was vacant. In the backyard, Adela stuffed the sacks under her blouse and wrapped her cotton sweater around the sacks. She then placed her blouse back over the sacks.

Adela knew the homeowners were away on vacation, and she also knew that the neighbors were at work. She reached into her left pocket and came up with a fake mustache, which she pasted above Peter's upper lip. Adela went into the shed and retrieved a rake and handed it to Peter.

They circled around to the front of the home. Peter started to rake, and Adela sat on the rocking chair in front of the abode. They heard the commotion in the distance. They saw the flashing of police lights and knew it was for them. Peter's palms began to sweat as he heard the sirens approaching the house. *They caught us*, Peter thought.

Peter listened keenly as the officer got out of the car, turned off the sirens, and approached the house they were pretending to possess. Peter continued to rake without looking up at the officer.

"Well, hello there, officer," Adela said in a bright and perky southern drawl. Peter looked over at his mother. She was standing now, caressing her money triplets that hid under her celeste blue blouse. The rocking chair still swayed behind her.

"Good afternoon, madam," the officer said to his mother. "Sir," the officer said to Peter. Peter nodded in acknowledgment. "Have you seen or heard anything suspicious today?" the officer inquired.

"The only thing I've heard today was the sound of those sirens in the distance," his mother replied, still very country. It was like Alabama had fallen upon her. "What's going on?" Adela inquired with obvious concern and oblivion.

"There's been a bank robbery just a few blocks away from here," the officer informed. Adela gasped. She rendered a flawless performance of being both perplexed and flabbergasted. Peter took in the show. *She is truly meant for the big stage*, Peter thought. *Maybe if she had pursued acting, our lives would have been different.*

"My word," Adela replied with her right hand placed on her chest in feigned shock. Adela then moved her hands to her protruding belly and caressed it with tender love and care. She really did love the occupants of her constructed womb.

"The two suspects fled the scene on foot, so we were asking around to see if anyone saw anything suspicious or any movement on their property," the officer added.

"We haven't, sir. But tell us what the suspects look like so we can keep an eye out," Peter heard himself say, trying to render a southern accent as well.

"The first suspect was identified as a slender, Caucasian man around six feet tall, with long black hair and blue eyes. The second suspect was identified as a plumb Caucasian female, around five feet six inches, with long red hair and brown eyes. If you see anyone that fits that description, please give us a call," the officer said on a final note.

"Will do, officer. You have a great day now," Adela said with a mixture of shock and perk. The officer waved goodbye, returned to his cruiser, and drove away. Peter resumed raking, and Adela sat back down on the rocking chair. Peter and Adela kept up the show for another hour; then, Peter joined Adela on their borrowed porch steps. *This is a real home*, Peter thought as he walked up the steps. Even in the midst of such drama, he was thinking of the dynamics of family.

"What are we going to do, Mom?" Peter questioned as Adela reached for and yanked the fake mustache off Peter's face. "We can't go back to the ditch car because that entire area is surrounded."

Adela got up from off of the rocking chair and walked around the porch in contemplation. The family and their neighbors would be home soon, and they had to think fast. Adela's attention then fastened upon the old vehicle in the driveway. Adela smiled, reached for one of the flowerpots that lined the front of the home, lifted it, and retrieved a silver key. She opened the front door of the picturesque home. Adela then instructed Peter to look for the key to the vehicle as she kept watch. Peter could not find the key anywhere, but he did take in the smell of apple pie that filled every corner of the house. He wondered about the family that inhabited that home. When he reached the living room, he saw a cross hanging from the wall. He stood there for a while, looking at it. Something about the tiny wooden cross stirred something inside of him. He was curious, then he was upset.

"Have you found it?" Adela called from the outside.

"No, I haven't," Peter answered, still taken by the cross and the little Jesus that hung from it. *What is it even about? What is religion even about?* Peter questioned internally.

"William," Adela called quietly and sternly. "Let's go," Peter glimpsed at the wooden cross once more before returning to the outside.

Adela locked the front door to the house and headed over to the idle car.

"But, Mom, I didn't find the key," Peter said. Adela reached for something in her pocket and began to work on the car door. In no time, it was open. Peter opened the fence gate while his mother started the car using the contraption from her pocket. Adela eventually got the engine rumbling and reversed out of the driveway. Peter closed the gate and jumped into the passenger seat. His mother had just hotwired a car. Peter didn't know that was a skill his mother possessed. He really didn't know the woman he was sitting next to, he thought.

"What are we going to do with the car?" Peter asked as they entered the ramp for the highway.

"Fix it up and sell it," Adela said with a smile. Peter couldn't help but catch the contagious grin. "We did it, Peter! The plan worked!" Adela said with childlike glee.

Peter laughed. "We did, didn't we? We did it! That was some rush."

"I'll say," Adela concurred. "Let's go out to eat tonight. To celebrate your birthday," Adela said gleefully. *She remembered*, Peter thought, seeing that she had forgotten his birthday for two consecutive years.

"You can get anything you want! I'll buy you the restaurant if you want!" Adela said, throwing her head back in laughter.

Peter chuckled and grabbed the wheel. "Watch the road!" He warned gaily. They laughed, truly enjoying each other's company.

"Dinner sounds good," Peter said.

****

"Nice watch, man," Jamal commented.

"Thank you," Peter said with a smile he could not wipe off his face. His mother had bought him the watch and presented it to him at dinner the night before. He and his mother had a wonderful dinner together at a nice brasserie. They dressed in their best and celebrated their successful robbery. They talked for hours. Peter had never felt so close to his mother. Her eyes were radiant and sober and green as the grass that lined the earth's floor. He loved her. She had her ways, but his love for her was undeniable.

"You must have been saving for a while for that," Jamal said, still commenting on Peter's watch.

"Actually, my mother bought it for me. It was my birthday yesterday," Peter said.

"Happy birthday!" Jamal said ecstatically. "You're legal! Drinks on me tonight!" Jamal said gleefully, to which Peter laughed.

The company phone rang, and Peter answered. "Good afternoon," Peter said.

"Happy birthday!" the voice exclaimed. Peter smiled. He knew who it was. "I tried to call yesterday, but they said that you weren't at work."

"Thanks, Marie. How are you?"

"You and me. Drinks tonight," Marie proposed.

"I have classes in the morning," Peter responded.

"So do I, James Will Chainsaw Peter," Marie said. The sound of his birth name caught Peter off guard, but then he remembered the night in the hotel. "We're going out. I'll send a driver for you, and don't worry, I'll have you home at an acceptable time." Peter could hear her smiling. He laughed at how direct she was. She always got what she wanted.

"Alright, Red Mane," Peter said with laughter riddled in his voice.

"What did you call me?" Marie questioned at the sound of her new alias.

"Red Mane," Peter repeated. There was a silence on the other line for a while, and Peter began to worry that he might have offended her.

"I like it."

****

They sported jerseys and drank like sailors. Marie had taken Peter to a bar not too far from where he lived. They talked, laughed, ate, drank, and watched the game on one of the many televisions that lined the sports bar.

"So, how did you spend your birthday?" Marie asked. Peter reckoned that her red hair, blue jersey, and pale white skin made her look like a living, breathing American flag.

"It was interesting," Peter replied as he lifted his drink to his lips. Marie was about to respond, but the breaking news on the television interrupted her.

There it was. Broadcast of the robbery that had taken place the day before. Peter watched as the media publicized his transgression for all the world to consume and regurgitate to others. Images of him and his mother sprung upon the television screen, taken from the security cameras, but they were both unrecognizable in their masks and getup. They had made the news. Peter knew they had made the news before for their other robberies, but that was the first time he was beholding his wrongdoings in public and in high definition.

Peter sighed in relief as the journalist reassured him that the bank teller, who was shot by his mother, was to make a full recovery. They had done it without even a trace of detection. A strange fusion of guilt and pride filled his heart. Peter leaned into the table so he could say his words privately to his friend.

"That was us," Peter whispered as he stared at his blue-eyed friend.

"What?" Marie said, unsure of what Peter was implying.

"My mom and I robbed that bank yesterday," Peter confessed.

Marie gaped at Peter in unbelief. She looked back at the television, then returned her gaze to her friend. "Whose idea was it?" Marie asked.

"My mother's," Peter answered quietly.

"Of course," Marie judgmentally said as her face reddened and disdain spilled from her lips. "You have to leave her, Peter. You have to leave her soon. Sooner than later, she's going to put you in a predicament that might get you killed, and I can't lose you. I love you," Marie said as she reached for Peter's hand and held it. She had said those three words again, and, for the second time, Peter was unsure as to how to respond. Peter bowed his head as if the weight of her words was overwhelming him.

"Peter, listen to me. I have a lot of money, which you know," Marie continued. Peter stared into her blue eyes. She had used the trigger word. She had his undivided attention. "Let me help you. Let me help you to run away. You have to leave her before she kills you!" Marie's voice had fluctuated to an extremely high and exasperated pitch. She was truly infuriated. Rage poured from her soul and pierced her eyes. She looked more wild than upset, and at that moment, Peter was frozen, unsure of what to do or say.

"Yes," slipped from his lips. "I want to leave her. I need to leave her for good," Peter heard himself say. *Maybe this is the way to get rid of Marie*, Peter reasoned internally. She was getting too close. Too wrapped up in their lives. She knew where they lived. She knew where he worked. She knew his deviant past. She knew too much. He had to rid himself of her constant pestering. "Please help me leave," Peter said with the best display of desperation he could enact.

"I can get you the money by the start of summer," Marie said with a tender smile. "You deserve a good life, Will. Far away from the controlling whip of that witch you call a mother."

The harsh words cut at Peter's soul, but he had to keep up the show as the battered child that wanted so desperately to leave his abusive mother. At that moment, Peter realized that his show had always been his reality. Peter leaned over and kissed Marie gently on the cheek. She smelt of expensive perfume and cheap liquor.

"Thank you," he said as he held the hand of his redheaded friend. At that moment, Peter knew he wouldn't leave his mother, but he was a little enticed by the tangible possibility.

****

"I am truly surprised that Peter told Marie about his past," Halia states.

"I guess he was really lonely," Olathe adds.

"Honestly, I think Jamal would have been a better confidant than Marie. Something about her just strikes me as being a little off," Perri interjects.

"Is it because she's a girl?" Olathe questions her brother.

"That's silly, Olathe. Of course not. Jamal just seems like the kind of person that would have shared some words of wisdom if Peter had opened up to him about his situation," Perri responds.

"True," Halia agrees. "I wonder if Peter will change his mind and leave his mother once he has Marie's grant in his hands," Halia questions while looking into her grandfather's warm eyes.

"He could easily take off without his mother's knowledge," Perri shares with vivid anticipation as he too looks to his grandfather for confirmation of his hypothesis.

"What does he do?" Halia, Perri, and Olathe ask simultaneously.

****

They sat comfortably on the settee, eating Chinese food and watching a comedy. The past few weeks had been one of peace and strange tranquility for Adela and Peter. They spent most waking hours together. Adela was no longer working, and all Peter's time outside school and work had been spent with his mother.

They spoke of their plans and dreams, made a possibility by their ill attained neo wealth. Without really thinking, Peter confessed, "I've been spending time with Marie." Adela turned and looked at her son with hurt and angered eyes, her mouth filled with Lo Mein.

"I told her a little about my past," Peter added. Adela's mouth dropped open, revealing its oriental contents. "No worries, it gets better. She wants to give me money to leave you."

Adela swiftly placed her boxed dinner on the table, swallowed her mouth's contents, and then turned to face her son. "I didn't know you were planning to leave me," Adela said with a sly smile. Peter returned the grin.

"No, you know I'm not going to leave you, considering I just told you that I've been given an offer to leave you," Peter said, to which they both laughed.

"But on a serious note, Peter. How much did you tell her?" Adela asked, her face grave.

"Not much," Peter lied. "But enough for her to offer to give me fifty thousand dollars to leave you."

"Fifty thousand dollars," Adela mouthed with shock and excitement. "So, what are you going to do?"

"I'm going to take it, Mom," Peter said, to which Adela laughed with glee, flopping her legs and clapping her hands like an excited child. "I'll tell her that I'm going back to England. We can move to another state and start over."

Adela leaned over and kissed the forehead of her son. "You are a genius."

For some odd reason, Peter could not wipe the smile off his face for the remainder of the night.

****

Peter felt out of place at the Cold Spring Hills country club. He sported white khaki pants and a white polo, but he still felt like a fish out of water. Marie had arranged for them to meet at the country club, and he could not quite understand why.

Peter entered the country club and looked around the lobby for Marie, but she wasn't there. He saw a lot of activity on the bright exterior, so he went through one of the large glass doors and entered the club's peripheral. It was stunning. To the right of him was a grand golf course that seemed to span for miles. He also saw people playing a game he had never before witnessed. A game played with sticks while on horseback. He observed the players for a while, but none sported the familiar locks. To the left of him was the grand and exceptionally posh pool area. He skimmed through the sea of beautifully trim women, then he saw her. She sported a red one-piece and was sunbathing on a beach chair. Peter journeyed to the entrance of the pool area.

"Marie," Peter called. Marie sat up and looked in the direction of the call. When Marie saw Peter, she smiled and journeyed over to him.

"Hi," she greeted. She opened the gate to the pool area and ran down the steps to embrace Peter. "Come with me," she said as she released him from the embrace and took his hand. Marie led Peter up the steps and into the pool area. She led him to the bar. Marie signaled to the bartender, and he began making two drinks.

"What are you doing?" Peter questioned.

"Having one last drink with you before you leave," Marie said as she reached for her drink and handed Peter his. "I'm really glad you decided to do this," she shared. After they had finished their drinks, Marie went behind the bar and pulled out a golf bag.

"Here's the golf bag that you left at my place," Marie said. Peter smiled as he placed the bag on his back. Peter pulled Marie close to him and embraced her. Peter kissed Marie gently on the forehead.

"I love you," he said as genuinely as he could enact. "Thank you." His breath lingering on her forehead.

Marie smiled. A tear fell from her eye and onto Peter's shirt. "I love you too," she said. Peter kissed her forehead again and let her go. He held on to the golf bag, exited the pool area, and journeyed to the golf course. He lingered for a while, then he exited the course, the main building, then he was off the country club premises completely. He took a moment to look inside the golf bag. Peter had to quickly close the bag for fear of currency blowing away from him.

Peter turned and looked back at the country club. He saw her in full red, the radiant sun behind her. She was waving goodbye. Peter reached into his pocket and took out his sunglasses. Peter placed them on his face and turned and walked away. Leaving the wave of separation behind him.

****

Adela and Peter packed the few things that they had into their new full-size vehicle. They started their journey. They decided to move to the south. They had settled their sights on South Carolina. Peter said goodbye to Jamal in the most meticulous of ways over ganja smoke and felines.

Peter and Adela stopped only for food and gas. They reached South Carolina on a bright Sunday morning. Their new apartment was much nicer than the one they previously resided in. They journeyed up the stairs to apartment 211. Peter was carrying a few things up the stairs when his neighbor opened the door. She was a petite young woman with brown skin and silky black hair that flowed like a fountain down her back. She wore a beautiful white dress and cradled a thick book in the nook of her right arm. She locked the door behind her and started to walk down the steps.

"Good morning," she greeted Peter with a radiant smile.

"Good morning," Peter said, passing her swiftly as he realized that the thick book she held was a Bible. She was one of them, he thought. Before he entered his apartment, he journeyed back down the stairs with his eyes and watched as the beautiful petite woman clicked away in her heels. He peered as she greeted his mother, then headed to her own vehicle. Peter opened the apartment door, rested the things in the spacious living area, and then went downstairs to help his mother once again.

"Our neighbors seem nice," Adela commented as they finished unloading the vehicle.

"So it seems," Peter replied. They retrieved the rest of their things, locked the car doors, and journeyed up the stairs once again.

"We're home, honey," Adela said with a smile. Peter smiled and hugged his mother, placing a kiss on her head.

They journeyed around the fair-sized apartment together. The living room was beautifully furnished. The kitchen sported a fancy fake marble countertop that Adela adored. The three bedrooms were decently sized, and the two bathrooms were surprisingly grand. It was quaint, but they deemed it acceptable. They began to unpack. They breathed in the new season filled with promise and hope.

Sheneen Monique Soares

****

Peter and Adela had comfortably settled into their new lives and routine. In just three weeks, Peter had a part-time job at the city's community center and had registered for fall classes at the local college. Adela scored another diner gig. She decided to stick with her original trade.

Those three weeks were peaceful. Peter was making friends easily at work. He still sported the William alias, but he didn't mind becoming William. Peter felt strangely free, and the feeling enticed him. After work, he enjoyed leaning against the apartment railing and looking out at the beautiful forest area that stood adjacent to the apartment complex. He daily took in the serenity of the birds as they flew carefree above the green canopy. The scene was mesmerizingly beautiful. He loved to feed the ducks that sometimes left the nearby pond to keep him company.

He saw his neighbor frequently. She always had a friendly greeting, a large smile, and an even larger Bible. Peter was intimidated by the Bible and its size, but her greetings were easily received.

After work one Thursday evening, Peter leaned against the railing of the apartment complex, looking out at the beautiful green stretch. Peter went back inside the apartment to grab a beer. He then quickly returned to the warm outdoors in order to watch the sunset. It was a show that was too vivid to be found on an electronic box. He stood outside, sipping his liquor as he watched the invisible hands paint pink and orange across the firmament. Akin to slumber, night came precipitously and consumed the sky. Peter stood there in the darkness, watching the ripple of the lake and admiring the slow glide of his feathered friends. Peter took another sip of his drink. He closed his eyes and breathed in the fresh air.

"So this is where you came," he heard a voice say.

Peter's eyes flung open. The voice came from downstairs. He knew that voice. His drink fell from the grasp of his hand and landed with a thud on the matted grass. Her red hair was wild and untamed. Her bestial eyes pierced him.

Marie looked at Peter with disgust as she made her way up the apartment steps. "You're such a liar," she said with contempt. "I took fifty grand out of my trust fund for you. For you to go back to England and start a new life. But you came here!" Marie exclaimed. She aggressively wiped her nose on her cotton sleeve. Blood and mucus smeared the sleeve.

As she stood there across from Peter, Peter got a good look at her eyes. There was barely any trace of the blue he had once known. He had never beheld such an extreme form of mydriasis. Even his mother's eyes had never carried such a horrifying guise. She looked hollow, uninhabited. She looked meager, much different from the slender girl he had left at the pool almost a month back.

"I didn't lie to you," Peter responded calmly.

"So, you're here alone then?" Marie asked, aggressively wiping her nose and scratching her skin violently. She was beginning to frighten Peter.

"No, she found the money and wouldn't let me leave for England. But it's fine now, Marie. I'm safe now, and it's all because of you, so I thank you," Peter said as he tried to gently lead Marie back down the apartment steps.

"No!" Marie exclaimed, thrashing her arms and pushing Peter off of her with all the strength she could muster. "I want to talk to her."

Before Peter could stop her, Marie had flung open the apartment door. Peter swiftly followed suit. Marie found Adela in the kitchen and began throwing vulgar insults at her.

"Get her out of the house!" Adela yelled, to which Peter grabbed Marie's arms.

"You're an abomination! You're a filthy low-life that doesn't deserve anything good! You don't deserve Peter!" Marie yelled as Peter pulled her outside.

"Get this maniac out of the house, Peter!" Adela yelled, clearly enraged.

"You can't handle the truth, huh?" Marie deafeningly spewed before Peter had completely pulled her outside. Marie staggered against the apartment complex railing, then began to mockingly laugh at Peter. Her physiognomy abruptly morphed into one of austerity. She placed her head back, gargled mucus, and propelled it onto Peter's right cheek. Marie laughed devilishly at Peter's angered expression. For a millisecond, Peter wanted to push her off the ledge, but then his reasoning returned to him. He wiped the multi-colored phlegm off of his cheek with the sleeve of his shirt, then gently grabbed Marie's arms.

"I know you aren't yourself right now, Marie. This isn't you. This has never been you. I know the real you. You're kind and smart, and you're my very best friend. You helped me leave New York. Even though my mother is here with me, it has been a much better life. We are living a normal life now, and it's all because of you. So, thank you," Peter said, then embraced his bewildered friend. The embrace tamed her demons. Her thrashing arms fell to her side. When Peter pulled away, she just stared at him, wordless. She broke the visual *tête-à-tête* and began to journey down the apartment steps.

"Bye, Marie," Peter said. Marie looked back at him for a moment with her dilated pupils, then continued to walk eerily down the stairs. For a moment, Peter saw a flash of the real Marie.

Peter went back inside the apartment. His mother sat at the kitchen counter, sipping red wine. Adela used her free hand to rub her aggravated temples.

"How did she even find us?" Adela questioned her son as he walked in.

"I honestly have not the slightest clue," Peter defended in his native tongue. "In the state she's in, Mum, I highly doubt she'll remember any of this," Peter said before heading to the bathroom. Peter washed his face thoroughly while replaying the last half an hour on repeat in the private theater of his mind.

Peter heard a commotion in the living room. Then a gun went off.

CHAPTER 10

Farook pauses dramatically and grabs his cup of tea. He slowly takes a sip. He places the cup back on the table. All three of his grandchildren now look upon him with avid anticipation. This portion of the tale is hard for him, but he has to act as if it is just a tale. Just a story. He has to act as if this is the tragic climax in the life of an unfortunate stranger.

This portion reminds him of the pain of tragic loss. Losing the one person who truly cared for him at that time. His heart begins to burn, but he has to stay strong for the children. He picks up his tea again and takes another gulp. He places the cup delicately back in its place, then repositions himself on his chair. He is ready.

****

The sound made Peter jump. He held on to the basin for dear life. He was frozen in space. He was frozen in time. He stood clinging onto the basin for a few moments. Numb and immobile. Trying to muster up the strength to place his hand on the cold doorknob.

Peter eventually opens the door, and the sight shatters his being. Marie stood over his mother with bloodshot eyes and a handgun dangling from her right hand. Peter just stared at Marie because he didn't have the strength to look at the blurred form lying on the ground in his peripheral vision.

Marie lifted her head and looked at Peter. Marie dropped the gun off to the right side of the lifeless form that decorated the apartment floor. The thud of the gun hitting the ground caused Peter to jump once again. He was frozen. He just stared at Marie. Marie wiped her nose with her sleeve and smiled. Marie lifted her arms. She looked like a dark bird in that sweater of hers.

"I did it for you," Peter heard her say. "I love you. You're free now," Marie said while smiling. Her eyes. Her eyes. Red. Her hair. Her hair. Red. The water. The water. On the ground beneath the lifeless form. Red. Too much red.

Peter felt sick. Marie approached him, repeating, "I love you. You're free now." She lifted her arms to embrace him, and he pushed her with all his strength. She crashed into the kitchen counter and yelped. Marie held her back in agony. In ire, Peter flung her out of the apartment. He wasn't sure if she was alright, but he didn't care. He slammed the door and stood with his face upon the cold wood and his back to the lifeless form. He heard as Marie struggled down the steps, bellowing in pain.

Peter's head was spinning. The room was spinning. He wanted to bolt out the door. To run past Marie. To run as far away as possible from the lifeless figure that lay on the ground behind him.

Peter eventually turned around, and streams fell from the safety of his eyes. Peter shut his eyes, trying to erase the image of his lifeless mother lying in a pool of blood. Peter punched the bookshelf to the right of him. Peter felt the warm contents of life drip from his knuckles, but he didn't feel a thing. He didn't feel a thing. Numbness had consumed him.

Peter dropped to his knees and wept for a few minutes. He was frozen. When he eventually thawed, he crawled to the left of the lifeless form. As he crept, he broke the wine glass that his mother was sipping from just moments ago. His knees were bleeding, but he didn't feel it. He just couldn't feel it.

Peter looked at her through blurred vision. Her eyes remained open. Green as the grass that carpeted the earth's floor. Peter gently lifted her onto his lap as if she were sleeping. Blood seeped into every nook and cranny of his clothes, but he couldn't feel it.

He held her and wept bitterly. Peter took her hands in his and bawled. Peter looked into her green eyes, blurred from his wet vision. He stared into her eyes for a while, then closed them with his red hand. He stared at his hand. Red. He hated red. Peter then noticed that her final facial expression was one of fright. She wasn't expecting to die. Death took whoever it felt like, whenever it felt like. Peter cradled her and rocked back and forth for what seemed to be an eternity.

In the eye of the storm entitled grief, Peter, through blurred vision, saw the gun just a few feet away from where he knelt, holding his mother. Thoughts that frightened his true self entered his mind. *Just do it*, a voice said. *No!* another yelled. *Life is going to end anyway*, grief and bitterness whispered. Voices swamped him. Peter raised his hands to cover his ears as if the voices were external. But it was in the blocking out of all exterior noise that the inner demons came out to play with his mind. *No!* he yelled at them. *Yes!* they yelled back.

Peter gently rested his sleeping mother back into her red pool. Peter got up and paced the apartment, trying to get rid of the voices. He knelt o'er next to the corpse and held her tight against his chest.

It was like a snap. Like something had suddenly consumed him. He let go of his unresponsive mother. She fell with a light thud into the pool of red. He stepped over the body and sat with his back against the bookshelf. Peter reached for the handgun and held it firmly with both hands. Peter closed his eyes and caressed his forehead with the muzzle of the revolver. The tips of his fingers slowly spun the cylinder in a horrid bout of Russian roulette. Tears escaped from his closed eyelids as the cylinder rotated.

Just do it. You have nothing to live for. You've only ever been who she created you to be. Your creator is dead. Your very identity lies before you, lifeless in a pool of her own blood. Look at her! Peter obeyed the voice and opened his eyes to behold his mother. *She is gone, and you're gone too*. He placed his finger over the trigger.

Do it. He shivered.

Do it. He grunted in pain.

Do it! He was about to pull the trigger when he heard movement outside the door. He tried to ignore it and stayed as still as possible. He didn't hear anything for a while, so he began to spin the cylinder as he did aforetime.

"Hello," Peter heard a soft voice say from outside the front door of the apartment. Peter opened his haggard eyes and looked right into the muzzle of the gun. He then shifted his attention to the green door. Green, like his mother's eyes. Peter closed his clamshell shutters o'er and waited for the person to leave so he could end it. Peter spun the cylinder.

Peter froze for a moment as he watched the doorknob turn, and the front door became slightly ajar. Peter didn't know what else to do, so he stayed still. The muzzle of the revolver remained connected to his forehead.

The door continued to open in increments until it was completely agape, and his neighbor stood just a few feet away from him. Peter held the gun tightly to his forehead as he stared at his neighbor. She was clearly taken aback by the sight of the dead body that lay on the apartment floor, but she did not run away. She didn't leave. She hadn't yet seen Peter. She stayed in one position near the front door and surveyed the quaint apartment. She kept looking until she began to move her head to the right, east of the front door. Then she beheld him, almost hidden from sight. The large apartment door had concealed him. He sat tucked away in the far east corner. A flicker of fright flashed across her face, then evaded. She stared at him. He gawked back at her with red, overused eyes that ran sad streams down the side of his face. He still had a firm grip on the gun. He wasn't going to let go of the gun; he had convinced himself. The voices had seemingly prevailed in the battle for his will.

After a wearisome time of gawking, Peter closed his eyes and began to spin the cylinder once again. His finger carefully over the trigger. He wanted to die. He didn't care if she was there. He was going to end his life. If she were wise, she would leave, he thought.

"There is a reason why you're alive," he heard her say. She was still there. He was still there and ready to evade the land of the living. Peter tried to let the subtle sound of the spinning cylinder drown out her words. *You don't have a reason to live*, a voice countered. In his state, he much preferred the latter attorney that was trying to win the case for his mind.

"I've seen you at the community center. You're so gentle and kind with the children. They appreciate that sacrifice of time more than anything. You're like a father to them," she said softly, not as one speaking to a child and not as one that was at all perturbed by the situation. She spoke with gentle confidence. She spoke with great assurance of her words.

Peter couldn't understand why, but her words soothed and bothered him. "How would you even know that?" he asked with needless abhorrence. His eyes remained closed, and the muzzle of the revolver continued to caress his forehead.

"I work at the Boys and Girls club. Most of the children you know are the ones I see almost every day. They brag about you. Some say you are the closest thing to a father they have ever had." The impact of her words caused tears to roll down Peter's cheeks. He meant something to someone. He had taken the job at the community center because he wanted to give back to the community instead of stealing from it. He wanted to mend as much as he could because of his own brokenness and guilt.

"They need you," she said. More tears escaped as his heart began to thaw, but it only lasted for a moment as he returned to his demented state.

"That's not true. They have people like you. They need people like you," he said with closed eyes. "What I did at the community center was a shiny spectacle to hide my mess. You do it from a pure heart. I did it because I wanted to feel better about myself. I wanted to know what it was like to be useful. I'm a piece of garbage that deserves to die. I've done things you can't even imagine. My blood is contaminated with depravity. I'm as inferno-bound as it gets. I'm unredeemable, and I'm going to end my life, so it would be wise if you left." Peter was sure she would leave. He was overtly unrefined in the way he spoke. He wanted to scare her away so he could do what the voices were compelling him to do.

Silence embraced the apartment for a moment, but to his annoyance, it was broken by the scuffle of tennis shoes. He heard as she sat right beside him. His eyes were still closed, but he knew that she was sitting to the right of him.

"I read a book about a man who lost everything. People around him thought he was cursed. He himself bought into the lie for a little while. He spent a lot of days angry and frustrated. He even rued the day he was born," she paused for a moment. Curiosity got the best of Peter.

"What happened next?" he asked wearily.

"Things got better for him. That's life. There are hard moments like this one. But life has a tendency to change for the better in the blink of an eye. Think of the seasons. Sometimes we think summer will never end, but it always does. Then fall comes, and all the color in our life fades and falls away. Then winter seems like it will never come to a conclusion, but spring always brings a ray of hope. Spring reminds us of the coming warmth. We remember the winter, but when spring comes, we no longer live in the frigid cold. You may feel this way now but now is not forever. This season will pass. You will make it through this," Anthea softly said.

Peter began to weep as her words saturated his bones, but he still held tightly to the gun. "You just don't understand. The girl…the girl I allowed into my life killed my mother," Peter said in between sobs.

"She killed my mother," he repeated with his eyes still sealed with no chance of opening. She cautiously and gently placed her hand on his shoulder. Her touch was comforting and unsettling. Peter hated and appreciated it.

"I let my mother's killer into my life," Peter continued. "I made that choice. I told her things I wasn't supposed to. I am the reason she started to hate my mother. She didn't even know the kind of person my mother was until I opened my large mouth. My mother warned me not to let anyone in, and I was stupid. I didn't listen," Peter said with self-directed rage. Peter dug the gun deep into his forehead; he wanted to pull the trigger. *What is stopping me from pulling the trigger?* he questioned internally.

"I don't deserve to live," Peter muttered through spittle and with his head bowed low. He still held the gun with both hands.

"I watched my dad die in front of me." The words forced Peter's eyes open, and he turned his head and looked at her. Blood glided down his forehead from the hole he had made with the schnoz of the gun. "It was two years ago. I'm alive. You can make it through this. I'm living proof that a person can survive after something like this." Her eyes radiated with tender care and brilliant truth, but a part of him didn't want to hear those words, so he shut his eyes and returned his head to its former frontal position. He began to spin the cylinder again.

"Your mother would have wanted you to live," she said with nonassertive confidence. He tried to fight it, but the tears ran away from his eyes. Peter opened his eyes and looked up at the ceiling with blurred vision. He tried to hold on to the gun, but his hands were getting weary. The revolver suddenly felt excruciatingly weighty. It felt like a load he had no business bearing.

He let go, and suddenly, the domino effect occurred. The gun fell with a heavy thud upon the cold ground, and weeping and weary Peter fell into the open arms of a stranger.

CHAPTER 11

Red, blue, and yellow. Anthea had called the police, and Peter vaguely recalled the red and blue lights that surrounded the apartment complex. Police and detectives sealed off the premise with yellow caution tape. They placed the gun in a plastic evidence bag. They cleaned the scene after carefully covering and removing the body.

Peter watched in disbelief as it happened. He just didn't understand. A couple of hours ago, he was fine. A couple of hours ago, his mother was alive. He felt so alone, but every time the feeling of loneliness tried to overwhelm him, he was made aware of Anthea's presence. She hadn't left him. Not even for a moment. She stood in the distance while he was being questioned.

Peter gave the officers a detailed description of Marie. After questioning, Peter felt as if he was going to be sick. He vomited behind a nearby bush and collapsed on the ground. He felt so tired. The last thing he remembered was Anthea coming to sit next to him.

He woke up to the smell of fresh blueberry pancakes. He smiled, but when he opened his eyes, he wasn't in Liverpool. He was in an apartment that wasn't his own. He was disoriented for a moment, but akin to an unforeseen tempest, all the memories of the previous day came rushing in like a mighty wind, and he wept. The pressure of the gloom that reality brought him caused his temples to throb erratically. He held his temples, trying to get rid of the pain. He desired the numbing lies of the third presence, but he had a feeling that he wasn't in a place conducive for such illicit activities.

She came out of the kitchen in a white cotton shirt and dark denim pants. She placed the food in front of him. Three pancakes, beautifully stacked with plump blueberries and a sultry river of syrup flowing from the brink of the sweet breakfast food. It was accompanied by a large glass of milk.

"I didn't know if you were a tea person, so I just played it safe and poured you some milk," Anthea said.

Peter felt like his eyes were in a hole, but he could see her clearly. "Thank you," he said, but his hands couldn't move to reach for the fork that sat patiently on the side of the decorated plate.

His stomach made a public declaration of hunger, and Anthea smiled. "Better answer your belly. Eat up," Anthea incited. Peter glared at her. Why was she being so nice to him? What did she want from him? She didn't even know him. Wasn't she afraid of being alone with him in her home, considering that he wanted to blow out his brains the night before? He pondered on these things.

He continued to eyeball her as he reached for the fork and had the first bite of the pancake. The honeyed taste did something to him; he inhaled the rest of the food and drank the milk in a flash.

"Do you want more?" Anthea questioned. Peter stared at her without any indication of a response. She got up, went to the kitchen, and came back with two more pancakes, scrambled eggs, and milk. He thanked her and began to eat yet again.

"They found her. Marie. She's in custody," Anthea said softly. The impact of her words caused tears to form in Peter's eyes. Anthea sat next to him on the sofa. "It's going to be alright."

Peter collapsed into her arms again. He was weeping beyond control, and he felt terribly embarrassed, but there was something comforting about Anthea's presence. He felt as if he knew her. He felt safe in her arms. He felt safe in her home. He felt secure and peaceful in her presence, but he sensed that there was another presence in that home. There was a potent atmosphere of peace that was inexplicable to him. There was a holy third in attendance.

In the midst of his crying, he heard her saying something, but she wasn't talking to him. She was praying for him. His weeping was out of his control, but he listened keenly to what she was saying. She was praying for peace. Peace in his mind. Peace in his heart. As he listened to her praying, the tears began to dwindle.

Peter had settled into a soft coo until Anthea began to pray for Marie. Peter pulled away from her and placed his head between his knees. *The audacity!* he thought. *Why would she ever pray for Marie? My mother's murderer!*

Anthea continued to pray for what seemed to be an eternity, with her hand on Peter's back as she did so. It was inexplicable to Peter, but he felt a strange sense of hope in the midst of his heartbreak.

"Let it be done. In Jesus's name. Amen," Anthea said to end her lengthy prayer. Peter still had his head between his knees and his arms over his head.

"I'm going to the store to get some groceries so I can make you a nice meal tonight," Anthea said with a smile. "Want to come with me?" Anthea asked. Peter emerged from the grief cocoon that he had built with his arms as the shell.

"Okay," he heard himself say. Anthea grabbed her purse and keys. Peter followed behind her like a zombie. His physical body was moving, but his inner man was dormant, numb, and indifferent. Peter was trying to achieve the ultimate level of indifference. That place of feeling nothing towards everything. He was trying, but he couldn't quite reach that place. His mother was dead. Tears escaped from his eyes as he followed Anthea down the apartment complex stairs.

Images of his mother lying dead in a pool of life resurfaced in his mind in vivid color. He collapsed on the steps and wept. Anthea turned and saw him. She journeyed back to the step where he had crumbled and sat next to him. Peter felt the brush of her shoulder against his. He didn't know her personally, but he was glad she was there.

After a few moments, Peter regained his composure and followed Anthea to her vehicle. Anthea played soothing music as they drove. Peter wept quietly in the passenger seat. They eventually reached the store and picked up the items needed for a lamb chop dinner.

They were driving back to the apartment when Anthea asked, "Would you like to sit in the park for a little while. It is extremely peaceful." Peter turned his gaze from the houses that were blurring by and focused on the mysterious stranger driving the vehicle he was currently sitting in. She waited for a response. Peter nodded, and Anthea slowed the vehicle and pulled into the park. Anthea parked the vehicle and found a bench to perch upon.

They sat in silence for a few minutes. Peter tried to find escape in the trees. Escape in the birds. Escape in the wind. He felt the wind caress his skin. He desired, at that moment, to be a windswept feather that moved swiftly and freely. Away from the place of potent misery. Thoughts that scared him entered his mind once more.

"You know it's my fault," Peter spilled. "It's my fault my mother's dead. I shouldn't have befriended Marie. She was bad news from the start, and I didn't take heed to any of the signs. It's my fault," Peter said through tears.

"I know you want to understand everything in this time of grief. You want immediate answers to all the questions that are roaming around in your mind, and because you don't have all the answers, you begin to blame the one person that you can consult about the situation—yourself. You find it easier in this time to blame yourself so you can feel something, but blaming yourself is harmful. Blaming yourself won't help your grieving process," Anthea said. Peter looked at the woman who shared the wooden park bench with him. "Trust me," she concluded assuredly. She didn't make any sense, but she made perfect sense.

He was blaming himself. He just didn't know what else to do.

They sat in silence for a few more minutes. "Let's head back. I have lamp chops in the trunk," Anthea said. Peter followed her back to her vehicle. She was a strange character, he thought. But there was something about her that made him feel secure. Anthea fostered a strength that Peter had never before experienced or seen in anyone else. Her words were sound and well thought out and exactly what Peter needed to hear. Anthea wasn't trying to be tough on Peter, but she also didn't want him to fall into depression by petting him in his anger and frustration.

Peter and Anthea made it back to the apartment, and Peter sat quietly on the settee. Peter wasn't sure where he belonged. *How am I going to survive without my mother?* Peter questioned internally. Peter knew of no other relatives. Peter knew that he must have had relatives out there somewhere; he just didn't know where.

As Peter sat and pondered these things, the smell of lamb caressed his nostrils, and his belly began to rumble. He wiped his tears and then journeyed to the kitchen. He leaned against the wall.

"Hi there," Anthea said without turning around. She sported a pretty yellow apron as she stirred her pot. "I hope you like lamb chops, green beans, potatoes, and white rice." Anthea turned around and gave Peter a smile, then placed her attention back on the steaming pot.

Peter wondered what Anthea saw when she looked at him. Peter hadn't seen himself since the night before when he stood before the bathroom mirror, holding on to the basin for physical support.

Peter walked over to the hanging mirror Anthea had in the hallway of her apartment. Peter's appearance frightened Peter. He looked awful. His eyes were wet, puffy, and carried a feeble guise. He was dirty. He had gotten the chance to change out of the gory clothes, but he was in desperate need of a bath.

Peter continued to stare at himself in the mirror. The mirror reflected an image of him, but he feared that the mirror was a compulsive liar.

He couldn't adequately identify himself. He felt lost. He felt empty. Peter turned from the mirror and returned to the kitchen. Peter watched as Anthea turned off the stove and started to serve the steaming food.

"Why are you doing all of this for me?" Peter was shocked at the fact that he had just spoken his thoughts aloud.

"Because someone did something even greater for me," Anthea replied smoothly.

"Who was that?" Peter questioned.

"Jesus Christ," Anthea answered with a smile as she shared the potatoes. Peter's immediate reaction was to roll his eyes, but rather he decided to look into himself. Did he even know anything about this Jesus called the Christ? He had made assumptions based on the false smiles he had received from the Christian group that had besieged his high school. Peter decided not to respond to Anthea's comment because he didn't know what to say. Peter knew nothing about this Jesus that people wore on crosses around their necks.

They ate in silence for a while. "Aren't you scared to be in an apartment with me at night?" Peter questioned, just to hear Anthea's response.

"Absolutely not," she retorted. "Eat up," she said, to which he obeyed. The food was delightful. Peter had no idea what he would be eating if he were alone. Then he reasoned that he wouldn't be eating anything at all because he and his mother would be in the same place.

His mother. Her eyes, green like the grass that surrounded those pink flowers in the lavish field that his six-year-old feet once trod. She was twisted and conning in so many ways, but she had loved him.

Long tears slowly made a path down Peter's face, caressing every follicle. He wasn't going to start bawling again. He couldn't. He had already made a fool out of himself before Anthea multiple times, and he couldn't do it again. He was trying to keep his composure and continue eating, but Anthea heard the sniffles.

"It's okay to cry. Let it out." Anthea scooted her chair closer to Peter's and placed a hand on his back as his fork and his tears fell from him.

****

The next day Peter met with the authorities. The court date was set for the thirty-first of the following month. He was in a daze, but he tried his best to respond when needed. Anthea had given him a note when she dropped him off at the station, but he hadn't opened it. He reached for it in his pocket. He rubbed his fingers against the folded paper.

Peter had received permission to return to his apartment earlier that day. Peter had gotten the opportunity to take a long luxurious shower. He wanted the water to wash all murky memories akin to how it thoroughly washed the filth from underneath his fingernails. As Peter stood in the shower, he decided to everyday act and pretend as if all that had happened wasn't real. His mother was in the next room plotting something brilliant. Or maybe she was on the sofa watching one of those romantic comedies she loved so much. Or maybe she was sipping wine while cooking up a delicious storm. Peter wanted it to be real. Peter closed his eyes and envisioned it all. Peter felt so consumed by his thoughts—like he was residing more in his mind than in reality. He was running away from veracity without a glimmer or desire of returning.

The authorities asked Peter more questions. They knew that he and his mother were not United States citizens. They knew quite a lot, but it seemed that Peter wasn't going to be charged with any of those crimes. Peter didn't really understand what was happening, but he went along with it.

When Peter finally decided to partake in the matters of reality, he heard one of the legal professionals say something along the lines of his crimes being expunged due to coercion and adolescent manipulation. *That sounds about right*, Peter stated internally before tuning out the meeting scattered with lawyers and detectives.

Anthea came back for Peter in the evening. She made him dinner again, then asked him if he was going to be alright alone. He said yes, while his heart was screaming out, *No!*

Peter wearily opened the apartment door and looked around. Everything had been spotlessly cleansed. Not a trace of criminal activity remained.

Peter ran to the bathroom and shut the door behind him. He held onto the basin as he did two days prior. Peter eventually released his grip on the basin and walked over to the tub. He placed the stopper in the drain and allowed the water to run free and fill the tub.

Peter returned to the basin and held on. Tears escaped as he thought of what he was being prompted to do.

What does it all mean? What is the point? These are the questions that popped into his mind.

Peter broke his hold on the basin, then stripped. As he took off his pants, a piece of folded paper fell from the pocket of his slacks. Peter stood there in his underwear, staring at the piece of paper that sat on the floor before him. *Should I read it?* he questioned within.

In defiance to all the voices compelling him to the overflowing tub, Peter picked up the piece of paper and unfolded it. It simply read, *You are not alone.* Like a robot whose mechanics were being controlled by another, akin to a marionette being governed by a sadistic puppeteer, Peter dropped the note and headed to the bath.

Peter sat idly in the tub for a long while, and then he slowly immersed himself in the bathwater. Peter gradually allowed his arms to join the rest of his body in full immersion. He held his breath for a while, then the struggle began. His lungs thrashed in his chest, grasping for oxygen. He opened his eyes underneath the bathwater. Everything within him burned. Images of his life appeared in high definition. He wondered if he was dying. He felt morbidly wonderful and miserable at the same time.

You are not alone. Peter propelled from the bathwater. He coughed violently. Water, saliva, and blood flew from his lips. He wiped his mouth with his bare arm. Why hadn't he gone through with it? He wondered.

It was a voice. A voice reading Anthea's note. Something had lifted Peter out of the water. And he knew what it was.

Hope.

****

Peter knocked softly. It was early, and he didn't want to wake her if she wasn't already awake. Anthea opened the door with a smile and allowed Peter inside the cozy apartment. He wanted to tell her of last night's events. He wanted to confess to her about the voices. He wanted to tell her about the suicidal thoughts and actions. He wanted to tell her about the sleepless nights, but he didn't. He let her prepare a meal for him, and then they ate in silence.

Before he left her apartment, she gave him another note. *You are loved*, it said. Peter watched from the railing as Anthea drove away. Anthea had a class to attend. Peter decided to take a walk to the park. He stayed there for a while, feeding the ducks and feeling the wind upon his tired face. He thought about running into the woods and letting the trees swallow him, akin to the cartoons of his youth.

Similar to an unforeseen embrace, exhaustion enveloped Peter, and he responded by traveling back to his apartment. He hadn't slept for more than forty-five minutes the night before, and he was extremely drained. Peter opened the apartment door, went to his room, and collapsed on the bed.

Sunlight streamed into his room, indicating the start of a new day. Peter lifted his head. He opened his haggard eyes and looked at the alarm clock. One thirty, the clock read. He had slept through dinner, breakfast, and lunch. He went to the bathroom to freshen up, returned to his room to change out of his sleeping clothes, and then journeyed to the kitchen. As he entered the kitchen, he stepped upon a piece of folded paper that had entered the apartment from the slit underneath the front door. Peter picked it up and read it. *You have a purpose*, it read. Peter placed the note in his pants pocket and proceeded to share cereal with himself. Peter felt better that day. Stronger. Peter was revitalized by the succor of sleep. Though Peter's heart was still aching, he felt it was a little more bearable. As soon as Peter finished his cereal, there was a knock on the front door. Peter opened it, and there she was.

"How are you today?" Anthea asked. She walked into the apartment with a smile and an arm full of groceries.

"I'm feeling a bit better, thanks," Peter said as he watched her fill his pantry and fridge with food. "You didn't have to do that. You didn't have to buy groceries for me," Peter said with weary gratitude.

"I did it because I wanted to," Anthea said as she continued to pack the refrigerator.

Peter watched for a while, then said, "I have a strange favor to ask of you." Anthea stopped unpacking and turned to give Peter her undivided attention. Peter continued, "The detectives will be finished with the body next weekend. Would you accompany me to the gravesite? I don't want to have a funeral; I just want to…I don't know. I would like it if you would accompany me to the gravesite. To lay flowers."

"I'll be there," Anthea said without hesitation.

"Thank you," Peter responded. "Thank you for everything." Anthea smiled. Peter curled his lips upward in an effort to return the smile; it was the best he felt he could do.

"I'm going to cook dinner for you now because I have to work tonight. What do you want to eat? Spaghetti? Salmon? Fried chicken?"

"Spaghetti is fine," Peter responded.

This woman is unbelievable, Peter said to himself. He watched as she placed the water-filled pot onto the stove, broke up the spaghetti, prepared the meatballs, and cut up the vegetables. Her little fingers chopped the onions with precision.

"So, what are your plans for today?" Anthea questioned Peter as she placed the broken spaghetti into the boiling water.

"I'll probably just venture to the park. I really like being out there," Peter replied.

"Oh!" Anthea said in sudden remembrance of something. "I forgot to tell you that I called the community center, and they gave you two months of paid leave." Peter didn't know what to say for a moment.

"Thank you," Peter responded. He felt as if he was going to cry, not due to the pressure of grief but the gravity of loving-kindness that worked upon the soft areas of his heart. Anthea was being kind to him for the sake of being kind to him. No ulterior motives. She just wanted him to be well.

Peter took a seat at the dining room table. He wanted to say so much more, but his tongue wouldn't let him. Peter decided to let his heart release the tears. He was so grateful. He was so very grateful.

"I figured you worked at the community center due to those bright orange shirts only employees sport," Anthea said with a smile.

"They are outlandishly orange," Peter said with a chuckle. The fact that laughter had tickled his lips felt so freeing at first, but then he was overcome by guilt. His mother had not yet been dead a week, and he was engaging in laughter. Guilt overwhelmed him, and in response, he set his face like flint. Peter and Anthea ate some of the food. Anthea placed the rest in storage containers.

"Would you like a ride to the park?" Anthea questioned.

"Sure," Peter responded. Anthea went to her apartment and grabbed her things; then, they headed out. They reached the park in no time.

"Did you see the note?" Anthea asked.

"Yes, I have it in my pocket," Peter responded.

"Good. Enjoy yourself today," Anthea said as Peter exited the vehicle.

"Thank you," Peter said. Anthea smiled at him before driving away.

Peter walked around the park for a while. He listened to the sound of nature and returned to his solace found in a sole wooden bench. He was alone for a while. He was learning to get accustomed to the isolation. There were a million things he was thinking of all at once.

Then Peter saw them. A little boy clinging to the hem of his mother's sundress. The youth didn't look more than three years old. Peter watched them. The mother knelt down and hugged the little boy, and he kissed her gently on the cheek. Tears flowed from Peter's eyes. His heart was burning again. He missed his mother. That was the first time he acknowledged that truth. She had put him through it, and there were times when he wanted to be away from her, but there were also times of laughter and glee. Times when they sat on the couch and watched movies together. Times of solidarity.

Peter began to watch them again. The mother was carrying her son now and walking in Peter's direction. Peter heard the little boy tell his mother he loved her as he draped his little arms around her neck. Peter bowed his head as they passed. They greeted Peter as they walked by. Peter looked up and turned his head in the direction that the boy and his mother had passed. The little boy locked eyes with Peter and smiled before laying his head on his mother's delicate shoulder.

Peter thought he was doing well, but again he began to weep. Peter got up from the wooden bench and sprinted away. Peter ran past the mother and her son. He ran out of the park. He ran to the apartment complex. He flung open the apartment door. He slammed it shut and cried over the spot where his mother laid those few days ago.

His head was pounding, and he realized how frail he was. Was time really going to heal him? He wondered. He wondered if the rest of the days of his life would be as such, broken and miserable and filled with unbearable loss.

Peter wept until he was sure he did not have any more liquids in his debilitated body. His migraine was getting perpetually worse, and the house was out of liquor. He went into the kitchen and flung open the cabinet doors. He grabbed a bottle of painkillers. He looked at the bottle. *Long-lasting pain relief,* it read on the seal of the bottle.

"That's what I need. Long-lasting pain relief," he said aloud, breaking the bottle's seal.

He poured four pills into his weak hand; then, he emptied the entire bottle. He stared at the fistful of white pills for a while, and then he poured himself a glass of water from the faucet.

He took the pills in series until they were all gone. He crawled over to the area where he saw his mother last. He skulked into fetal position and fell asleep.

CHAPTER 12

Peter was conscious, but he couldn't open his eyes. He couldn't speak. He couldn't move. He heard the bustle of a congested place. He knew he wasn't in the apartment anymore. He knew he wasn't lying on the ground in a fetal position over the area where his mother left him. He felt a touch. Someone was holding his left hand.

"You're going to make it out of this." It was Anthea. She was there. Wherever he was, she was there as well. "You have so much within you. At this time, you may feel like all hope is lost, like everything is gone, but there's a reason you didn't die Thursday night, and there's a special reason why you aren't going to die now. This isn't it for you. God is for you. God loves you with an everlasting love. The love humans have for each other may fade or become conditional, but God's love is pure and unconditional. He loves you, Peter. You have to live. You have to get to know this love," Anthea said before she started to pray for Peter. She prayed a lengthy and audible prayer.

Peter heard a rustling. A door was being opened, and he listened keenly as heavy footsteps neared him. A male voice greeted Anthea and began to talk with clear and debonair diction. His voice was grand and slightly domineering. Peter didn't hear everything because he was going in and out of his comatose state. One minute he heard everything with clarity, and the other minute, there was a deafening silence. He did hear when the man said, "In the state he is in, we just have to wait it out. He is being properly and regularly nourished. All opiates have been pumped out of his system. It's a miracle he's alive. You found him right on time."

They talked for a little while longer, but Peter could not recall the ending portion of their conversation. Peter tried his best to piece everything together in his debilitated state. He concluded that Anthea had found him after he blacked out and that he was in a coma and lying in a hospital bed. The reality of his state brought in the visitor of fright, but he noted that panic was probably not the best option in such opaque situations.

"Did you hear that, Peter?" Anthea said to him. They were alone once again. Peter hadn't heard when the man left, but it was obvious that he was gone. "Even the doctor knows that it is a miracle that you are alive. You have to fight. You have to fight." Those were the last words Peter heard before he was sucked deeper into the portal of debilitation.

****

The children eat their lunch without a thought about what they are consuming. Perri, Halia, and Olathe are completely mesmerized by the tale. They sit around their grandfather's grand mahogany table and try their best to digest their lunch, but the mellifluousness of the tale that drips from their grandfather's lips seems much sweeter to them.

"I cannot believe Adela has died," Halia says. Halia dangles her uneaten sandwich.

"It is unfathomable that it is Marie who has killed her," Perri states with his mouth full of potato salad.

"It is despicable!" Olathe says with her usual dash of zest. Farook, Perri, and Halia all laugh in unison at the wit of their youngest companion. "Marie was sketchy from the start," Olathe states in antithesis to her former stance on Marie.

"Drugs were a key factor in her decision," Perri adds.

"Drugs amplify feelings that have already taken root in the life of an individual. Rage and bitterness towards Adela must have been brewing in Marie's mind for a while. Incoherent or not, she acted upon the seeds that were germinating in her heart," Halia states.

"What do you mean?" Olathe questions her sister.

"What I mean is that Marie was already angry, and the drugs she took only amplified her anger and gave her the ungodly courage to act out her deep dark thoughts," Halia retorts.

"Gotcha," Olathe says with a mouth full of potato salad.

"Thank God for Anthea, who's such a great help to Peter, who is in such a weakened predicament," Perri inputs in between bites.

"It is so strikingly beautiful how Anthea has become this pillar in Peter's life. It just shows the fluctuating nature of this life that we live. One day life looks one way, and the other day it looks another way," Halia says with conviction.

"Brilliantly expounded upon, my child," Farook says to Halia from across the large table. Halia gives her grandfather a radiant smile. "That is the nature of this life. Ever-changing. In the blink of an eye, lives are altered forever. It is of utmost importance that we have moments like these. Times of face-to-face communication, which is becoming such a rarity in our modern society. You may never remember a post on the internet, but a smile, a word, or the presence of another human being can never be erased. God sent Anthea to be a part of Peter's life, not virtually but physically. God is using Anthea's presence as comfort for Peter."

"It is sad that Peter was at a place where he felt like life was no longer worth living," Perri shares.

"I believe it all comes back to identity," Farook adds with his hands clasped over a full plate of untouched food.

"How so, Grandpa?" Halia inquires over her untouched food. Farook and Halia consume words, while Perri and Olathe consume bread.

"Those voices that were haunting Peter were feeding off of Peter's fears. He was so unsure of who he was without the covering that was his mother. Those suicidal voices were hitting at his identity because he didn't know who he was. For so long, his mother had been forming him and dictating the course of his life. When Adela tragically died, Peter was left questioning his identity. He got to a place where he felt as if he no longer had an identity because his mother was gone. When a person places their identity in things on this earth, they are left stranded and desolate when those things leave or fade away," Farook says with conviction.

Halia processes the words of her grandfather. Perri and Olathe have almost finished their meals.

"Grandpa," Olathe says after wiping her mouth with a napkin.

"Yes, my dear," Farook responds with a smile.

"Does Peter survive?"

****

Anthea quietly opened the hospital door. Room 401. She took one of the two chairs that sat quietly against the west hospital room wall and pulled it close to Peter's bed. She opened the blinds, allowing sunlight to pour into the small room.

She turned and looked at Peter lying in the hospital bed. Comatose. "They can't have you cooped up in here without any sunlight," Anthea said as she made her way to the chair she had pulled near to Peter's bedside. With a heart filled with faith, Anthea began to pray for Peter.

"Lord," she commenced. "I come to You in the name of Jesus. I come to You as humbly as I know how. My Lord and my King. You are faithful and true. When You say You are going to do something, I am fully persuaded that You are able to perform just that. God, Peter is lying here in this hospital bed, and my request is for You to bring him out of this coma. You are the one that led me to him last Thursday night. My

King, you are the one that convinced him to put that gun down. You are the one that confirmed that he was meant to live. You are the only wise God. My King, I ask that You please bring Peter out of this coma and let him come out of the coma with a new heart. A heart that is turned towards You. I pray that You rip away that hardened heart. I pray that he will arise with Your peace. The peace that passes all understanding. The peace You gave me when I lost my father. That supernatural peace that cannot be explained. I pray he wakes up a new person, and I pray that he will get to know You, the true and living God. In Jesus's name. Amen."

Anthea opened her eyes and looked at Peter. "Peter, you will live in Jesus's name. There is a reason you are still alive. You're going to live and live life with identity and purpose."

There was a gentle knock on the door; then, a doctor walked into the room. His heavy footsteps and orotund voice caused Peter to be thrown back onto the shore of consciousness. He could hear them, but he remained immobile and unable to indicate his ability to listen in on the conversation.

"How is he doing, doctor?" Peter heard Anthea ask.

"He's stable," the doctor answered in an extremely honeyed voice. "He was experiencing severe heart palpitations late in the night yesterday. Right now, we are just monitoring him."

"How long does it usually take an individual to come out of a coma?" Anthea inquired.

"It varies. After two to four weeks, there is a high possibility of permanent brain damage leading to a vegetative state." Silence filled the room as the doctor checked on Peter's vitals and scanned all the machines Peter was connected to.

The doctor said his farewells to Anthea and left the room. "You have to fight Peter. You have to fight. Fight for life. Fight to live."

Peter's brain then took him for a whirl. He couldn't hear Anthea anymore. He was in a field. He was in a field of vibrant pink flowers that seemed to span for miles. It was a beautiful field rimmed with a luscious green forest. The sun was just beginning to rise, and the flowers basked in the golden wonder and lifted their glimmering petals in its presence.

Peter felt extremely peaceful in the field. He sat in the field, moving his arms over the petals of the delicate flowers. The flowers moved majestically in the wind. They looked as if they were dancing. He began to sway with them. He closed his eyes as he swayed with the dancing flowers.

Then he heard it. He heard her. He heard the audible voice of his mother calling him from the forest that lined the immense field of pink flowers. His eyes flashed open at the sound of her voice. He stood up with a start and began to run towards the vast green stretch that seemed so far away. As he ran, the delicate pink flowers began to grow spontaneously around him at rapid speeds. The flowers continued to germinate until they were towering over him. All Peter could see were tall green stems that seemed to span in every which direction. Peter decided that he was going to keep moving.

Peter sprinted around the stems that had stopped growing once they reached eight feet in height. Peter looked up to behold the dance moves of colossal flowers. It made him smile, but he didn't stop moving because his mother's voice hadn't ceased calling him. Towards the trees. Towards the green. Green like the stems. Green like the grass beneath his feet. Run away from the pink, press toward the green.

Peter kept running. He realized that he wasn't experiencing fatigue. He wasn't tiring at all. Once he realized that, he began to run with even greater haste toward the trees. He ran straight into a tree, but instead of falling backward, he cantered right through it.

Then he saw her. Adela. She wore a long white dress sprinkled with gold accessories. At that moment, Peter knew his mind was tricking him. She looked far too glossy to be real. She spoke with a slick tongue, and while the being looked and sounded like his mother, he knew it wasn't her. Peter knew it was a trick from the depths of his psyche.

"Stay with me," she beckoned with her arm outstretched; the gold bangle on her arm glittered in the sunlight that seeped through the trees. The trees acted as a canopy for the forest.

Peter walked towards her and tried to take her hand, but his hand grasped at nothing. His hand went right through her hand. He looked into her eyes. They were outlandishly green.

She wasn't real. He knew she wasn't real, but he wanted to stay with her. He knew she was a fragment of his imagination, but he wanted the fib instead of the truth. She sat modestly on the ground, and he sat down next to her.

"Stay with me," she kept repeating. "Stay with me."

Peter wanted to respond, but he could not. Peter tried to speak, but he was wordless. Nothing was forthcoming from his lips. It was in that time of realizing that he could not verbalize his thoughts that he began to understand the mirage.

The flowers in the field were tangible. He could feel them. He could pluck the petals. Everything in the forest was translucent. His hand moved right through all obstacles in the forest. The mirage of his mother and the trees that surrounded her seemed opaque, but when touched, they proved to be completely transparent.

He stared into her green eyes. "Stay with me," she kept repeating. But then Peter heard another voice. It was coming from the field. He walked over to the edge of the forest and peered upon the vast field. Peter heard the voice again. The voice was telling him to fight. The voice was telling him to fight for life. The field was absolutely radiant, but the sound wasn't coming from the field; it came from the sun. Peter began to journey back to the field.

"Stay with me," he heard her say from behind him. He turned around and looked at the vision of his mother. He looked at all the green. What did it all mean? He wondered. What was his mind trying to show him?

What were his emotions erecting in this highly vivid mirage? Peter desired to speak. He wanted to respond to her, but he couldn't. He couldn't speak. But he had to. He began to fight for the ability to speak.

After standing there, staring at the image of his mother and trying to verbalize his thoughts, he finally let out a word. "Goodbye."

The image of Adela vanished once the declaration of separation was made. Peter turned his back to the forest and walked towards the voice. He walked towards the prompting to live.

Peter noticed that the flowers in the field had returned to their regular size. Peter walked through the field as he cautiously approached the sunlight. Peter walked until he stood in front of the sun. Peter stared right into it. Peter placed his hand on the sun, and the yellow hue began to distort, revealing images of the real world, images of reality. Peter saw himself, his legs covered with a hospital sheet.

Peter moved his hand through the sun once again. He saw tubes and intravenous fluids. Peter moved his hand again. He saw Anthea sitting to the right of him.

"You have to fight for life, Peter," he heard her say.

All of a sudden, the mirage vanished, the field and forest and all. Peter was completely aware of his surroundings. He moved his right hand and squeezed Anthea's hand.

Peter opened his eyes.

CHAPTER 13

Peter slept for two days. He got up only to use the bathroom and to digest a handful of food. Peter loved the sweet escape that sleep brought him. Sleep had become his abscond ever since the demons of suicide had evaded him.

The bright Thursday morning sun brought a ray of hope. Peter was highly disoriented as he pulled out of the succor of sleep. The delusion only lasted for a moment. Akin to an unforeseen tempest, all the memories of last week came rushing in like a mighty wind, and Peter wept bitterly. The pressure of the gloom that reality brought him caused his temples to throb spasmodically. He held the sides of his head, trying to get rid of the pain. He desired the numbing lies of the third presence, but he didn't have access to it, and he didn't have the strength to seek it out.

Peter had graciously been moved to an apartment on the first floor, but it still felt strange to him. He was still in the same apartment complex. All of the apartments were built with similar design and architecture. The apartment he was in looked identical to the apartment he shared with his mother. Every time he went to the kitchen that overlooked the living room, his mind concocted an image of his mother lying on the floor, dead. Every time that happened, Peter went back to bed, allowing sleep to eat at his consciousness afresh.

Handfuls Of Yesterday

That Thursday morning, Peter searched for sleep o'er and could not find it. His body was trying to communicate its need for cognizant activities. When Peter realized that sleep had truly evaded him, he got up and took a cold shower. Bitterness gnashed at him, and he wept bitterly under its intimidation.

Peter got dressed and then stood in the living room like a statue. He was unsure of where he belonged. He was unsure of what to do. He grabbed his keys and walked outside. The air was fresh, and sunlight seeped into his pores, filling them with its much-needed vitamins.

Peter stayed there for a while, just taking in his favorite show. A few tears eluded his eyes, and he swiped at them quickly. He was tired of crying. He began to walk. Peter reached the curtain of the green stretch that he had beheld from a distance for the past few weeks. Peter stood there for a moment, taking in the wonder and beauty of the slim statuesque trees that moved gracefully in the wind. The difference between that stretch and the one his mind had created while he was in a coma was the tangible nature of the trees before him. The trees in the stretch were completely opaque.

In the midst of his gawking, Peter realized that there was an entrance. There was a discreet path that he had not yet seen until that moment. Peter looked around at the apartment complex. No one was there. No one was watching him. Peter entered the green abyss. Peter gasped at the beauty he beheld. Everything was teeming with life. Rich, beautiful life. Birds and butterflies spun through the sky in a flawless performance. The path he walked was extremely narrow, but ahead he beheld a wooden bench. Peter sat upon the bench and breathed in the fragrance of nature.

Peter sat there for a while. Trying to clear his head. Trying to turn off his thoughts. He knew what he needed to help him to do so. He searched his pockets in a quest for the relaxer. He found the joint and searched for a lighter in one of the many pockets that lined his khaki pants. He found a red lighter in his lower left pocket. Peter wanted to throw the lighter across the green plain because of the crimson hue he now detested, but he reasoned that it was unlikely he was going to find another lighter in his pocket. Just as Peter was about to light the joint, he heard footsteps approaching the bench. There she was. Anthea, with an arm full of different kinds of food.

"I thought you might be hungry. I saw you enter the opening, so I grabbed some food from the pantry and I followed you. I promise I'm not a stalker," Anthea said with a smile as she approached Peter. Peter gave a slight smile in response to Anthea's stalker comment. He realized that he was still holding the joint and lighter. He quickly concealed the drugs and paraphernalia.

She reached the bench, plopped the food in between them, and then took a seat. She opened one of the bags of chips and started to eat. Anthea took notice that she was the only one eating.

"Don't be afraid to dig in. There's a lot of food here," Anthea prodded. Peter was indeed hungry. He grabbed a handful of chips and munched.

"Your name is Peter, but the children at the community center call you Will. Why is that?" Anthea asked.

"It's a long story," Peter replied.

"I hope one day you will find the time to tell me that long story," Anthea said. Silence reigned for a moment as they both gazed into the immense green display. "How are you holding up?"

"Honestly, I'm not. But I'm alive. That must count for something."

"That counts for everything," Anthea said. Peter looked at Anthea, and he couldn't help but smile and thank her with his eyes. Silence overtook them once again.

"So, did you really lose your dad, or was that something you said to deter me?" Peter asked. He kept his eyes on her, waiting for a response.

"That was real. Everything I said to you is the truth," Anthea said as she opened a tin of cashews.

"How'd it happen?" Peter asked

"Why do the children call you Will?" Anthea countered.

Peter shook his head and smiled. "How about we do this. I ask a question, then you ask a question with a promise to be truthful with one another," Peter proposed.

"Sounds feasible," Anthea agreed. "You can begin by answering my question," she said.

"My name is Peter. My alias is William," Peter confessed. He had nothing left to lose, he reasoned.

"Why do you have a pseudonym?" Anthea asked.

Peter shook his head while munching on freshly chopped fruit. "You are not abiding by the question for question guidelines," Peter scolded. Anthea held her hands up in a comical display of remorse and surrender.

"Go ahead then," Anthea said.

"What happened to your father?" Peter questioned.

"My uncle killed him," Anthea replied with a straight face. Peter gazed at her. He didn't know what to say, but he was extremely taken by her strength.

"I'm sorry," Peter said.

Anthea nodded in acceptance of sympathy. "Why do you have an alias?" Anthea inquired.

Peter sighed and ran his right hand through his curly mane. "Because I've lived an extremely dishonest lifestyle. I have a lot of demons I'm constantly running away from. Like the one that killed my mother," Peter said as thick disdain flowed from his tongue. Just speaking of Marie enraged him. Peter was about to get sucked into the portal of malice when he realized that it was his turn to ask a question, and he zealously wanted to solve the enigma that was Anthea.

"The uncle that shot your father. Was it your father's or mother's brother?" Peter inquired.

"It was my father's brother. His own brother killed him," Anthea shared. She took a break from eating to ponder upon her next question. "Why'd you move to South Carolina?" Anthea inquired.

"The girl that killed my mother gave me fifty thousand dollars to leave New York City," Peter replied. Peter looked at Anthea to see if she was at all shaken by their discussion. She looked as shaken as a mountain. He hated to admit it to himself, but Peter loved having someone to talk to about real things. It had been a while since he had a real conversation with a temperate individual. Even though the motifs of their queries were deep and personal, the conversation seemed to flow naturally. He felt safe around Anthea, and he didn't know why. Peter couldn't quite put his finger on the reason why he was letting all his guards down with ease when he was around her. Was it because he had no one else? No, that wasn't it, he reasoned. Was it because she was a woman, and he had always been more comfortable opening up to women? No, that wasn't it either, he whispered internally. Peter couldn't explain it to himself, but he just knew he could trust Anthea. There was something extremely genuine about her. She carried a warmth that radiated from within that caused Peter to feel liberated in his transparency. When Anthea looked at him, Peter could tell that she genuinely cared for him, and he couldn't quite understand why.

"You don't have to answer this one if you don't desire to, but I'm going to take the risk and ask you anyway. Why did your uncle kill your father?" Peter asked with his eyes glued to Anthea.

Anthea continued to eat her cashews. "That answer requires quite a lot of backstory. Can you handle that?" Anthea asked. She looked into Peter's eyes, waiting for a retort. Peter nodded. Anthea straightened her posture on the old wooden bench. "Okay," she said.

"My uncle killed his own brother because my father took the blame for the Bible he found in my room when I went to visit my family in Saudi Arabia. My relatives already looked down on me because I had a darker-hued skin tone than the rest of my family, so if they had found out that the Bible was mine, they would have killed me in a heartbeat. My dad found the Bible and questioned me pretty harshly about it. When he went to dispose of it, my uncle and other male relatives were coming over for dinner. They saw the Bible. They asked him who it belonged to. Some of my cousins started to yell my name and share that I had been acting strange and not praying with the family as I used to. They were about to march into the house for me, but my dad convinced them that it was his, and they killed him. I watched from an opening in the curtain that lined the living room windows. That was the last time I'd been home," Anthea paused to take a drink of water. "It's not safe to go back because my family now knows I'm a Christian. They blame me for my father's death."

"I'm sorry," staggered out from Peter's lips.

"You're the first person I've shared that with," Anthea said. Peter and Anthea stared at each other for a while, engaging in nonverbal conversation.

"Anyway," Anthea said, breaking the silence. "Is it not my turn?" Peter nodded. Anthea took in a big breath and exhaled. "What's your happiest memory?" Anthea asked, with an extremely pleasant expression on her face.

Peter was slightly taken aback by the change of tide in their conversation, but he couldn't help but smile, then laugh. "Well, that was an unexpected turn in the motif of our questions. Let me think," Peter took on the position of one deep in thought. "I would have to say that my happiest memory was when my mother took me out for dinner for my twentieth birthday. That was my happiest memory because it was one of the rare occasions where neither of us was drunk or high on something. We just ate and talked. It was nice." Peter closed his eyes and reflected. He saw his mother every time he closed his eyelids. He missed her.

Peter opened his eyes, cleared his throat, and looked at Anthea with smiling eyes. "My turn," he said.

"And so it is," Anthea seconded.

"Why would you give up your family for a religion? If you were already religious, why would you take on another religion? Aren't they all the same thing?" Peter questioned. He greatly anticipated her retort to his inquiry.

"Wow, way to hit me with the serious questions," Anthea said with a beautiful smile. Peter returned the smile. A day ago, Peter never thought that his physiognomy would ever engage in the freeing activity of smiling anytime in the near future, if ever again. But there he was, grinning off his face next to an angel who had been a stranger a week prior. The stranger had become the only person in his life. It was startling to him how life could change so drastically without the slightest of warnings. Peter and Anthea had wordlessly passed each other for weeks. They had only given quaint greetings to one another for those weeks, but life had pulled them together so intimately. There they were, Peter and Anthea, in the deep belly of nature, solving the mystery that was one other. Looking at Anthea, Peter couldn't believe that those small arms held him so grandiosely last week. Those small arms held him as he wept like the abandoned child that he was. Those small arms had held him as he laid comatose in a hospital bed. An undeniable bond had formed between them that day.

"I didn't take on a new religion. I simply embraced truth. I traded in rituals and rules for a Savior who loves me enough to die for me. I didn't give up on my family. I would love to hear their voices again. To see them again. I would love to go home and spend time with my family again. I would do it in a heartbeat. But my family has given up on me. They have chosen to disown me. What my family believes and what I believe are completely different. Jesus Christ has freed my heart. He teaches me to love as He loves. Jesus Christ is the only way to God because He is the Son of the Most High God. A popular phrase I hear people say often is, 'Only God can judge me,' and that is true. Almighty God is the true and faithful judge, and the judge will forever favor His Son. I have put my faith in Jesus Christ so that when I stand before the judge, I will be accepted into heaven because the judge always...."

"Favors His Son," Peter finished.

Anthea smiled. "Exactly," Anthea said.

"I've never seen it like that before," Peter said, deep in thought. "I have never seen it at all, actually."

Anthea smiled at Peter's comment. "Do you have any other family? What has become of your father?" Anthea questioned.

"Absolutely no one. I have no idea who my father is, and my mom never introduced me to any other family members. I really don't know if my other family members knew that my mother had a child. I have no idea why my mother was so secretive. I guess that will be an unsolved mystery," Peter answered as he reached for more food. "Alright, my turn. What's your happiest memory?"

Anthea smiled and breathed a sigh of relief. She waved her arms in the air. "Finally, a freebie!" she exclaimed. Peter laughed. He laughed as one that was free. Peter couldn't recall a time when he had laughed so vivaciously. He laughed as one who hadn't been through loss. He laughed as one who was learning what it meant to live after he thought life was through for him.

"My most joyous moment was when I gave my heart to Jesus Christ," Anthea said with a smile. "My happiest moment was with my father when I was ten years old. He woke me up early one morning before the sun came up, and we climbed onto the roof of our house and watched the sunrise. That moment meant so much to me because I was being brutally bullied at school for my skin color, and at home, I was treated like an outcast, but my father was always kind. When he brought me onto that roof, hugged me, and gave me the most radiant smile, my heart melted, and I barely saw the sunset because I was so blinded by the love I saw in his eyes. It was so comforting to know that someone loved me for me."

"He seemed to have been an excellent man of character," Peter said.

"He truly was," Anthea agreed with a smile. "Okay, my turn," Anthea said as she poured more cashews into her hand. "Where are you from originally? You speak as one who is trying to conceal an accent," Anthea said with a knowing smile. Peter looked at her in disbelief. She was reading him like a book.

"Wow, you're good at this," Peter said. "I'm originally from Liverpool, England. Would you like for me to speak in my native tongue for the remainder of this conversation?"

"I would be most delighted," Anthea said in her best rendition of an English accent. Peter's vivacious laugh pierced the trees. "It's a pity I didn't bring crumpets, but I do have a large selection of tea that I can bring to our next excursion," Anthea adds.

"You amuse me," Peter said with laughter in his eyes.

"As do you," Anthea said before filling her mouth with cashews. "I believe it is your turn."

"Alright," Peter said as he changed his position on the wooden bench. "This Jesus that you speak of. This Jesus that you have given up everything for. What makes Him different than all of the world's religious leaders?"

"I believe Jesus Christ is God in the flesh. I believe that faith in Him is the only way to God and to heaven. I believe Jesus Christ to be the way, truth, and life. Not just one of the ways, but the only way. What makes Him different is that He is fully God and fully man. He is able to relate to everything we go through because of His humanity. He suffered loss like us. He's gone through all the different stages in life, but He's still at a higher place than we are because of His divinity. So, when I pray in the name of Jesus, and I confess my sins, He is at the place of understanding the temptation to sin, but He Himself has never sinned. So, He was tempted like us to do things that are wrong; that's the humanity part. But he did not and cannot sin because of the divinity part." Anthea looked at Peter, who appeared to be deep in thought. "I know that's a lot."

"No, it's fine. Do you mind if we pause the game for a bit and I ask you a few more questions?" Peter inquired.

"Sure," Anthea said.

"So, how do you believe the world was created? How did humans come into being?" Peter inquired as he stared at Anthea.

"According to the Bible, which is the Word of God that I stand upon, Almighty God spoke all things into existence and formed man from the dust of the ground and breathed His mighty breath of life into his nostrils and man became a living soul," Anthea said with a smile.

"I've heard that before," Peter stated. "So why did God have to put on flesh and come into this world?" Peter inquired.

"Well, in the beginning, when God created the heavens and the earth and all that lives therein, He gave man a command, and that was to abstain from consuming the fruit that was dangling from the tree of the knowledge of good and evil. Eve, the first woman that was created, was coerced into eating the fruit from the tree of the knowledge of good and evil. Adam, the first man that was created, saw what had taken place and chose to eat from the tree as well. That conscious choice was what started the sin problem that the world has. From Adam, everyone else was born sinful. The Word of God explains that the wages of sin is death. So, Adam and Eve, who were meant to enjoy the pleasures of a life free from pain, guilt, and suffering, were condemned to death," Anthea stated.

"Just because of eating fruit?" Peter asked, perplexed.

"No, not just because of eating the fruit, but because of the act of disobedience. God had given them so much and withheld only one thing from them, and they disobeyed His command. God was trying to establish a father and child relationship with His people, but due to disobedience, that perfect relationship was tarnished," Anthea added.

Peter thought long and hard of her words. It made sense, but it didn't make sense. Peter felt as if he was embarking upon something so much greater than himself and his finite understanding. Questions swarmed his mind like bees in a busy hive.

"So, if God spoke everything into existence, why couldn't He just have said 'Sins be gone' or something else along those lines to eradicate the sin that Adam and Eve had committed?" Peter inquired.

"Well, God never goes back on His Word. God had spoken to Adam and Eve, letting them know that the wages of sin is death. God had warned Adam and Eve, prior to their sin of disobedience, that if they were to indeed disobey, they would surely die. God doesn't go back on His Word. God is sovereign. He rules over all. Think of an earthly ruler; when they declare something, they are held to their word. God could not go back on His Word, so that is why He did not say 'Sins be gone,'" Anthea elaborated.

"So how does Jesus fix the sin problem if we still have sin and see sin so rampant today?" Peter inquired.

"What Jesus did is He came and died for our sins. Before Jesus came to earth, God's people were sacrificing animals as sin offerings to God because—"

"The wages of sin is death," Peter finished.

"Precisely," Anthea said with a radiant smile. "Those animal sacrifices were a foreshadowing of the sacrifice that Jesus Christ would make for us on the cross. Jesus came, lived for thirty-three years upon the earth, and then died for us on the cross. He died in our place. Our blood was stained with sin. Stained with depravity," Anthea looked at Peter, and Peter turned and stared into her eyes, remembering the words he had spoken in his suicidal state. "The blood of Jesus Christ is perfect, and because of Him, we no longer have to sacrifice animals. Jesus Christ has purchased our redemption, and we get to know God as intimately as Adam knew God before sin entered the world."

Peter and Anthea sat in silence for a few moments.

"I think I'm going to hold off on the questioning for a little while. That's a lot to process," Peter said as he leaned against the wooden bench.

They sat in silence once again.

"Wait, I lied. I have a few more questions," Peter said. Peter and Anthea shared a time of short laughter.

"Go ahead," Anthea said with a kind smile.

"Last Thursday. Did you hear the gunshot? Did you hear when Marie killed my mother?" Peter asked.

"No, when you heard me outside your door, I was just coming in from work. So no, I didn't hear the gunshot," Anthea shared.

"Then how," Peter paused to gather his thoughts and contort them into words. "Then how did you know to come over to the apartment if you hadn't heard the commotion? Did you see Marie walking away from the complex?"

"I didn't see Marie. God was just prompting me to knock on your apartment door," Anthea said. Peter stared into the green abyss; the weight and mystery of Anthea's words were overwhelming. "I was coming home from work. I walked up the steps, and I felt God just pulling me to your apartment. I knocked softly and didn't get a response. I was going to walk away, but the Lord was just telling me to stay where I was. I kept repeating 'Hello' from the outside, but I didn't receive a response. I really wanted to leave, but God wanted me to stay where I was. Then God led me to open the apartment door. I was extremely resistant at first, but I did eventually open the door. When I opened the apartment door and saw your mother, I wanted to flee the scene, but God gave me the strength to stay. Then I saw you. Being human, all these thoughts were going through my mind as you sat before me. I wondered if I was going to witness a suicide. I wondered if you were going to hurt me. God reassured my fluttering heart and gave me supernatural peace at that moment; then, He just started to speak through me." Anthea paused and looked at Peter, who hadn't taken his eyes off of her for a moment.

"Peter, if you aren't sure about anything else, just know that God loves you. Jesus Christ loves you. God loves you so much that He would send a petite woman who is terrified of guns to minister to you. Jesus Christ wants you to know that you have a purpose. God sent me because He knew that I could reach you with my personal testimony of overcoming loss," Anthea said. Peter processed her words.

"I'm so glad we could talk today," Anthea continued. "I'm not going to lie to you and tell you that it's easy. It's not. There were times after my dad died that I didn't want to get out of bed. I didn't want to talk to anyone. There were times when I didn't know if I could make it, but I was constantly reminded that even though life's tempest may blow frigid winds, I'm never alone. Peter, you are never alone." Peter looked away from Anthea with filled eyes. A tear escaped. Peter swiftly swiped it away.

"Thank you," wearily escaped from Peter's lips. Anthea placed her left hand gently on Peter's back as they stared into the green terrain. Peter's tears as water for the soil.

****

"Anthea is an angel," Olathe says with a glowing smile.

Farook's smile gives light to the entire dining room. "She surely is," Farook says with love and agreement.

CHAPTER 14

Peter stood in front of her door. She had done so much for him already. Peter was starting to wonder if his constant presence may be imposing. He knocked anyway. The door opened, and the smile she gave him broke down all his reservations.

"Hi, Peter," Anthea said from the doorpost.

"Hi, I was wondering if you wanted to grab some food. Have you eaten already?" Peter asked.

"No, I haven't eaten. I would love to grab some food. Let me get my sweater and keys," Anthea said before leaving the doorpost. She quickly returned, and they journeyed down the apartment stairs.

"Do you like Big Joe's diner?" Peter asked. Big Joe's was one of the few diners in the area that Peter knew about. The diner was just a few blocks down the street, east of the apartment complex.

"If by like you mean love, then yes," Anthea responded with her usual warm smile.

"How was work today?" Peter asked as they began to take the short walk to the diner.

"It was tiring. Working with children drains every ounce of energy out of your body," Anthea replied.

"They are a handful," Peter seconded.

"How was your day today?" Anthea asked.

"Much better. I thought a lot about our conversation yesterday. I thought about your past, your family…Jesus." Peter looked at Anthea, who sported a radiant smile. He couldn't help but smile along with her. "Why are you grinning like that?" Peter asked.

"You said you were thinking about Jesus. That's why I'm grinning," Anthea said as she began to skip along the sidewalk, which made Peter giggle like an adolescent. Peter didn't understand it, but there was a beautiful feeling of freedom and a potent connection he felt with Anthea that he had never experienced in all his days.

"You really love your religion, huh?" Peter said.

"Not more than I love my relationship with Jesus Christ," Anthea said with a smile as she ceased skipping and continued to stroll alongside Peter.

"Relationship?" Peter questioned.

"Yes, I have a relationship with Jesus Christ," Anthea said as she looked at a perplexed Peter.

"How does one come into a relationship with Jesus Christ?" Peter asked.

"Well, first, you believe in Him and what He's done on the cross. Then you begin to read the Word of God, pray, and worship. It's amazing when God begins to speak to your heart. It's the best! My relationship with Christ is more intimate and candid than any earthy relationship because Jesus Christ will never leave me. He remains constant," Anthea said with a love that was enigmatic and never before experienced by Peter. Peter had never heard anyone else speak about God with so much love, passion, and adoration. It really did seem as if Anthea was describing the most intimate of relationships. *She is the most sublime of conundrums*, Peter said within himself.

"Is that what God did last week? He spoke to your heart, and you responded by coming to my apartment?" Peter questioned.

"Exactly," Anthea answered as Peter opened the door of the diner for her. They were gleefully greeted by a waitress who zealously took their drink orders. Peter and Anthea took a seat at one of the booths near the large windows that lined the diner.

"So, how does God speak to your heart?" Peter inquisitively inquired.

"It truly is inexplicable. It is something that must be experienced. One thing I can say assuredly is that when God speaks to your heart, it's not a mind thing. Most of the time, your mind has no clue of what's going on. God speaks to your inner being. Your true self," Anthea said with radiant conviction.

Peter nodded and began to survey the menu. He was looking at the menu, but he wasn't processing anything. Anthea was introducing him to a world he didn't want anything to do with. *Had God truly spoken to her about finding me in that apartment those nights ago?* Peter thought. *If so, does God truly love me?* Peter wondered.

This world of avid discussions of God, Jesus Christ, and faith was so new and foreign to Peter. He felt as if he had been plunged into this new world without warning or caution. A part of Peter was curious and knew that what Anthea was saying was the truth, but another part of him wanted to run from the unknown waters like a drenched cat. Peter knew that if he were to run away—if he were to completely end all communications with this woman that spoke so highly of her God—that it wouldn't change the mighty impact she had left on his life. Thursday night was forever painted upon the doorpost of his heart. Peter could never forget that moment. Peter could never forget the petite woman that sat across from him in Big Joe's diner.

"What looks appetizing to you?" Anthea asked.

"I'll probably just get a burger and fries," Peter replied.

"I think I'm in the mood for chicken," Anthea said. Just as they made their decision, the waitress came and took their orders.

"Are you in school?" Anthea asked once the waitress left.

"I am," Peter responded. "Second year. Undecided. How about you?"

"I'm in school as well. I'm going into my third year as a psychology student," Anthea answered.

"So, how long have you been in the States?" Peter inquired.

"I actually came here for college. So, two and a half years. In all of this, I've seen God's hand so prominent in my life. I was always a nerd. My head was always in a book, and because of that, I excelled academically. I was the head student in my class back home. Here in America, that academic position is called valedictorian. I was given the opportunity to receive an American university education. I gave my life to Christ in the first semester of my freshman year. I went back home for winter break, and the day before I was to return to the States, my father was killed. The following weekend, after returning to the States, I received an e-mail from my uncle in Saudi Arabia. He was letting me know that the family found out that the Bible was mine and threatened that if I ever placed a foot on Saudi Arabian soil again that I would be killed. God had made a way of escape for me. It was hard for me. It is still hard. I wept like a baby. I haven't heard from any of my family since. I haven't spoken to my mom or my four sisters in almost two years," Anthea shared.

"Do you have any family in the States?" Peter questioned.

Anthea shook her head. "No, I don't. Do you think you have family in the States?" Anthea asked.

"I don't know due to the ambiguity that is my father. I don't know whom else may have escaped from his loins," Peter said. He watched as Anthea covered her mouth and smiled. Peter gave her a questioning look.

"It's the way you speak—with such eloquence. You should consider English or communications as your major," Anthea said, to which Peter smiled.

The waitress approached with large plates of food. The waitress shared the dishes and departed. Anthea and Peter ate in silence until they were satisfied and sated. Only a handful of fries and half glasses of iced tea remained between them.

"How do you cope with being alone?" The question that had been weighing heavily on Peter's heart finally escaped from his lips.

"Some days are really hard. Some days I don't want to get out of bed. Some nights I cry like the disowned child that I am. Even though I'm a believer, I still go through the pain of loss like anyone else, but Christ is my refuge. Jesus is my hiding place, so I may be perplexed but never in despair. I've had times of extreme loneliness, but Jesus never lets me stay in the cocoon of lonesomeness. He picks me up out of the state of despondency before despondency gets the chance to bring me back to a state of depression," Anthea said confidently.

Her words were surreal to Peter. Everything Anthea was saying was reaching deep into the core of Peter's being.

"I'm learning," Peter said as he moved his straw around in the almost depleted glass of iced tea. "I'm learning how to live again. I'm learning how to live without my mother. It had always been my mum and me. She was indubitably my best friend. I miss her green eyes, and I think that's the reason why I love going into the green stretch behind the apartment complex. My mother wasn't perfect, far from it, actually, but she was always there. She was my constant, and in that apartment last week, I felt like everything was gone. Voices had swamped my mind telling me to pull the trigger," Peter shared while looking out the large diner window and trying to keep his composure. He felt tears forming, and he was excruciatingly tired of his constant displays of frailty in front of Anthea. He quickly swiped at his eye, catching the raindrop before it fell from its succor and onto his face.

"You don't have to pretend with me," Anthea said softly as she placed her lovely petite hand over his. "If that's how you feel, let it out."

Peter looked at Anthea with hurt and angered eyes, but those emotions were not directed at Anthea, and she was wise enough to know that. "I hate her," Peter said through wet eyes and clenched teeth.

"Who?" Anthea questioned, her hand still over his for comfort.

"Marie. I hate Marie, but Marie would not have known my mother if it wasn't for me. So, I hate myself," Peter blurted with ease.

"I know that this may be hard to hear right now, but I'm going to say this because I care," Anthea said as she held Peter's hand. "You have to learn to forgive Marie."

Peter's head shot up from its bowed state and stared into the eyes of the one person that cared about his existence. Peter pulled his hand away from underneath hers. How could she tell him that? He thought. He was truly hurt, even though a part of him knew she spoke the truth.

"Malice and bitterness are two forms of poison that kill persons daily. I know that this may be difficult to hear, but you have to start the process of forgiveness," Anthea said softly. "Malice and bitterness are gateway drugs to depression, and getting out of the grips of depression is hard. This is coming from someone who knows."

Peter looked at her. She had suffered from depression as well. She just seemed far too confident and joyous to have ever gone through anything, but Peter was beginning to realize that everyone had gone through something. Even a baby in a stroller has gone through something. Maybe the infant got their feeding late and was extremely hungry for a lengthy period of time; that's going through something. At that moment, Peter was learning that everyone has been through trials. Peter was learning not to judge and deem people who have overcome trials as the exempt ones, but rather to praise their strength and learn to thrive as they do.

"Also, surrendering to Christ Jesus is a wonderful step to make. He promises peace. Real peace. For your mind and heart. This is coming from someone who knows," Anthea said with a smile.

Peter looked at her. He wanted to smile back. He wanted to agree and hold her hand and have her pray one of those lengthy prayers over him, but he felt his head shake, and his mouth spewed, "I'm not ready."

****

Farook, Perri, Halia, and Olathe return to the fourth-story living area. The children take their seats on the topaz carpet. Perri and Olathe sport full and satisfied stomachs. Halia and Farook hardly touched their food; they filled themselves with words.

"Grandpa, does Peter have a funeral service for Adela?" Olathe questions.

"Remember Peter told Anthea that he was just going to lay flowers at the gravesite," Perri answers.

"Maybe Peter feels as if no one will attend the funeral but himself and Anthea, so he wanted to save the heartache and just lay flowers," Halia interjects.

"I believe that is exactly how Peter felt, my dear. Alone and abandoned. A funeral service would just have further amplified his loneliness," Farook adds.

"It's a good thing he has Anthea," Olathe states.

"My dear, it is a wonderful thing," Farook seconds.

"Grandpa, I'm going to make an educated guess and say that the flowers Peter lays will carry a pink hue, continuing the strange but mystifying motif," Halia brilliantly states.

****

The drive to the cemetery was torturously long for Peter. He wanted to get there quickly, and he didn't want to get there at all.

Peter stared at the flowers in his lap, and then he returned his attention to the car window. Peter turned and looked at Anthea, who smiled at him. He smiled wearily and then returned his gaze to the car window. Flashes of last Thursday began to swamp his mind. Holding his mother for the last time. Red everywhere.

They drove into the cemetery and parked. The parking lot was barren save a small vehicle that sat idle near the cemetery entrance. Peter and Anthea beheld a petite woman standing before a tombstone, talking and laying flowers. Peter felt as if he was going to be sick.

"You can do this. I'm right here. I'll be right here," Anthea said. Peter looked at her and saw genuine compassion swimming around in her eyes. Peter felt the arms of safety wrap around him like a blanket. He looked at the flowers in his lap, he stared at Anthea again, and then he placed his right hand over the car door handle.

Peter walked out into the wind. The flowers flopped their petals in response to the caress of the waft. Anthea walked next to Peter, on his right side. They walked towards the third row of graves.

There it was. The grave of his mother. Overcome with emotions, Peter lifted his head in the air and allowed the tears to roll down his face. Anthea's hand graced Peter's back.

Peter gently placed the pink flowers next to the tombstone. "She was only forty years old," Peter spewed with spittle and tears.

Peter felt as if he was going to be ill. His legs buckled underneath him. He felt like he was having an out-of-body experience. *Maybe this is another mirage concocted by my mind*, he thought. To Peter's dismay, the wind that slid across his face reminded him of the reality of the moment. His mother was gone. *How does someone live after something like this?* He whispered internally. Thoughts that terrified him began to plague his mind. Hate swathed itself upon his emotions.

Peter's knees buckled under him. He collapsed and wept. *How does someone live after something like this?* He repeated in his mind. The wind blew his tears across his face.

Malice. Like an army invasion, malice marched into Peter's heart. The bitterness he felt started to taste like bile in his mouth. *How does someone live after something like this?*

Her touch. Anthea's touch reminded Peter of something. *She is alive, and she's been through loss.* Peter thought it frightening how quickly the pain of loss could paint the world as a place where you are the only person that is being inflicted by its sting.

Anthea knelt beside Peter and placed her hand gently on his back. "You're going to be alright." Peter collapsed into her arms. "You're going to be alright," Anthea whispered as she held the broken man.

CHAPTER 15

Olathe's hand sits politely over her heart. Her face wears an expression of heartbreak. "Poor Peter," she utters.

"I agree with Anthea. I believe Peter is going to be alright," Perri states.

"I stand with you on that one," Farook seconds.

"Well, if the storyteller affirms your statement, Perri, you must be correct. I stand with you too," Halia says with a smile.

"Didn't you say there was to be a trial, Grandpa?" Perri inquires.

****

The jury was chosen from venire. Twelve unknown faces sat on wooden benches preparing themselves to give a verdict regarding the remainder of another person's life.

The case had been hurried by Marie's family, who didn't want the media to eat it up, so they pulled a few judicial strings and started the criminal trial way before any other criminal trial had ever commenced.

Peter's hand twitched as he sat on the wooden bench outside the courtroom. He had been there, in the courthouse, for so long. As he sat there, he glanced at the clock. Ten in the morning, it read. The trial was set to begin at ten thirty. Peter looked down at his tie. The tie had navy and green stripes. Peter wondered if the tie was too festive for such a solemn gathering. Peter was highly flustered and was trying his best to keep his mind off the one thing that kept pestering his psyche. Marie. He was going to see Marie. He was about to look upon the woman who told him she loved him, then killed his mother. He was going to see his mother's murderer. Red was about to smash against his vision. The striking red of her hair, which would remind him of the red pool his mother lay in. The deeds of red had painted red on his apartment floor. The deeds of red had opened the door to voices that tempted him to do unthinkable things to his own self. The deeds of red had caused him to yield to temptation o'er and o'er. The deeds of red. Peter hated red.

Peter bowed his head low and held his head with his hands. Peter wasn't sure of his ability to speak when called to testify. How could he speak about his mother's death that was still so fresh in his heart and mind? Peter thought. The trial seemed to have come way too soon, but Peter didn't have a say in its delay or expedience.

Peter sat alone on the bench for a while. Anthea entered the courthouse in a gray dress suit. Anthea walked right over to where Peter was sitting and sat down next to him.

"I like your tie," she complimented. Peter lifted his head and smiled through the mind brawls. Anthea had that effect. "How are you feeling today?" Anthea questioned.

"I don't think I can do this, Anthea," Peter spilled from his heart. "I don't think I can do any of this. I don't think I can be in the same room as her. Breathe the same air," Peter finished with detest.

"Lessons learned from my youth are ministering to my present self," Anthea said softly.

Peter was absolutely flabbergasted. "What are you trying to say? What does that statement even mean? How is that applicable to me and my situation?" Peter asked as he lifted his head to look upon Anthea.

"Lessons learned from my youth are ministering to my present self. Meaning that the things that I have already gone through have molded who I have become and am becoming. Every moment, the good and the bad ones leveled, has a teaching element. I have learned that there are experiences that one won't necessarily want to engage in, but it is of utmost importance. Take today, for instance; you are the key witness in this case. You didn't see the act, but you witnessed the aftermath and Marie's incoherent state. You have to testify. It may be difficult, but you have to give the jury a clear and genuine understanding of that night's events so that they can give a fair verdict," Anthea said as Peter soaked in her every word.

"I know this may be exactly the opposite of what you may want to hear," Anthea continued as Peter looked at her, "but sometimes you have to completely defy your feelings in order to do what must be done."

Peter shifted his attention to the grand clock. Ten twelve. "What did you feel like doing when your dad died?" Peter questioned, without thought of the inquiry.

"I felt like staying with my family. I wanted to stay for my father's funeral, but I knew I had to defy my feelings and leave the country without ever looking back. My dad knew I had to live for a specific purpose; even though he didn't know what it was or understood it, he still knew, and that's why he took the blame for the Bible. You have to stay strong, Peter. I'll be here for the entirety of the case today. Defy your feelings and testify. Do what you must because my life may just have been spared so that you could live."

Anthea's last sentence pricked Peter's heart. *Could that really be true? Could Anthea's life really have been spared for my sake?* Peter questioned in the fortress of his mind.

Peter didn't realize what he was doing until he did it. He was holding Anthea's hand. Anthea was a little taken aback at first, but she let him hold her left hand. They sat on the bench for a long sixty seconds. Hand in hand. Wordless.

Ten fifteen.

"Maybe we should go in now," Anthea turned to Peter and said. Peter nodded, and they rose from the bench. Breaking their hand hug. Peter opened the large wooden South Carolinian courtroom doors. Peter and Anthea walked in. The place was packed.

An expensive-looking couple that shared equally haggard eyes turned their weary necks to strain to see who was entering the courtroom. Peter looked at them. They were sitting on the first wooden bench over to the left of the courtroom, right behind the bar and very close to the well.

The couple stared at Peter for a while, then the eyes of the man widened, and Peter suddenly felt highly exposed and recognized. The man quickly looked away, then began to speak in hushed tones to the woman next to him.

Peter was a little taken aback and disoriented at that moment, but as he and Anthea found a seat, he began to process his surroundings.

That couple must be Marie's parents, Peter shared with himself within himself. It made sense to Peter. The staccato glares and pointed whispers. Peter constantly felt eyes on him in those fifteen minutes. Every time Peter turned to look at the couple, their eyes would quickly flutter away.

Peter took in the actions and movements of the well. Two attorneys, who sometimes turned around to talk to Marie's parents, sat with exceedingly great posture over to the left of the courtroom's well. The attorneys looked just as expensive as Marie's parents. The male attorney was a lengthy man with pale skin and a confident demeanor. He sported a silky black suit that competed with his silky black hair that seemed to hold more grease than any fast-food restaurant. On him, even the hair grease looked expensive. He also wore a red tie. Red. Peter hated red.

The female attorney sported a gray pants suit and a pink ruffled blouse that stayed confined by her gray jacket. The attorney's dark skin and light-colored eyes were strikingly beautiful to Peter, but then he rebuked himself for even considering the beauty of the attorney who was preparing to defend his mother's murderer. The female attorney read what appeared to be her notes as her partner reasoned with Marie's parents.

On the other side of the well sat the two attorneys that Peter had been speaking to for weeks. The prosecution attorneys. The first attorney was a Hispanic man who had kind eyes and brilliant legal skills. This attorney wore humility like a cloak, and it was so refreshing for Peter to be around him. The second attorney was a short Caucasian man who sported a dark brown suit and a cream-colored tie. Both prosecution attorneys had been very kind and helpful to Peter, and it was sort of comforting for Peter to see them there. Peter knew that no matter how expensive the defensive attorneys looked, the prosecution was well prepared and ready for the courtroom proceedings to commence. Peter watched as the prosecution attorneys sat and spoke in hushed tones to one another, going over notes and watching the grand clock that sat powerfully over the bench. Everyone in the courtroom seemed to be glancing at the clock. Ten twenty-three.

Peter looked over at Marie's parents, who cast their eyes away from him. Peter wondered about them. Peter pondered upon the vastness of their material privilege and power. They had been able to conjure a trial in less than a month and keep the media completely at bay. The amount of money that they must have spent to keep the trial under high confidentiality wraps must have been astounding, Peter thought. Strings hadn't been pulled for the early trial; an entire net had been hauled up for the commencement of such a high-profile criminal case. The media would have loved to devour the story of a rich mogul's daughter who murdered a middle-class woman out of her twisted version of love for the woman's son. That would have been the headline for weeks, if not months. They would probably have started a television drama based on such a story, but the courtroom was barren of cameras. Not one camera was in the courtroom, and not one camera was allowed in the courtroom.

Peter continued to stare at Marie's parents. Neither of them had red hair. Marie's mother kept tugging at her sleeve and turning the rim of her watch. She looked drained.

Peter began to examine the well once again. The stenographer sat patiently off to the right side of the well. The stenographer's blonde hair was in a neat bun atop her head. The stenographer's small green eyes glanced around the courtroom from behind large glasses that seemed to be trying to swallow her face. The clerk of court and the judicial assistant seemed to be reviewing something riveting.

The courtroom wasn't loud by any means, but there was a buzz as so many groups of individuals tried to engage in quiet conversation. Peter looked at the clock.

Ten twenty-seven.

Peter looked down at his folded hands that sat on his lap. His hands began to sweat as he came to the realization that the trial would commence soon. He would have to speak soon. He would see Marie. Soon.

The double doors adjacent to the well suddenly opened. There she was. Marie. Her blue eyes were sober but glued to the courtroom floor. She was escorted in by officers on either side of her. She wore an orange jumpsuit. The chains around her legs and arms made noise as she walked in. Her red hair was in a neat bun, and her face was dressed in light makeup.

The visual was confusing to Peter. How was it that her family and the attorneys looked so expensive and untouchable while Marie looked like a glamorized criminal? Marie's makeup and hair looked like illegal residents on her body. They were outliers. They didn't belong with such a getup. *Were her parents not able to pull the net completely out of the water?* Peter questioned within himself.

Ten twenty-nine.

Peter felt eyes on him. He looked over at Marie's parents. Peter caught the gaze of an extremely exhausted-looking man. He tried to swiftly look away, but Peter's eyes had caught his a millisecond before he zipped his eyes away from being processed and deciphered. Peter saw something in the eyes of the man Marie was to call her father.

Shame.

You spent no time with your daughter, and now you wear her as your shame, Peter thought.

"All rise," an extremely muscular bailiff bellowed from the well. Everyone stood at attention like army trainees who were ready to comply with their general's demands. The bailiff looked like he owned all the world's masculinity with his authoritarian voice and strong arms that were coated in a beautiful brown hue. "The honorable Judge Lemear presiding," the bailiff concluded.

The judge immerged. He was a lean and fairly tall man. The judge's face looked fresh and youthful, like a man in his early forties, but his graying and balding head increased the hypothesis regarding his age. The judge took his lofty seat around the bench. His black robe matched with the black wall behind him, and without the visibility of his hands, he looked much like a floating head.

"You may be seated," the judge said. His voice was surprisingly slivery.

Peter sat gingerly. He was feeling highly uncomfortable. He didn't want to be there. He wanted to run through the courtroom doors and keep running until he was in Liverpool with his mother again, but she was gone. He saw the grave. It had become a reality.

Peter was becoming overwhelmed by emotions when he felt a little hand on his. Anthea. Peter turned and looked at her. Anthea beckoned, with her eyes, for Peter to look in his hand. Anthea gently placed a piece of ripped paper in Peter's right hand. Anthea placed her hand back on her lap after delivering the note.

Peter sat with the note clenched in his hand for a while; then, he opened his clenched fist. *You are not alone*, the note read. Peter looked at Anthea and gave her a weary smile.

Peter needed that note. Anthea beckoned for Peter to look at the back of the small note.

I am with you, but most importantly, Christ is with you, it read.

Peter had no clue what it meant for Christ to be with him, but there was something peaceful and comforting about knowing that he had physical and spiritual company that was for him and on his side. Peter placed the note in his pocket and leaned back against the hard wooden bench as the trial began.

* * * * * * * * * * *

"Good morning, Your Honor, Clerk of Court, and members of the jury…," the attorneys began their opening statements, their roadmaps that they would want the jury to venture down.

Both the prosecution and the defense attorneys were clear and articulate in their speech, but even through the grand diction, there still remained an eerie stillness.

Peter felt eyes constantly trying to pry him open. He was the motherless child. He was the one that was to be pitied.

He didn't like it. He didn't like being the victim. He didn't like the eyes of strangers deciphering him.

Peter felt like a frog that was split asunder and left exposed for people to prod with the non-disposable scalpel of their eyes. Peter was grateful, in that moment, for the lack of cameras. He didn't want genuine and artificial lenses filming his every move in the courtroom.

Peter sat through the open statements for what seemed to be an eternity. *These attorneys should be sued for the length of their statements*, Peter thought.

The attorneys continued their eloquence contest, and Peter became highly irritated. He was annoyed by the constant gaping and molestation by the eyeballs of so many. Peter was annoyed by the constant yammering that the lawyers were partaking in, which he deemed highly unnecessary. He was annoyed with the judge for not telling the attorneys to be quiet. He hated Marie. He was annoyed by her red bun that sat awkwardly atop her head. He was annoyed at how big the clock was that hung from the wall above the bench. Everything annoyed him. Peter concluded that he detested courtrooms and the strange stench of manmade power that made a public spectacle in the godforsaken place.

The one thing that kept him sane was Anthea's presence. She had promised to be there, and she was there. She was also court-ordered to be there, as she was a witness to the mala in se crime after the fact. Peter so desperately wanted to commit the mala prohibita of walking out of the courtroom, but he stayed put.

The opening statements came to a tedious end. Peter felt compelled to applaud the attorneys back to their seats, but he was trying his best to clothe himself in the demeanor of indifference. Peter wanted to appear nonchalant so that the pestering of eyes would cease. To his dismay, more eyes swarmed him every millisecond, and he felt like he was on fire in his suit.

The first witness was called. He was a forensics expert. The prosecution began a direct examination of the witness. The forensic expert confirmed, in many high-flowing words, that Marie was indeed the murderer. The expert went into the specifics of his findings from the crime scene. The expert presented the revolver that remained cocooned in its evidence bag. In Peter's opinion, the courtroom proceedings could have ended there, and the jury could have gone into deliberation. Marie was without a doubt the murderer, so what was the need for all the theatrics? Peter thought, in exasperation and grand vexation, that he was trying his best not to emanate upon his face.

The defense declined the offer to cross-examine the expert witness. The case progressed. The prosecution called their next witness. The one man who saw Marie grab what he describes as a dark object from the tree lining around the apartment complex. The witness stated that he could not make out what was in her hand, but he could see that she was clearly incoherent. He stated that he watched Marie fumble up the apartment steps. The witness, who was a tall, well-built man with orange-red hair, stated that he heard something that sounded like a gunshot, then he saw Marie awkwardly running out of the apartment complex. The prosecution was surprisingly short with their questioning. Breaking their lengthy motif. The female defense attorney cross-examined the witness, and then the male attorney took a word stab at him. The defense was trying their best to question the validity of identifying Marie as the murderer, but their pursuit wasn't bearing fruit.

Anthea was then called to the stand. She stood and walked boldly into the well, taking her seat behind the witness stand after affirming her truthfulness in the upcoming speech.

She looked so calm in Peter's eyes. *She is extraordinarily strong*, Peter said to himself.

"Good afternoon, Ms. Boutros," the attorney greeted Anthea as he prepared to swarm her with questions.

"Good afternoon," Anthea politely responded.

"Ms. Boutros, the police affidavit pointedly states that you were a witness of the aftermath of the crime after the defendant fled the scene. What is it that you witnessed once inside of the apartment?" the attorney queried.

"I beheld the victim's corpse in the living room area, and I beheld the victim's son, who was evidently distraught," Anthea coolly replied.

The prosecution continued to ask surface questions to help the jury to get a full understanding of the night's events. Peter tried to tune them out. He didn't want to relive that night when he was just learning how to live since that night. The suicidal pull was still trying to pester him, but Peter felt a stronger pull from the other side that was advocating for his life. Peter chose life.

The male defense attorney took the opportunity to cross-examine Anthea. "Ms. Boutros, to repeat the words of the counsel, the police affidavit pointedly states that you were a witness of the aftermath of the crime after the defendant had fled the scene. My first question for you is: did you see the defendant?" the attorney probed.

"I did not," Anthea truthfully answered.

"Ms. Boutros, was there a noisy commotion coming forth from the apartment of Mr. Davies?" the attorney questioned.

"No, there was not, counsel," Anthea retorted.

"So, Ms. Boutros, how did you know to go into Mr. Davies's apartment?" the attorney queried.

Anthea shifted a little in the witness stand chair. She discerned that the words she was about to say were going to fall on stony ears, but she said it anyway, "Well, counsel, I didn't know to go to Mr. Davies's apartment. It was God who led me to the apartment."

The posh lawyer was taken aback at first, and then he sported a crude smirk. "God told you? I asked for an honest answer, Ms. Boutros. This isn't a joke."

"Counsel, beware of your tone," the judge reprimanded.

"Yes, Your Honor," the proud attorney retorted at the reprimand. "Ms. Boutros," the attorney began again, turning his attention back to Anthea, "in your statement, you specified that when you entered the apartment, you witnessed an extremely downcast Mr. Davies. Was it not the murder weapon that he held in his hand?" the attorney questioned, with the same smirk that infuriated Peter.

Peter didn't like how Anthea was being questioned and treated, but there wasn't much that he could do except sit on the uncomfortable wooden bench and wish himself to be elsewhere.

"Mr. Davies was holding a gun," Anthea meticulously answered.

"Please answer the question, Ms. Boutros. Was it or was it not the murder weapon that Mr. Davies held in his hands?" the attorney probed.

"I later found out that it was," Anthea answered.

"Ms. Boutros, if you found Mr. Davies with the murder weapon in hand, would you not deem it possible for him to have been the murderer?" the attorney asked, his eyebrows raised. The way the attorney was towering his eyebrows annoyed Peter. The stench of pride filled the nostrils of all who sat in the claustrophobic courtroom beholding the pompous attorney.

"No, deeming something plausible does not make it the truth," Anthea retorted.

The pompous attorney smirked and shook his head. "How can you say that when you just told the court that your imaginary friend told you to enter a closed apartment?"

Gasps flowed around the courtroom. The Hispanic prosecution attorney shot out of his seat, "Objection, Your Honor. Relevance."

"Sustained. That was way out of line, counsel," the judge rebuked.

The attorney looked upon Anthea with a look of belittlement. He smirked his arrogant smirk once again and uttered, "I have no further questions, Your Honor."

The prosecution declined the offer for redirect examination of the witness. Everyone in the courtroom could feel the dragging nature of the courtroom proceedings when there was only one witness that truly needed to testify.

"Counsel, please call your next witness," the judge facilitated.

"Your Honor, I'd like to call Peter Davies to the stand."

****

Peter stared at the prosecution attorney whom he had been meeting with for the past few weeks. Peter took note that the eyes of the attorney were kind, but the reality of the situation was that he was behind a witness stand, in a criminal trial, across from an attorney who was trying to achieve the maximum punishment for a girl Peter once called his friend, who murdered his mother. It was all too disturbing for Peter.

"Mr. Davies, what was your relationship with the victim?" the kind attorney began questioning.

"She was my mother," Peter answered, his left hand tightly holding his right hand behind the stand. He was nervous beyond belief. Sweat was forming in the palms of his hands and under his armpits. Peter was hoping to survive the questioning without morphing into a ball of sweat.

"What is your relationship with the defendant?" the attorney inquired, never breaking eye contact with Peter. Peter believed that the attorney was trying to comfort him, to make him know that he was safe and that it was going to be alright. Peter could not apply the message that was being conveyed through the eyes of the counsel.

"She was my friend," Peter answered. Peter took a quick glimpse at Marie and instantly regretted it. Marie's sober eyes carried shame, and she looked as if she was about to cry. Peter hated it. Peter would have preferred to see a deranged Marie, snarling and gnashing at him, so he could continue to hate her, but that's not who Peter saw. He saw his friend. He saw the girl that called him Chainsaw. He saw the girl that walked him to all of his classes in high school. He saw the girl that he thought he might have loved. The guilt in Marie's eyes was confusing Peter.

"Mr. Davies, where were you when the gun went off?" the counsel questioned.

"I was in the bathroom," Peter answered, his sweaty hands still fighting one another.

"Mr. Davies, would you kindly expound upon your version of the events that took place that night? That way, the court can have a live testimony and a clearer understanding," the attorney kindly asked.

Peter quietly sighed and cleared his throat. "I was leaning against the apartment railing on the date mentioned. I had just finished watching the sunset, and I was enjoying the fresh air. I heard a familiar voice begin to speak to me from the sidewalk. I couldn't see the defendant at first because it was dark, but I knew it was the defendant based on her voice. She then proceeded to approach the apartment. She began to walk up the stairs toward my apartment. It was clear that she was under the influence of extremely potent drugs. Her pupils were dilated to what I would deem as maximum capacity. She was obviously enraged. She stormed into my apartment and started hurling insults at my mother. I got her out of the apartment, and I thought she was gone, so I went to the bathroom. That's when I heard the gunshot. I came out of the bathroom to behold my dead mother in a pool of her own blood on the living room floor and the defendant over my mother with a revolver that was still issuing gun powder. The defendant then proceeded to drop the gun, and she tried to embrace me and tell me that she had just freed me from a tyrant, but of course, you know that in such a predicament, one wouldn't be in the mood to embrace the person who has just killed their mother. I threw her out of the apartment, and that's that."

"We are sorry for your loss, Mr. Davies," the attorney said with genuine remorse, to which Peter nodded in acceptance. "So, Mr. Davies, you confirm the defendant to be your mother's murderer?" the attorney asked for repetition's sake.

"Yes," Peter coyly answered.

"No further questions, Your Honor," the prosecution attorney addressed the judge before taking his seat. The judge shifted his attention to the defense attorneys.

"Counsel, would you like to cross-examine the witness?" the judge processioned.

"Yes, Your Honor," the ruthless attorney retorted. As the attorney rose from his seat, he swiped at his shiny, over-gelled hair. That very act nauseated Peter.

"Mr. Davies," the supercilious attorney addressed with the same ungodly smirk. "Why is it that the defendant was so upset with you and your mother?" the attorney asked, tilting his head slightly to the left. There was a stillness in the courtroom. "Please remember that you are under oath to answer all questions truthfully," the attorney smugly reminded.

Peter's sweaty left hand became even more violent with his right hand as he squeezed the circulation out of three of his right hand's fingers. This was the moment of truth. This was the moment of confession. *No more lies. No more lies. No more lies.* Peter recited in his mind. No more lies. Peter had been told that all criminal charges that he should have been charged with had been expunged, so he had nothing to hide and nothing to oppose. So why was he so nervous? Peter questioned within himself. Peter looked at the puffed attorney who was waiting for Peter's retort to his inquiry.

"The defendant was upset with my mother because I had shared with the defendant some of my mother's shady past, and I believe a resentment for my mother started to germinate in the defendant's heart. The defendant was upset with me because she had given me quite a sum of money to leave my mother, but instead of leaving my mother, I left the state of New York with my mother. I believe the defendant was also upset because of the fact that I did not go to the place where I had told her I was going," Peter answered honestly.

"Mr. Davies, what was your relationship like with your mother?" the attorney asked, his head still slightly tilted.

"It was…" Peter paused to find the words to describe the relationship he once had with his late mother. "It was complicated, but we were close," Peter answered painfully and truthfully.

"Mr. Davies, if you had a close relationship with your mother, why would you take money from the defendant to leave your mother? Did you really intend to leave your mother, or were you just going to take the money?"

"I thought about leaving my mother, but I knew that my intentions were to keep the money and stay with my mother," Peter answered.

"Mr. Davies, was not anger an emotion that was warranted by the defendant?" the attorney asked, his head still slightly tilted. Peter wondered if the counsel was ever going to straighten his cranium.

Peter shifted in his chair, then looked into the eyes of the proud attorney. "Anger was warranted, but malice never was. Murder should never be something that's easily justifiable. Marie should not have killed my mother." As the words left Peter's mouth, his eyes automatically fluttered to Marie. Her head was down in shame, and he saw a tear fall from the haven of her eyes and then upon her lap. Something in Peter moved.

Peter shifted his attention to Marie's parents. They stared back at him for a little while before shame compelled them to break their stare. Peter looked over at Anthea. Anthea nodded at Peter, and her eyes whispered, "You are not alone." The courtroom was silent for a while.

"Mr. Davies," the attorney continued, breaking the deafening silence. "The forensic expert identified the defendant as the murderer due to the scientific evidence previously presented. Your testimony also elucidates the defendant as the murderer, but the expert also stated that your fingerprints and the fingerprints of Ms. Boutros were also found on the murder weapon. Why is that?"

Peter dropped his head. He was about to expose his inner demons to a courtroom filled with strangers. Peter lifted his head and sighed as he prepared his mouth to say the words his heart didn't want to hear or repeat. His heart wanted to keep those secrets between him and Anthea. Strangers were about to hear of his weaknesses, but he didn't have a choice. Peter looked down again at his uneasy fingers.

"I was going to kill myself," Peter heard himself say. The courtroom was hushed. "I was going to kill myself with the same revolver Marie used to kill my mother. After holding my dead mother for a couple of minutes, I reached for the revolver. I leaned against the bookcase and placed the muzzle to my forehead. I spun the cylinder, mentally preparing myself for death. I didn't see the point of living without my mother. That's why my fingerprints were found on the gun. Anthea, the woman you mocked earlier, was led by God to walk into my apartment and stop me before I blew my head off. Ms. Boutros eventually convinced me to put down the gun and pushed the gun far from my reach; that's why her fingerprints were found on the gun. So, counsel, just because you do not understand the ways of God doesn't mean you have to mock the wonderful and caring things that God does through people. Counsel, your pestering of Ms. Boutros earlier was insipid. You were trying to belittle a lifesaver. Even with your lofty education and high-flowing words, you lack discernment. You'll defend a murderer and chastise a hero because you do not understand the way in which Ms. Boutros reached my apartment. Is Ms. Boutros not to be applauded? If it wasn't for her, I wouldn't be sitting here. I would be in a grave, next to my mother, with a self-inflicted gunshot wound to the head," Peter paused for a moment to catch his breath. "Don't just increase in knowledge, increase in wisdom," Peter concluded.

It was as if someone else had spoken through him. Peter, and the rest of the members of the courtroom, were all taken aback by the dynamism of his words. Peter looked at the attorney. A glimmer of shame ran across the attorney's face before the infamous smirk returned.

The attorney eyeballed Peter for a moment and then turned his attention to the judge. "I have no further questions, Your Honor."

"May we approach, Your Honor?" the prosecution inquired. The judge nodded and voiced his approval of the approaching of the bench that was perched before him. All four attorneys made their way to the bench. They spoke in hushed tones for a minute before returning to their seats on either side of the well.

"Any redirect, counsel?" the judge inquired of the prosecution attorneys.

"Yes, Your Honor," the stocky attorney answered. The prosecution attorney got up and approached the witness stand.

"Mr. Davies," the attorney began when he reached the witness stand. "It has been made known to us that this act is something that the defendant had been planning for weeks. She had journals filled with different scenarios that ultimately would lead to the death of your mother. The defendant committed first-degree murder, which is worthy of the death penalty in this state. Were these details made known to you? Did you have any inclination that the defendant may have been planning the murder?"

Peter's eyes fluttered to Marie. Marie's eyes were filled with tears, and she mouthed the words, "I'm sorry." Peter looked away. He looked down at his right hand that he had been strangling with his left. Marie had been planning to kill his mother for weeks. That explains why she was able to retrieve a gun so quickly after Peter had kicked her out of the apartment. She had hidden the gun in the tree lining. She had planned it all.

Peter continued to look down at his hands. The court was waiting for a response. The judge was waiting for a response. The jury was waiting for a response. Peter wanted to bawl, but he denied himself. He couldn't cry. Not there. A display of waterworks would work on the heartstrings of the jury, but it would embarrass him. He couldn't. He swallowed the tears and went on a pursuit of his voice.

"I didn't know that," Peter commenced. "I didn't know she planned it—" Peter choked. The tears were trying to asphyxiate him. Peter fought back and regained his composure. "That is premeditated murder.... That is first-degree murder." Peter paused for a minute. The attorney gave him time as he mustered up the strength to say what he had on his heart to say.

"Don't kill her. I know in South Carolina this crime is eligible for the death penalty, but don't kill her. I know Marie. She's an extremely troubled girl. She has a lot of struggles and insecurities, and she has used various drugs for as long as I've known her. I am in no way condoning what she did. Her actions were dubious and evil, but killing her won't solve anything. It wouldn't give her a chance to get better. To get clean. It wouldn't give her a chance to soberly reflect on what she's done. It wouldn't give her a chance to change. It wouldn't give her a chance to become physically and mentally sober. Death is just an escape from facing the consequences of one's decisions. I don't even know if I'm allowed to say this, but…," Peter said. Peter turned to look at Judge Lemear, who was unmoving, neither affirming nor denying the legality of Peter's speech.

Peter continued, "I miss my mother every day. My mother had her ways, but she was my best friend. Killing Marie won't rectify what has happened or bring my mother back to me. Justice would not be served with such a verdict; justice would be missed. True justice would be giving Marie the chance to change and become repentant. True justice would be giving Marie the chance to learn how to live with the decision that she has made."

Justice would not be served with such a verdict; justice would be missed. Those powerful words lingered in the hearts and minds of the members of the courtroom. The courtroom fell silent. No one moved as the words moved them. A sound escaped from the lips of Marie's mother as she wept in the arms of her husband. Marie's father wore a stern face, but his true feelings rolled down his face in the form of tears.

Marie was taken aback by Peter's statement. She wept. She couldn't wipe her tears with her shackled arms.

Anthea gently nodded her head in agreement with Peter's profound statement. Peter watched Anthea as she nodded, and peace overtook him. *I'm not alone*, he thought. *Anthea's here. Christ is here.*

"I have no further questions, Your Honor."

CHAPTER 16

The jury deliberation lasted four days as they strived for a unanimous verdict. Marie was sentenced to life in prison with the possibility of parole. Peter was at peace with that sentence.

As they took Marie away and people began to exit the courtroom, Peter and Marie's father's eyes met. Marie's father did not look away that time. The eyes of Marie's father were red and fatigued. He looked Peter square in the eyes and mouthed the words, "Thank you." Peter nodded. Marie's father gave Peter a weary smile, and then he and his wife exited the courthouse.

Peter understood. Peter knew that the things he had said in the courtroom four days ago had moved the hearts and the minds of the jury. It was clear that the jury was siding with the prosecution in regard to capital punishment, but Peter, the key witness, had changed their judgment.

After the trial was over, Peter and Anthea started to spend most of their time together. One evening they sat in Big Joe's diner, enjoying the deceptive taste of fast food.

"You know," Anthea said in between bites, "I never got the chance to thank you."

Peter looked at Anthea lovingly and wondered what it was that he had done to warrant thanks. "I never got the chance to thank you for defending me in court," Anthea said. Anthea slid her arm across the diner table and placed her hand over Peter's, "It meant so much to me."

Peter could feel his face reddening, so he looked down. He smiled, then lifted his head and said, "Ms. Boutros, it took you three months to thank me?" Peter said with his head tilted ever so slightly to the left. He was trying to imitate the unrefined attorney.

Anthea's laughter shook the restaurant. Some of the customers turned and looked at her. Some smiled. Some looked annoyed. Anthea held her stomach and laughed all the more. Finally, when she was able to regain her equanimity, she said, "That was a great imitation of him."

Peter smiled. "Anything for you, Anthea. He shouldn't have spoken to you in that manner."

"So, I have a question for you," Anthea said with a smile.

"I think I know what it is," Peter responded prematurely. "I'll go," Peter retorted before the inquiry was enunciated.

"Really?" Anthea said with a brilliant smile.

"Yes, I'll go to church with you this weekend," Peter said. "I knew you were going to ask for the hundredth time, so I've decided to go with you."

"Excellent," Anthea said with a smile.

****

Peter was nervous as he stood outside the church doors. He'd never before stepped foot in a church. He didn't know what to expect.

Peter and Anthea walked into the church and stepped into the lobby area. Anthea introduced Peter to a few persons, all of whom greeted him politely.

Peter observed that there were persons who wore black and white and had name tags. They approached and welcomed Peter and Anthea. They opened the large doors that led to the main sanctuary.

What Peter saw surprised him.

There was a band on stage, and a tiny woman was singing her heart out as she lifted her left arm to the sky. The majority of the congregation had their arms lifted as well. There were even persons kneeling. The large screens towards the front of the church read: *Praise and Worship*.

This is intense, Peter thought. Peter and Anthea found a seat in the middle section of the congregation. Peter noticed that Anthea had her arms raised and eyes closed as well. Peter wasn't sure of what to do. He didn't want to lift his arms because he didn't know why he would be doing that.

Peter began to read the words on the screen in an attempt to get a better understanding of what was taking place. The words Peter read didn't make sense to him.

Why are they rejoicing over someone dying? Peter thought. *Who died?* he whispered within himself.

The worship leader then began to repeat the name of Jesus. It was then that Peter realized that it was Jesus who had died. Peter felt ashamed about not knowing who it was that had died. Peter and Anthea had discussions about Jesus Christ many times, but being in a place where hundreds of people were all calling upon the name of Jesus was a new and overwhelming experience for Peter.

Peter looked around the church. Peter saw three persons that were looking around akin to him. Peter started to feel a bit better about his lack of participation.

The intimate worship eventually ended after two more selections. Peter took his seat next to Anthea. A man in a white button-down shirt and black slacks walked onto the stage. He greeted the congregation, then he prayed. After he prayed, he opened his Bible and began to speak.

"Identity," he said. He didn't hold a microphone, but his voice was amplified. Peter then noticed the small microphone attached to his shirt. "Where does your identity stand? That's the topic and the question God placed on my heart for this week. Where does your identity stand?"

Is this how church usually is? Peter wondered. *Do you walk in and get hit with deep and personal questions on the spot?* Peter questioned within himself. Peter wondered if he even knew where his identity stood. *Isn't that what everyone is searching for?* Peter queried within himself. *Does anyone truly know?*

"Turn with me to Philippians chapter three and verse nine. When you've all found it let us stand for the reading of God's Holy Word," the pastor said. The congregation responded by rising from their seats, Bibles in hand. Peter glanced over at Anthea's Bible, and she pointed out the scripture verse to him.

"The Word of God says, 'And be found in him, not having mine own righteousness, which is of the law, but that which is through the faith of Christ, the righteousness which is of God by faith.'" (Philippians 3:9, KJV.)

"Amen," a concerto of voices echoed after the reading.

"You may be seated," the pastor instructed, to which everyone yielded to the directive. "The apostle Paul was writing to the church in Philippi when he penned these words. Paul was speaking to believers about the importance of having their identity hidden in Jesus Christ. So, what does that mean? That means that our identity should not be found in material things. Our identity should not be found in our homes. Our identity should not be found in our earthly achievements or successes. Our identity shouldn't even be found in the persons closest to us. Our identity should be found in Jesus Christ and what He has done on the cross. The same Paul writes to the church in Galatia and encourages them in the Lord by stating in chapter six and verse fourteen, 'But God forbid that I should glory, save in the cross of our Lord Jesus Christ, by whom the world is crucified unto me, and I unto the world' (Galatians 6:14, KJV). And what Paul was saying here is that everything that he achieved, and that was a lot, meant nothing. Paul understood that everything that he saw, everything he achieved, would fade away, but he knew that the Lord Jesus Christ reigns forever. Paul understood the folly of placing his identity in temporary things. Paul understood that if his identity were to be found in temporary things, all of his emotions, feelings, mindset, and entire being would be hinged on things that would eventually fade; hence, he would fade with the temporary things. God revealed to Paul that persons can have everlasting hope and identity in Jesus Christ because He will never fade away or fail."

Peter wasn't sure about what was taking place within him, but he felt a strange stirring in his heart. He was starting to become uneasy as the message pricked his heart and pierced his soul. He had never before considered his identity or what it was being placed in.

"You may be wondering, why should my identity be found in Jesus Christ? What has this Jesus ever done for me? Well, I want to let you know this morning that God loves you. If you've never heard it before, I want to let you know that God loves you. God loves you so much that He sent His Son Jesus Christ to die for you. He died for your sins. He died for all the wrongs that you have done and ever will do. All He is asking for you to do is to put your faith in Him."

Peter was embraced by a holy presence, and tears fell from the safety of his eyes. Someone had died for all his wrongdoings. Someone had died for all his mistakes. Someone had died for the brokenness he felt so often. Someone had died for the pink flower that he had picked all those years ago.

"Hebrews nine and verse twenty-seven reminds us that it is appointed unto humans once to die, then after death comes the judgment. Without believing in Christ Jesus, none of us can stand before God. Our sins will capture us at that moment, but if we put our trust in Jesus Christ, we will stand righteous before God. If our identity is hidden in Christ Jesus, we will stand righteous, holy, and pure before God Almighty."

Peter's heart was racing. His palms were sweating. This was the time of reckoning.

"So, you see, it doesn't matter what you have done. It doesn't matter how far gone you think you are. Christ Jesus died for you, and you are free through Him and Him alone. I know this message was a short one, but God wants me to give the altar call now. If you are here and you would like to know Jesus Christ. Come. If you are here and you want your identity to be hidden in the One who is eternal. Come. 'It is appointed unto men once to die, but after death comes the judgment.'[1] Without Christ, you cannot stand before God. Without Christ, there will always be a fear of death. Accept Jesus Christ and start living without fear."

At that moment, flashes of Peter's life appeared before him. The field of pink flowers. The begging. The physical abuse. The thievery. The con-artistry. The drugs. The alcohol. The lies. His mother. Marie. Red. His suicide attempts. Peter, at that moment, realized that the reason why he had wanted to kill himself those months ago was that he didn't know who he was without his mother. Peter realized that he didn't know who he was at all. He didn't know where his identity stood.

He heard the words of the pastor as he called for persons to join him at the altar. The pastor was telling them to come as they are. *How could I ever come as I am?* Peter thought. *What would Jesus ever want with me?* Peter thought as he bowed his head. Peter had decided to stay in his seat.

"God is calling a young man this morning. A young man who thinks he cannot come to Jesus Christ," the pastor said. Peter looked up. Even though there were approximately fifteen persons already at the altar, the pastor was still beckoning for another.

"You know who you are. You think you're unworthy. You've tried to take your life because you didn't know who you were. God is beckoning for you to come and accept the free gift of His Son. God is calling you to surrender to the freedom that comes only through Him. God is calling you to surrender to liberty. You don't have to understand it all, but if God is moving upon your heart, young man, come," The pastor beckoned with his arm outstretched. The pastor had left the stage and was now on ground level with the congregation. He stood with his back

[1] See Hebrews 9:27

to the persons at the altar, calling for one more soul.

Peter noticed that most of the church had their heads bowed in prayer. Peter looked over at Anthea. She was praying as well. Peter looked at the pastor. Peter could barely see him because of the blurred vision that his tears had induced. Peter wasn't sure of what was happening to him. There was an inexplicable stirring in his heart.

Peter continued to quietly weep in his seat. Peter looked up again and looked at the pastor. Peter thought that maybe if he sat in his seat long enough, the pastor would return to praying for the fifteen that knelt at the altar. Peter bowed his head again. He looked up, and the pastor was still there.

Peter, every time you look up, I will be there. I will never leave you.

That wasn't the pastor. That wasn't his mind. Peter held on to the church pew with his left hand. What was happening to him? He thought. Someone had just promised not to leave him, and he was weeping uncontrollably in response to the promise.

"That voice you just heard, that was the Lord. There isn't a place where His grace cannot find you. There isn't a place where His love cannot surround you. He'll never leave nor forsake you. Come," the Pastor beckoned with his arm still outstretched.

Peter's heart was overwhelmed. Peter lifted himself from his seat. He held on to the pew for a while until he finally let go and staggered down the aisle until he collapsed in the arms of the pastor. The pastor held him as he wept.

"I surrender," Peter muttered, still embracing the pastor. Tears and snot flowed down Peter's face like a stream. "I want to be found in Christ."

The pastor embraced him, and Peter felt the potent presence of Almighty God. At that moment, Peter knew that God was using the pastor as the vessel in which to tangibly embrace him. Peter felt a kind of love that surpassed anything earthly.

Peter felt depression lift from him. He felt malice lift from him. He felt peace. He felt joy, but most importantly, he felt a supernatural flow of freedom as he surrendered to the liberty found only in Jesus Christ.

The embrace ended, and Peter collapsed at the altar, leaving a pool of phlegm and tears on the pastor's shirt. The pastor cared not about his marred shirt.

An explosion of worship commenced as the pastor, with arms lifted, walked the new believers through the prayer of repentance and acceptance of Jesus Christ.

Anthea opened her eyes. She realized that the seat next to her was empty. *Where's Peter?* she thought. She looked around for a moment, and then she decided to look at the front of the church. She scanned the altar.

There he was. Prostrate at the altar. Weeping before God. Tears formed in Anthea's eyes, and a grand smile spread itself across her face. Anthea fell to her knees in worship. Anthea thanked God for His faithfulness.

Anthea had just witnessed the answer to the prayers she had been praying for the past four months. Anthea's prayer was for Peter to have a personal encounter with Jesus Christ, and there Peter was, enjoying the sweet embrace of Almighty God.

Tears streamed from Anthea's eyes. Her friend was finally free.

The pastor still had his arms lifted in worship as he said, "If you are here at this altar and you have decided today to dedicate your life to Jesus Christ, please repeat after me."

"Father God," the pastor commenced.

"Father God," repeated an exuberantly liberated Peter.

"I come to You in the name of Jesus," the pastor led.

"I come to You in the name of Jesus." Peter smiled as he repeated the name of the God he had just fallen so desperately in love with.

"Lord, I choose this day to surrender my life to You," the pastor said passionately, with eyes closed and arms lifted.

"Lord, I choose this day to surrender my life to You," Peter said. Peter was now on his knees with his arms lifted to God. He understood now. He understood why people knelt. Peter understood why people cried during worship. He now understood why they lifted their hands. It was because God is good and gracious, and His love is infinite and freeing. Peter now understood the things that Anthea had been trying to share with him.

Peter tilted his head back as the tears streamed down his face. With arms lifted, Peter surrendered to freedom. With a broad smile, Peter inhaled the love of God and exhaled worship. He breathed in liberty and exhaled praise. God was changing him. God was mending him. His heart had been so bitter. His mind had been so warped. But in that place, God's presence met him, and he soaked up the liberty like a thirsty sponge.

"I believe that You sent Your only Son to die for my sins," the pastor led.

"I believe that You sent Your only Son to die for my sins," Peter followed.

"I confess with my mouth and believe with my heart," the pastor prayed with a smile on his face. The pastor wept under the potent presence of God.

"I confess with my mouth and believe with my heart," the altar and a few from the congregation followed.

"That You rose Jesus Christ from the dead," the pastor prayed.

"That You rose Jesus Christ from the dead," Peter said with joy.

"Amen," the pastor ended.

"Amen," the altar echoed. The church erupted in a session of passionate praise and worship. Peter stayed where he was. He stayed where he was at the altar and worshipped. Perpetual tears streamed from his face as he worshipped his Savior and friend. Jesus Christ had been there all along. The freedom that he had been trying to find in people and in drugs had been in Christ Jesus all along. Peter realized that the void that was in his life was far too vast to be filled with temporary pleasures. The void sought an eternal fix. The void sought for Jesus Christ.

Peter remained at the altar even after the worship team had left the stage. Even after people started leaving the sanctuary. Peter stayed. He was afraid of losing the freedom if he stood up.

The pastor came over to Peter and gently placed his hand on Peter's back.

"Welcome to the family of God," the pastor said to Peter with a smile. He helped Peter to get up from his knees. Peter was going to say something, but he just ended up embracing the pastor once again. The pastor's wife and Anthea began to rejoice. Peter eventually let go of the pastor and joined in on the worship.

The pastor gave Peter new believer's material which consisted of a Bible, a devotional, and contact numbers for the ministers. Peter was still overwhelmed as the pastor and his wife left the main sanctuary, hand in hand. Only Peter, Anthea, and the ushers remained in the main sanctuary.

Peter turned to Anthea. "Thank you," Peter said through tears and with a radiant smile. "Thank you for caring about me. For never giving up on me. Thank you for being obedient and coming into my apartment that night and for staying with me in the hospital. Thank you for being there every day. Thank you for every encouraging note you've ever given me. Thank you for staying with me all throughout the trial. Thank you for never ceasing to invite me to church. Thank you for leading me to Jesus Christ, who is my beautiful Savior." Peter's voice began to break, "Anthea, thank you for loving me."

Anthea tried to keep her composure. She was trying to keep herself together, but tears fell wildly from her eyes. Peter pulled her in for an embrace.

"I love you," he uttered from the depths of his heart.

"I love you too," Anthea replied as she closed her eyes and laid her head on Peter's chest.

****

Halia and Olathe wipe tears of joy from their faces. Perri tries his best to keep his equanimity, even though the tale is moving upon his heartstrings.

"This story is so beautiful, Grandpa," Halia voices through sniffles. "At first, Peter's life seemed so hopeless. Especially after his mother died, but there's always…hope." Halia stumbles through before her voice goes on vacation because of the influx of tears.

"Grandpa, I just feel so grateful," Olathe says. "I feel so overwhelmingly grateful for my parents. I'm so grateful for you, Grandpa, and for Grandma. I'm grateful for you, Halia," Olathe says as she hugs her sister.

"I'm grateful for you, Perri," Olathe says as she walks over and hugs her brother. Perri plants a kiss atop his sister's head.

"You do have a lot to be grateful for," Farook says to his granddaughter as she approaches him for a hug. He embraces her with a full heart. "But always remember to be grateful every day for the people around you. Continue to pray and give thanks for all the wonderful people God has placed in your life," Farook says, to which Olathe nods and hugs her grandfather again. The door opens, and Zahra steps into the room.

"Speaking of wonderful people," Farook says as he beams at his beautiful bride of forty years. "How are you, dear?" Farook inquires of his wife.

"I'm well," Zahra responds as she takes a seat on the carpet next to Halia. Halia places her head on her grandmother's shoulder.

"I've been back for a little while now. I hurriedly prepared dinner because I wanted to catch the end of the story," Zahra says.

"Grandma, the story is so captivating," Halia says.

"You missed most of it, Gran," Olathe states as she leaves her grandfather's arms and takes her position in her grandmother's arms that form a warm nest around Olathe.

"Is that so?" Zahra questions Olathe with a smile. Zahra wraps her arms around her granddaughter and gently squeezes her, which makes Olathe giggle.

"Yes, but I'll catch you up on the story at dinner," Olathe says, to which Zahra smiles. Zahra shifts her attention to Farook.

"My husband, where in the story have you reached?" Zahra inquires.

"I have reached the portion where Peter and Anthea marry," Farook says, beaming at his beautiful wife. The children stare at Farook with wide eyes.

"Peter and Anthea marry!" the children exclaim simultaneously.

"Yes, they do," Farook says with a sweet smile.

Zahra gleams at Farook. "I like this part. I'm sad I missed the portion where Peter gives his life to Jesus."

"I know! That was my favorite part. Grandpa spoke with such passion. It's like he was there!" Olathe dramatically gestures as she speaks to her grandmother. Zahra smiles and kisses Olathe on the cheek. Olathe giggles and rests her head on her grandmother's shoulder.

"How does it end, Grandpa?" the children inquire.

"Yes, Grandpa, how does it end?" Zahra inquires with a knowing smile. Farook returns the witty smile.

Farook reclines in his chair as he prepares to vocally deliver the end of the tale.

****

Three years had passed since Peter gave his life to Jesus Christ. Peter spent most of his time in prayer, worship, and reading the Word of God. Peter had finished college with a major in social work. He kept his job at the community center and received several promotions throughout the years. The children at the community center loved him, and he thoroughly enjoyed being a mentor to them. He enjoyed being their father figure.

Peter and Anthea continued to spend all their free time together. They had become young adult leaders in the church after two years of training. They enjoyed the ministry, and they enjoyed each other's company. One evening, as they sat in the park eating sushi, Peter spontaneously said, "I love you."

"I know you do," Anthea said with a smile. "I love you too. Finish the sushi," Anthea said as she returned her attention to her meal.

Peter got down on one knee. "Anthea Boutros," Peter said as he pulled a little velvet box from his pocket. Anthea's chopsticks fell from her, and the sushi she had meaningfully placed on her lips sat on the park floor. "I love you," Peter repeated as he looked into Anthea's now streaming eyes. "Ever since you came into my life, the light switch turned on, and I could finally see. You're my angel. You're the one God sent to me to keep me sane. You're the one God sent to me to lead me to Him. God has used you to teach me what love is, and I have fallen in love with the angel He has sent to me."

Anthea swiped at her tears. Peter continued, "This relationship has grown into something more beautiful than either of us could have ever imagined, and right now, I want nothing more than if you would grace me with your hand in marriage. Will you marry me?"

Anthea, lost for words, nodded and embraced Peter. They filled the empty park with laughter.

****

"This story is so beautiful, Grandpa," Halia says as she glares into her grandfather's eyes with love.

"This is my favorite part," Farook says with a smile.

"Mine too," Zahra adds.

"I never want this beautiful tale to end," Olathe says with a sigh.

"All good things here on earth must come to an end, my sweet girl," Zahra says as she kisses her granddaughter once more.

"Good thing Jesus went back to heaven then," Olathe states, to which everyone smiles.

"So, Grandpa, how does Peter fare?" Perri asks.

****

Peter stood mesmerized as he beheld his beautiful bride. Anthea walked down the aisle in the radiant white gown that seemed to span for miles behind her. Her wardrobe was beautiful, but it was the smile that she gracefully wore that lit up the room.

As Peter and Anthea stood across from each other at the altar, they thought about their lives. They were so different. They each had their own unique story to tell. Peter and Anthea never expected their lives to have come together so intimately. They reflected on that Thursday, that dreadful Thursday almost four years prior. Peter would have never guessed that the woman who God led to talk him out of taking his own life would become his bride.

As Peter and Anthea held hands and exchanged vows and rings, Peter's mind fluttered to the fact that they were both without parents for their wedding. Peter looked out into the pews. He saw the beaming faces of church family, but neither of them had immediate family in which to invite. At that moment, Peter thought of his mother. He missed her. He reasoned that she would have loved Anthea.

Peter placed his attention back upon his bride. She was so radiant. Peter looked at the pastor, the man that had held him all those years ago, as he wept and gave his heart to Jesus Christ. The pastor smiled at him.

"I now pronounce you man and wife. Mr. Davies, you may kiss your bride," Pastor McCloud said with enamor.

Peter was extremely nervous as he neared Anthea's face with his own. It was the start of their new life together. The start of a life Peter never knew could be his. A life without lies and everyday acting. A life without paranoia. A life of freedom. A life with Jesus Christ and a beautiful wife who loved and respected him.

At that moment, Peter felt full. His past would always be his past, but he no longer lived in the past. He no longer lived in the hurt. He no longer resided in the pain of loss. He wasn't the little boy that picked the pink flower. He had been born again. He had been given a new life. A life filled with hope and promise.

A couple of weeks afterward, Peter and Anthea walked past a suicide prevention center, and Peter felt led to sign up to be on staff.

For the next two years, Peter and Anthea continued to serve in the ministry. Anthea had started the doctorate program and was studying and writing deep into the night.

"Anthea, are you still writing?" Peter asked as he entered their small living room.

"Yes," Anthea answered with a smile amidst her books that had formed mountains around her. Peter placed a sandwich and a tall glass of iced tea in a small space he found available on the busy desk.

"Thank you so much," Anthea said with gratitude as she looked up at Peter from behind her glasses.

"You're welcome, love," Peter said as he kissed her atop her head. "I'm going to get some air and leave you to your work," Peter said as he headed to the balcony of their small apartment.

"Okay, enjoy the air. I'm going to join you just as soon as I finish these two thesis statements," Anthea said.

Peter walked out onto the balcony. He allowed the cool breeze to caress his face. He had made it in time for his favorite show. The sunset. He watched as the invisible hands painted streaks of pink and orange in the firmament. Peter was pleased that he had gotten the chance to get to know those invisible hands. Peter now knew that it was Almighty God, the creator of heaven and earth.

Peter closed his eyes and seeped the wonder and majesty into his pores. He smiled as he felt the arms of God wrap around him.

"Lord, I thank You for Your faithfulness," Peter bowed his head and prayed. "I thank You for—" The phone in his pocket stopped his prayer abruptly as it alerted him that someone was calling. Peter had a mind to silence it, but he decided to take the call. Peter looked at the phone screen. It was an overseas phone number. Peter answered the phone.

"Hello," Peter said into the device.

"Hello," a seasoned Englishman greeted back. "Is this Peter Davies?" the voice questioned.

"Yes, it is. May I ask who is calling?" Peter curiously inquired.

"Peter, this is Brian Davies. Your father," the voice retorted.

The force of the words caused silence to reign for a moment as Peter processed what he had just heard. *My father?* Peter questioned in introspection. Peter had so much he wanted to say, but his voice had failed him.

Peter stood with the phone pressed against his ear but failed to utter a word. *My father?* he repeated within the tower of his mind. Peter listened to the heavy breathing of a fatigued man that dominated the phone line.

"Peter, I know you weren't ever expecting to hear from me. I don't even know if your mother ever told you who I was," the Englishman said. The man then ushered a series of loud, phlegm-filled coughs. "Peter, I've been searching for you for a year now. Last year it was made known to me that I had a son. I tried to search for Adela, but I then found out that she had died. I'm sorry for your loss, Peter." The man paused for a moment and took a few long and heavy breaths.

"Peter, your father is dying. My heart wishes that it had the knowledge of you before such a tragic end to my journey…but my son, I must see you. I must see my offspring before I die," the man said.

"Where would you like to meet me?" Peter heard himself inquire.

"I cannot travel, but I'll have my secretary book a flight for you to come and see me." The man paused to cough violently. "I found out that you are a married man," the Englishman struggled to project. "I can arrange a flight for your wife as well."

Peter's vocabulary had been dramatically reduced to only a handful of words. He was in shock.

"Where exactly would my wife and I be meeting you?" Peter eventually spewed.

"1112 Lakeview Lane."

"1112 Lakeview Lane. In England?" Peter inquired.

"Yes," the man responded.

Peter held on to the railing. 1112 Lakeview Lane. That was the address of the mansion. The mansion with the field of radiant pink flowers. That was his father's home.

Handfuls Of Yesterday

****

Peter and Anthea stepped out of the vehicle. Peter was in shock as he beheld the house. It was just as he remembered. The rich dark-hued brick covered the mansion, and the light pink curtains blew in the wind from the fourth-story windows. The house had many visual banquets to devour, but nothing compared to the field. Peter walked over to the field and placed his hands atop the petals. The flowers moved in the wind and caressed the palm of his hand. Peter looked out on the portion of the field that sat next to the sidewalk. He looked at the place where he stood twenty years ago. He thought of his mother. Peter felt a hand hold his. He turned and looked at the beautiful woman that graced his side.

"Is this the field?" Anthea asked.

"Yes, it is," Peter somberly responded.

"Mr. and Mrs. Davies," a woman called from the front door of the mansion. Peter assumed that she was his father's secretary. "Mr. Davies would like to see you now."

Peter and Anthea walked hand in hand towards the house. They walked into the grand home that looked more like an enclosed football field. They followed the secretary as she led them to the east elevator. Even the elevator reeked of posh.

They traveled to the fourth floor. The elevator doors opened, and the kind secretary led them around the stairs and down a long hallway. She stopped in front of the last door on the left.

"Please wait here for just a moment," the secretary said before opening the room door and closing it behind her. Peter looked out the grand window that was slightly agape. He took in the fluid motion of the light pink curtains as they swayed in the wind. He looked down at the field that swayed in sync with the curtains as if they were in cahoots.

Peter closed his eyes and breathed in the fresh air. Peter took a moment to ask God for the strength to speak to his father. Peter asked God to fill his mouth with words because his heart was feeling vulnerable and frail.

As if on cue, Anthea asked, "Would you like for us to pray together?"

Peter opened his eyes and looked at his wife.

"I could sense the anxiety, my husband. Let me pray for you." Peter smiled as he wrapped his arms around her. She began to pray.

They heard the door open. They opened their eyes. The secretary beckoned for them to enter the room. "Mr. Davies will see you now," she said. Peter and Anthea entered the room hand in hand.

"Thank you, Alexandra," Brian Davies weakly said to his secretary as she exited the room. As Peter neared his feeble father, he realized that the resemblance between them was uncanny. He bore his father's light brown eyes and matted curls. Brian's facial features had been rewritten verbatim upon Peter's face.

"I feel as if I'm looking upon a photograph of my youth," Mr. Davies weakly voiced with a feeble laugh that propelled him into a fit of coughing. "You are undeniably my son," Mr. Davies said after his series of coughs.

Peter smiled as tears formed in his eyes. He and Anthea took seats next to the bed of the enervated man.

The room looked much like a hospital. Mr. Davies was connected to oxygen tanks. Intravenous lines slowly dripped their liquids into his system.

"Hello, Anthea; it is a pleasure to meet you," Brian Davies greeted with a faint smile.

"Likewise, Mr. Davies," Anthea answered with a genuine grin. Anthea's heart was overjoyed at that moment as she watched her husband meet his father for the first time.

"You have a wonderful wife, my son," Brian Davies complimented.

Handfuls Of Yesterday

Peter nodded in agreement.

"Come closer to me," Mr. Davies requested of his son. Peter and Anthea moved closer to the man who lay uncomfortably in his bed.

Brian grabbed the hand of his son and held it as tightly as he could. "Peter, I wish I could have been there for you. I wish I could have been the father that was present in your life. Your mother—" Brian coughed violently into the napkin that he held in his left hand. The napkin was laced with blood. "Your mother never told me of you," Brian Davies continued. "I employed her as a housekeeper after she completed grade school. Our romantic relationship commenced shortly after she began working for me. She only worked here for four months. I had to fire her after I caught her stealing money from my room. She never told me she was pregnant. She never spoke to me again."

Mr. Davies took a break to cough. "Last year, my secretary brought an article to my attention. The article was about a man named Peter Davies who was working as a volunteer at a suicide prevention center. The striking resemblance caused me to start a search for you. When I found out you were Adela's son, I knew you were my son as well."

Brian Davies looked at Peter, "You are undeniably my son."

Tears streamed down Peter's face as his father held his left hand and his wife held his right. The love in the room was enveloping Peter in an overwhelming embrace.

"Peter," Brian Davies continued. "I have rewritten my will. You are the sole heir to my entire estate. You will be in charge of the family business when I pass. My secretary will become your secretary. This house will be your house. Everything that I possess is yours. This moment makes my heart exuberantly jubilant. For so long, I thought I was to die alone. I was convinced this time last year that I was going to die without an heir, but here you are, my son."

Mr. Davies painfully coughed into his napkin, but the joy that filled his heart was unmistakably pronounced upon his face.

"Come closer to me, my son," Brian Davies requested.

My son. Peter soaked in the words as he embraced his father.

Peter and Anthea stayed with Brian Davies until he died three weeks later. They made the decision to permanently move into the mansion so that Peter could run the family business.

As Peter moved his things into the grand home, he realized, at that moment, that the thief had always been the heir.

CHAPTER 17

Farook, Zahra, and the children stand in the frigid cold with warm, food-filled bellies and sweater bundles. They watch as the familiar blue minivan waltzes up the long driveway. The bright van lights pave an illuminated path up to the west portion of the mansion.

Niran cautiously parks the van in the snow, pulling up the handbrake. Niran and Nadya exit the vehicle, and a procession of love, mingled with hugs and kisses, takes place as the children say goodbye to their grandparents.

"Thank you so much for keeping them on such short notice, Mum and Dad," Nadya thanks.

"We truly appreciate it," Niran follows.

"It was our pleasure," Zahra retorts.

"Today was such a beautiful day, Grandpa. Thank you," Halia says as she hugs her grandparents, then goes and takes her seat in the minivan.

"At first, I thought today was going to be somewhat of a drag, but it turned out to be the best day we've ever had together, Grandpa," Perri says as he embraces his grandparents, then follows the trail of his sister into the van.

Olathe dramatically places a hand on her chest. "How can I say thanks," she commences. "For such a fantastic day filled with vivid adventures," Olathe concludes. "Thanks for such a great day," Olathe says as she embraces both grandparents at once. Olathe carefully skips to the vehicle and takes her favorite seat, sandwiched between her siblings.

Niran and Nadya embrace Farook and Zahra. The adults engage in small talk before splitting.

Zahra and Farook watch as Niran and Nadya join the children in the van, then eventually make their way down the vast driveway. Zahra and Farook stalk the vehicle with their eyes until the moving cocoon that holds their prized jewels is a mere smug in visual range.

Nadya's smile lights the entire vehicle. There is something about being in her parent's presence that causes Nadya's heart to be overjoyed.

"How was your day today?" Niran inquires of his children.

"It was delightful," Halia responds for her siblings and herself.

"Excellent," Niran says with a smile as he attentively watches the thoroughfare. "What did you do today?" Niran questions.

"Grandfather told us a riveting tale," Olathe retorts with theatrical hand gestures.

"Grandmother was busy with a patient for most of the day, but she joined us for dinner and for the latter portion of the story," Perri informs his parents.

Nadya soaks in the words of her children. "Grandpa told you a tale?" Nadya asks and turns around in the van's plush seat to look at her children, who nod at her rhetorical question. "What was it about?" Nadya curiously questions as she mentally prepares herself for the response. Her father was always kind and loving, but Nadya also knew him to be a particularly secretive man. The fact that her father would tell the children such a long tale intrigues Nadya.

"It was about a boy named Peter," Perri begins. "His life was one of hardship, crime, violence, drugs, physical abuse, and redemption."

"Drugs?" Inquires Niran.

"Physical abuse?" Nadya follows.

"Yes," Halia responds. "Grandfather didn't go into detail about some of the areas of Peter's life because he understood his audience, but he was very real and open with his storytelling. It was as if Grandpa had a front-row seat to Peter's life. Grandpa is a wonderful storyteller. He wore his emotions on his sleeve as he spoke. His face carried all the sentiments we would imagine that Peter must have felt."

As Nadya listens, she wonders who her children spent the day with because it didn't sound like they spent it with the kind and reserved Christian father she knew.

"Tell me more," Nadya requested.

"Well, it's a very long tale, but we'll give you all the highlights," Olathe says with a radiant smile that Nadya graciously returns.

"The story begins with a boy named Peter standing in a field of radiant pink flowers," Halia commences. The sound of radiant pink flowers sets off a subconscious alert as Nadya listens attentively.

"His mother coerces him into stealing a flower from the garden of a beautiful mansion," Olathe follows.

"That's where it all began," Perri fills in.

"That does sound captivating," Niran states.

Nadya looks at her children, but she isn't looking at them. She's thinking of the significance of the tale and why her father would choose to tell such a riveting tale to the children. Nadya knows her father to be a man that does everything with a specific purpose. Nadya has never known her father to be an impulsive man; he always thought everything through meticulously. Every word he ever said to her growing up was calculated and punctiliously delivered.

"What's the name of the boy's mother?" Nadya inquires.

"Adela, and she…," Halia is still speaking, but Nadya is consumed by her own thoughts.

Adela. That was the name of her grandmother.

The children are still speaking, and Nadya is trying to listen and process. Adela. The mansion. The field of pink flowers. *Could it all be coincidental?* Nadya questions within herself, but knowing her father, she knows the internal inquiry is rhetorical.

Could he really have given the children a story of himself without their immediate knowledge of the true identity of the main character? Nadya questions as she listens to the children. The things they are sharing with her are connecting like a large puzzle in which she has been given a key. She listens and reflects on the secretive nature of her father throughout the years. He had never shared anything regarding his past with her. *Was shame the reason why he was so secretive?* Nadya questions introspectively. *Why now? Why open up now?*

For the next hour, Nadya soaks in the tale being so dramatically presented by her children. *Is mother Anthea? She must be!* Nadya inwardly discusses.

As the garage of their home opens, Perri, Halia, and Olathe hurriedly finish the latter remnants of the tale. The children are all quite pleased with their cohesive storytelling.

Is Papa Peter? Nadya deliberates from the *château* that is her mind. Nadya tries to decipher every portion of the tale and translate each alias. The children bolt inside the house, excited to get back to their electronic distractions.

For the next hour, Nadya busies herself with housework, but her mind busies itself with the salient tale delivered to her by her children, straight from the mouth of her father. Was the tale truly about her father? She questions while doing laundry. Many things the children had mentioned were answers to questions Nadya had for a long time.

Why did he feel the need to withhold all these details of his life from me? Nadya discusses within herself. Nadya pours more fabric softener than warranted into the machine.

Later in the night, as Nadya lays in bed, her mind continues to pedal as it processes all that she heard from the mouths of her children. Niran snores loudly beside her. Nadya knows what she must do.

She quietly gets out of the bed, changes, grabs her keys, writes a note for Niran, and then heads downstairs to the garage. She gets in the car, opens the garage, and then reverses into the night. She closes the garage and then speeds off into the frigid abyss. The drive seems shorter due to her pondering.

Nadya reaches the house in less than an hour. Nadya commences the tedious security process to enter the mansion of her parents. She punches in the digits for the gates. She patiently waits as the scanner reads her fingerprint. The gates eventually open, and Nadya drives her small red car up the extensive driveway.

Nadya slows the vehicle as she approaches the house, then she parks. She sits in the car for a while as she processes what she is to say to her father, then she exits the vehicle. Nadya walks with caution on the slippery ground.

Nadya eventually reaches the grand west entrance to her father's mansion. She rings the fourth-story doorbell and waits. A few minutes later, the grand door opens, and out steps Farook. He stares questioningly at his daughter.

Nadya's speech fails her. She raises her hand gently to touch her father's face. She swipes at his matted curls that strategically cover his forehead. She searches for it. She finds it. The scar.

"You got a haircut when I was seventeen," Nadya says with her hand still upon her father's forehead. "That's the one and only time I saw your scar," Nadya says before lowering her hand from her father's forehead. Silence dances between them.

"Papa, are you Peter?" Nadya asks.

Farook feels a mixture of fright and relief. Nadya knows, and he isn't having a panic attack in response. Farook is surprised at his own self and his tranquil response. Farook is slightly taken aback but joyous simultaneously as he looks at his daughter, who still sports love in her eyes.

"Yes," Farook truthfully answers. "Peter was my first alias. It's the alias I liked the most," Farook freely shares.

Nadya digests the new openness that has suddenly swallowed her father whole. So many questions race through her mind.

"Why didn't you share your story with me, Papa?" Nadya inquires.

Farook breathes in the cold air as he beckons for his daughter to walk with him alongside the house. "I was ashamed, Nadya. I have always been ashamed of my past. Of my decisions," Farook confesses.

Nadya soaks in the shift. The transparent shift in the glass ceiling of their relationship, whose wake has shaken them both.

"I have so much I want to ask. I have so much I want to say to you, but everything is so jumbled in my mind right now," Nadya shares.

"Well, when you're ready, I'm here to answer your questions. I've decided that it's time my family knows all about me. The good and the bad. I've decided that I'm not going to live life in fear of you not loving me if you were to truly know of my past," Farook says.

"I could never stop loving you, Papa," Nadya says as she grabs the hand of her father.

Farook smiles as he lovingly squeezes the hand of his daughter. They stop walking to look out upon the field. Copious quantities of images of her and her father standing, hand in hand, in this same spot, resonate in Nadya's mind.

She looks up at the east wing of the house and spots the one light pink curtain swaying every so elegantly from the agape fourth-story window. Nadya takes a moment to piece the puzzle together and to take everything in from a new and enlightened perspective.

"So, this is the house?" Nadya inquires.

"Yes, this is the house. This is the field of pink flowers."

The End

ABOUT THE AUTHOR

Sheneen Monique Soares is an author, recording artist, worship pastor, preacher, teacher, writer, and musician. Sheneen Monique Soares currently resides in Dallas, Texas, where she works as a worship pastor and high school teacher. You can learn more about Sheneen Monique Soares at her website: **www.sheneenmonique.com**.

CPSIA information can be obtained
at www.ICGtesting.com
Printed in the USA
BVHW051133050123
655630BV00008B/399